SUMMER WARRIOR

Book One in The Clan Donald Saga

REGAN WALKER

This is a work of fiction. Names, characters, places and incidents either are the product of the author's imagination or are used fictitiously. Any resemblance to actual events, locales, business establishments or persons, living or dead, is coincidental.

SUMMER WARRIOR

Copyright © 2020 Regan Walker

Paperback ISBN: 978-0-9979905-9-1
Print Edition

PRAISE FOR REGAN WALKER

"The writing is excellent, the research impeccable, and the love story is epic. You can't ask for more than that."

—*The Book Review*

"Regan Walker is a master of her craft. Her novels instantly draw you in, keep you reading and leave you with a smile on your face."

—*Good Friends, Good Books*

"Ms. Walker has the rare ability to make you forget you are reading a book. The characters become real, the modern world fades away, and all that is left is the intrigue, drama, and romance."

—*Straight from the Library*

"Walker's detailed historical research enhances the time and place of the story without losing sight of what is essential to a romance: chemistry between the leads and hope for the future."

—*Publisher's Weekly*

"…an enthralling story."

—*RT Book Reviews*

"Spellbinding and Expertly Crafted…Walker's characters are complex and well-rounded and, in her hands, real historical figures merge seamlessly with those from her imagination."

—*A Reader's Review*

ACKNOWLEDGEMENTS

I am indebted to photographer Paul Marriott for the magnificent cover photograph taken from the Isle of Man where he lives and works and where my story begins. You can see more of his talent at PaulMarriottphotography.com. In addition, because of all the places named in the story, I commissioned a map by illustrator, Bob Marshall, who did a wonderful job at helping my readers get a feel for where the story will take them.

The Clan Donald clan badge is used with the gracious permission of Clan Donald's High Commissioner, Bill McDaniel.

As always, I must thank my splendid beta readers who help me get things right. These include Dr. Chari Wessel for all things to do with ships, even longships, and Liette Bougie, one of my readers who lives in Montreal and speaks French as well as English.

SCOTLAND AND THE
KINGDOMS OF THE ISLES

CHARACTERS OF NOTE

Somerled MacGillebride, Lord of Argyll, Kintyre and Lorne
Ragnhild Olafsdottir, Princess of Man
Olaf the Red, King of Man and the Isles, Ragnhild's father
Domnall, cousin to Somerled
Angus MacGillebride, Somerled's brother
Affraic, daughter of Fergus, Lord of Galloway, and wife to Olaf the Red
Rognvald Kali Kolsson, Earl of Orkney
Abbot Bernard, a Savignac priest and Abbot of Rushen Abbey
Sweyn "the Skullcrusher" Asleifsson
Maurice MacNeill, foster brother of King Olaf
Ruairi MacInnes, one of Somerled's galley captains
Liadan MacGilleain of Islay, Somerled's self-appointed guard
Cicely, Ragnhild's handmaiden
David I, King of Scots
Hugh de Morville, Deputy Constable of Scotland, and his wife, Beatrice
de Beauchamp
Goubert d'Harcourt and Aubri de Mares, French stonemasons
Duncan MacEachern, blacksmith on Islay
Fergus, Lord of Galloway and his wife, Elizabeth
Edward Siwardsson, Lord High Constable of Scotland

Somerled's parentage was noble, of the Kings of Dublin, the royal house of Argyll and the great *Ard Ri*, the High Kings of Ireland. But when the Norse invaded Argyll and the Isles, his family's fortunes fell with those of his people. When all hope seemed lost, he rose from the mists of Morvern to rally the Gaels, the Scots and the Irish.

Sweeping across Argyll and the Isles like a fast-moving storm, brilliant in strategy and fearless in battle, Somerled began retaking his ancestral lands, driving away the invaders and freeing the people from the Norse stranglehold. In doing so, he would win the title *Somerle Mor*, Somerled the Mighty, Lord of Argyll, Kintyre and Lorne and, eventually, Lord of the Isles.

This is the unforgettable saga of his path to victory that forged the Kingdom of the Isles and won him the heart of a Norse king's daughter.

It is no joy without Clan Donald,
It is no strength to be without them;
The best clan in the world;
To them belongs every goodly man.

The noblest clan ever born,
Who personified prowess and awesomeness;
A people to whom tyrants made submission;
They had great wisdom and piety.

A brave, kind, mighty clan,
The hottest clan in the face of battle,
The most gentle clan among women
And most valorous in war.

A clan who did not make war on the church;
They feared being dispraised.
Learning was commanded
And in the rear were
Service and honor and self-respect.

A clan without arrogance, without injustice,
Who seized naught save the spoils of war;
Whose nobles were men of spirit,
And whose common men were most steadfast.

~ From the poem by Giolla Coluim mac an Ollaimh, 1493

CHAPTER 1

Off the coast of the Isle of Man, summer 1135 A.D.

FROM THE DECK OF HIS GALLEY, rocking gently in the waters off the coast of Man, Somerled let his gaze stretch out across the azure sea to the green hills that sloped to the shore. He had paused in his voyage from Dublin back to Morvern in Argyll to give the crew a respite from the oars.

The sun-warmed grass of early summer blanketed the land like green velvet, beckoning to him. On the cliffs some distance away, a colony of cream-colored gannets with their black-tipped wings made raucous, throaty noises. Taking to the air, their cries became quieter as they flew to great heights and then plunged into the waters of the Irish Sea, catching fish.

Glancing behind him, he saw his men lazing at the oars. Their conversations faded into the background as he turned back to the green isle to consider the one who reigned there as king.

Somerled had never met Olaf the Red but he had heard much about him.

Olaf Godredsson was an unusual Norseman, the younger son of the

1

King of Dublin, who had succeeded to a throne initially meant for his eldest brother. For his protection, Olaf had been raised in the court of King Henry I of England. Known for his skill in diplomacy, Olaf's many alliances had kept him in power and his kingdom at peace for decades.

Somerled was jarred from his musings by the sight of a white horse galloping across the sloping green hills. On the back of the magnificent palfrey, her hands entwined in the horse's mane, rode a girl with long red hair. The horse's mane and tail whipped about in the wind as he drove on, his mistress' dark blue mantle flying out behind her.

She did not seem to notice the galley resting just offshore as she sped north.

If the fire in her eyes matched her wild abandon and her command of the horse, she would be a woman to covet.

Who might she be?

"Best keep your eyes in your head," said his cousin, Domnall. "That one is not for you."

"She rides like she owns the isle," he said, tying his long hair at his nape to keep the wind from blowing it about his face.

Domnall chuckled. "Aye, she might as well. She's Ragnhild Olafsdottir. The king's *only* daughter."

Watching her, Somerled recalled what he had heard about the daughter of the King of Man. Men spoke of her beauty, wisdom and intelligence, valued by her father no matter she was young and female. Around the night fires, they speculated on the man to whom Olaf would give such a prize.

"She looks to be sixteen or seventeen summers," Somerled muttered.

"Aye, thereabouts."

Without turning from the vision, he said, "Doubtless she will be bartered for lands and wealth—or peace with the Norse or even the Irish." Such was the way of things.

"Aye, and a man must have all those in hand to offer for her."

Somerled could offer nothing, having lost his lands and his family's title to the Norse pirates who had long pillaged the shores of Argyll and the Western Isles, forcing the Gaels into slavery or worse. Even his father had fallen to a Norseman's axe in an attempt to retake what was theirs. Somerled and his brother, Angus, had fought fiercely at Gillebride's side, their faces splashed with the blood of their enemies, but to no avail.

When the girl was gone from sight, Somerled heaved a sigh and turned toward his men, shouting the order that would take them north into the Irish Sea.

"*FLJÚGA!*" RAGNHILD HISSED in Fairhair's ears, urging him on. His hooves pounded the earth as she bent low over his neck, her fists clenched in his mane. It felt good to ride with the wind, as if in fleeing Castle Rushen she could flee the fate her father hinted he would inflict upon her.

She would not wed Rognvald Kolsson, the Norse warlord who was Earl of Orkney—a man she knew to be a murderer. Having tried to wrest control of the islands from Earl Paul, his second cousin, he had attempted to lure the people of Orkney to his cause with a promise to build a great cathedral. Yet behind the scenes, he had Earl Paul kidnapped and spirited away from Orkney, never to be seen again.

Ragnhild remembered the lustful glances the earl directed at her last eve while he and his men dined in her father's great hall. The earl's leers sent chills down her spine. Doubtless he would embrace evil to accomplish his ambitions.

Rognvald looked at her as if she were yet another isle to conquer, another land to possess. Nay, she would not wed such a man, no matter her stepmother's plotting to be rid of her. If she were to marry at all, it would be a man like her father, clever and wise, a man who listened to her even if he did not always agree.

As she neared the rocky promontory above Niarbyl Bay, she reined in Fairhair and slid from his back, sending a hare running through the grass. Around her, summer's green was broken only by patches of amethyst-colored heather, brilliant in the sunlight.

She left Fairhair to nibble on the grass and, telling her racing heart to calm, took a deep breath and stared out to sea. In the distance, she spied a galley, half the size of her father's longships, its red sail unfurled to the wind. It was unusual for such a vessel to sail so close to their isle. She wondered at its purpose for only a moment before her thoughts turned back to the predicament that had troubled her for days.

Idly, she watched the gulls circling the bay, their harsh shrieks echoing her inner protests. At times like this, she missed the counsel of her mother. The pain of Ingibiorg's loss was still sharp. As the daughter of the powerful Earl Hakon, who had ruled Orkney before Ragnhild's birth, Ingibiorg grew up around fierce warlords appointed by the King of Norway. She would have known what to do.

In the years since her mother's death, Ragnhild had grown into womanhood surrounded mostly by her father's men and the castle's servants. It was only natural she should assume the role of Rushen's chatelaine, serving as hostess for her father. Organizing his household and entertaining his many allies pleased her, for his court drew important men who made for interesting conversations.

She had often accompanied her father on his voyages, sailing to the Hebrides, Ireland and Galloway.

She had no desire to leave. But she knew her stepmother wanted to be rid of her troublesome stepdaughter. Affraic was only a few years older than Ragnhild but not so pretty as Ragnhild's mother had been. The queen was jealous of the respect and freedom Olaf bestowed upon his only daughter. Why, Ragnhild could not imagine. In truth, Affraic wanted little to do with the duties of running the castle that Ragnhild embraced.

But she knew her father's thinking. An alliance with Orkney's earl, particularly Rognvald, who was closely aligned with the King of Norway, would assure there would be no interference by the Norse in the affairs of Man and the Isles.

Fairhair nudged her shoulder, nickering.

"What am I to do?" she asked, turning to gaze into his obsidian eyes. "My father's wife would have me gone, and now that she has given birth to a male child, Father will not gainsay her." The look in Fairhair's eyes seemed to convey sympathy, or mayhap it was pity.

Feeling the sun's warmth on her back, Ragnhild brushed her fingers over the soft skin of Fairhair's muzzle. "For certes, she is behind this unseemly match that would send me far from the shores of Man." Using a rock as a step, she lifted herself onto the horse's back, knowing she must return. "Had I not promised Father I would oversee tonight's feast for the earl and his men, I would ride the twenty miles to the other end of Man and never return."

On the bank of the river Gear Abhain, Loch Aline, Morvern, later that summer

SOMERLED EYED the large salmon just beneath the surface of the river Gear Abhain at the headwaters of Loch Aline. Its silver scales glistened in the pale afternoon light as it neared the surface of the dark waters, tempting him mercilessly.

The elusive creature had managed to avoid his spear these past many days, but he was determined to have it for dinner this night.

"Should I bring forth the remnants of last night's meal?" asked Domnall with a raised brow and sarcastic tone as he stepped toward the riverbank.

"Nay, I shall have the great beast this day or die trying." Somerled and his men had returned to Morvern where he lived simply in a cave near Loch Aline. After the battle that had robbed him of his father and so many of his clan, Somerled had not sought to return to Ireland. There, the son his wife had borne him before her childbed death, lived with his mother.

The boy was too young to follow a warrior, even a defeated one.

At the moment, Somerled had no other ambition save to catch this elusive fish.

Just as he was about to thrust his spear into the suddenly still salmon, the sound of heavy footfalls coming through the brush brought his head up and his spear to the fore.

"There you are!" said his brother. Angus resembled Somerled, save he was younger and his hair was a dark gold, his short beard brown, and his eyes a deeper blue.

Somerled lowered his spear.

Behind his brother stood a half-dozen MacInnes men with whom Angus had been sojourning, their clothing marking them Gaels. "We've news."

Somerled waded from the waters to greet the men and join his brother on the riverbank. "What is it?"

The somber look his brother gave him spoke of tragedy. The faces of the men with him confirmed Somerled's belief the tale they brought to him would not be welcomed.

When Angus spoke, his tone was solemn. "Our cousin, the Mac-Innes chief, has been slain by the Norse pirates raiding Argyll."

The news hit him like a blow and a heaviness settled into his chest. Another chieftain lost to the pirates. And this one had been not only his cousin but a good man, one respected by all.

A MacInnes man in trews and a saffron-colored linen shirt and wide leather belt, stepped forward. Somerled recognized Ruairi MacInnes with his long brown hair and short beard. "The tribes could not agree on which of their chiefs should lead us. A wise elder recalled that the MacInneses left the field of battle in good order, led by a young man valiant in the fight. He named you, Somerled, and that choice was acceptable to all. So, we have come to ask for your help to rid Morvern of the wretched Northmen once and for all."

"They remember your skill with a sword," explained Angus, "and your way with men. They will follow you as they might not another."

"Aye," said Ruairi. "We remembered that our chief's cousin lived, one who was raised in the old ways, untamed by the Norse tyranny— Somerled, son of Gillebride the Brave."

Somerled met the stern gazes of the MacInnes men and registered each nod, pleased to see the spirits of their fathers rising in them.

Finally.

He glanced back to the river where the big salmon swam unconcerned and recalled a story his Culdee priest once told him about a great general. "I put to you a challenge."

"Tell us," said a burly man behind Angus. "We will meet it."

"If you can catch the large salmon that has escaped my spear these past many days, I will consider your request." Like Naaman in the Bible, asked by God's prophet to do something he considered ridiculous to cure his leprosy, the MacInnes men grew angry, grumbling among themselves.

Somerled recalled that when Naaman finally succumbed to the pleading of a servant girl to do as the prophet asked and wash in the river Jordan seven times, he was cured. Mayhap if these prideful men, who thought this request beneath them, would agree, they might accept without question his orders to follow.

"That is hardly a challenge for a warrior!" growled a harsh-looking man, one whose face was red with anger.

"Yet the fish has eluded me," said Somerled with a wry smile. "Only best me at this task and I will look favorably upon your request that I should lead the clans against the Norse."

"Very well," said the one who had spurned the challenge. Raising his spear, he stepped into the dark waters up to his knees and waited. The men on the shore watched in silence as the salmon swam around before diving deep as if teasing them.

Then, suddenly, the salmon rose to the surface of the dark waters and the MacInnes warrior struck fast, his spear a blur. After some struggle by the powerful fish, with a broad smile, out of the water the MacInnes man pulled the largest salmon Somerled had ever seen—more than two feet in length. "A good omen," pronounced the MacInnes man.

"It seems God has favored your request," said Somerled. "Come, let us dine on the fish and discuss this cause of ours."

Angus let out a huge sigh as the men trudged back to Somerled's camp, startling a flock of crows that had settled into the branches above them. "I might have known you'd have them seek a sign, Brother."

Somerled laughed, batting away the midges that swarmed about his face. "Or, mayhap I am merely hungry for a salmon dinner."

CHAPTER 2

Castle Rushen, Isle of Man

RAGNHILD ALWAYS BELIEVED she was safe behind the stone walls of her father's castle but no longer. With her stepmother determined to be rid of her and Orkneymen lounging in her father's great hall, she felt on shaky ground. Seeking to avoid them, she occupied herself with directing the servants preparing the evening meal. Now summoned by her father, she could no longer avoid what the evening portended.

Quietly, she came through the door to the great hall and paused when she heard Earl Rognvald's deep voice reciting yet another of his tiresome poems.

In appearance, the earl made a vivid impression, for he took pains with his person. No fold of his tunic out of place, no hair of his chestnut head allowed to separate itself from the others to fly about his face. Arrogant and bold, his dark eyes gleamed as he spoke.

At nine skills I challenge—
A champion at chess:
Runes I rarely spoil,

I read books and write:
I'm skilled at skiing
And shooting and sculling
And more!—I've mastered
Music and verse.

To that, his kinsmen lifted their tankards and cheered, "Rognvald! Rognvald!"

Disturbed from their sleep where they lay by the hearth fire, the deerhounds that had been a gift to her father from the Lord of Galloway, raised their heads, suddenly alert.

Ragnhild silently uttered an oath and went to the hounds, whispering assurances to them as she stroked their narrow heads. 'Twas a truth that the Lord of Orkney liked to hear his own voice. His pride might be understandable for he was accomplished at many things, yet to recite his skills for all to hear made him appear the braggart.

He had accepted the Christian faith, as had the Norwegian king, and attended Mass these past several days at Rushen Abbey, but he still sought knowledge in the pagan runes, boasting of his power to read them. How could God honor such a man?

She was convinced Rognvald could not imagine anyone else as the Earl of Orkney save himself. Even murder had not been beneath him to gain the title the King of Norway wanted him to share with Earl Paul. He might not have done the deed himself. Though, if the rumors be true, Rognvald had a hand in it.

The earl and his Orkneymen had lingered on Man for nearly a week, taking advantage of her father's hospitality. She had not been privy to all of his conversations with her father so she could not discern his entire purpose. Mayhap they spoke of the alliance that had been in place since before Ragnhild's birth.

The King of Man and the Isles was favored by all, including the English, Irish and Scots. An alliance often involved a marriage between two families to make fast a bond. Her dowry would be a rich one and the Earl of Orkney would want sons. But if he thought to take her with him when his dragonships sailed north, he was mistaken. She had made her dislike of him known to her father. Surely Olaf would not force her to go.

Affraic, her father's wife, gowned in pale gray silk that did nothing for her black hair and colorless eyes, sidled up to Ragnhild. "You should draw near to Earl Rognvald and smile," Affraic whispered. "Your admiration would greatly encourage him."

The daughter of Fergus, Lord of Galloway, and one of King Henry's illegitimate daughters, Affraic considered herself above Ragnhild. The marriage of Affraic to Olaf made both men happy but it had changed Ragnhild's life.

"As I would fear," said Ragnhild with a frown, "which is why I'll not do it. The earl has enough admirers among his men. I would not become another."

At one end of the hall, a raised dais would welcome the royal family for dinner but, now, it was empty as her father and Earl Rognvald and his men sat at one of the trestle tables that stretched out before the raised platform.

Affraic's face twisted in a pained expression as she spat out, "You are the Princess of Man, Ragnhild! You have a duty to wed according to the king's will."

"Yet the king's will may change," said Ragnhild. It was her fervent hope.

"Too long you have run free," she hissed. "Marriage is honorable and expected but you will never find a husband harboring such an attitude."

"Mayhap not." Ragnhild raised a skeptical brow. "Did I say I wanted one?"

"Ah, Princess!" The Earl of Orkney, having spotted her, interrupted his recitation. "Come here and I will favor you with a poem. An ode to your beauty."

With a groan, Ragnhild stepped out of the shadows. Did he think she was vain? She wanted to ask but, instead, to honor her father, she dipped her head and said, "You are too kind, my lord." She came forward and took refuge at her father's side where he sat enjoying his ale at the end of the table.

Rognvald began another poem, his intense dark eyes never leaving her. His voice faded as she shifted her gaze to the men of Orkney sitting around him held in rapt attention. They were all mail-clad warriors, long-haired and bearded, battle ready with swords and great gleaming axes hanging from their belts. Had they been the ones to murder Earl Paul? Had they pillaged as they sailed south, leaving cottages burning in Argyll and the Isles? One named Sweyn, when drinking deeply, had boasted of his battles and the women who satisfied his lust.

Rognvald's booming voice drew her attention to where he stood. Not as tall as some of his men but well-proportioned and strong-limbed, his chestnut hair fell in waves to his shoulders. Even before his arrival she had heard he was a man who gave great attention to his person and his clothing.

In her father's great hall, where the rushes were herb-scented and always fresh, where tapestries hung on the stone walls that spoke of the Kings of Man, Earl Rognvald wore his finery, bright with color and the fabrics rich. His mantles of fine woolens were clasped with gold brooches carved with Norse symbols. She suspected that was not what he wore beneath his mail when he engaged in battle, which, by all accounts, had been often.

She knew from her mother that Orkney's history was one of petty grievances, feuds and warring factions. The stories often involved betrayal and murder, of cousins, friends, even brothers. She wanted no part of it.

OLAF PATTED his daughter's hand as her fingers rested on his shoulder as she sighed beneath the weight of Rognvald's many words. The tension she conveyed in her touch was uncharacteristic of his fearless, spirited daughter. Mayhap it was the grin the earl gave her as he spoke of her beauty, one that hinted of possession and nights under the furs. Olaf could see the earl was pleased with the possibility of having her to wife. Any man would be. The flame-haired Princess of Man had grown into an emerald-eyed enchantress, beautiful and keenly intelligent, but one who was slow to accept another's will, even Olaf's own.

Still, he needed this alliance.

The Norse sea-raiders gave little heed to anything save their own pleasure and lust for wealth. Word had reached Olaf of their pillaging, raping and burning as they sailed south, coming ever closer to Man where great treasure lay. Olaf took comfort in his warriors and his many longships resting in the harbor but he feared a stealthy attack. A great force of Norse could overpower his men.

His marriage to Ingibiorg, Ragnhild's mother, had brought peace for many years as the Earls of Orkney kept the villains at bay, but would this new earl observe the old alliance? Earl Paul, who had ruled Orkney before Rognvald, had been a man like Olaf, one who preferred peace to war, one who was loved by his people. Alas, he was gone, replaced by this capable, though pompous Norseman whose axe, dagger and sword spoke of battle. Could Olaf give his beloved daughter to such a one? Did he have a choice?

THE NEXT MORNING, Ragnhild lengthened her stride as she hurried toward the abbey her father had built several years before. She had to speak to Abbot Bernard, her confessor, counselor and closest friend. Not even her handmaiden, Cecily, was privy to the secrets she shared with the priest. When the Savignac abbot first came to the Isle of Man, she could speak Irish, Norse and English, but he had taught her to write as well. They had shared many hours by the fire as he read to her from ancient manuscripts and spoke about God, encouraging her to trust her future to the Master of the Heavens.

The priest met her at the door of the wooden abbey, wearing the gray robe of the Savignacs that was nearly the color of his tonsured hair and short beard. "What is it, child? You seem greatly disturbed."

"Indeed, I am," she confirmed. "Do you know who my father has been entertaining at the castle this past sennight?"

"'Tis known the Earl of Orkney visits the island."

"Not just a visit. I think my father means to make a match between us! I cannot bear the thought of being wedded to a man so full of his own conceit."

"Yet you are both Norse."

She averted her gaze. "We are not the same. You know as well as I the King of Norway has little to say in the affairs of Man. Some of the Norse still hold to their pagan traditions while my father is a man of reason and learning, a man of God, closer to King Henry than Norway's king."

"Yea, 'tis true," Abbot Bernard said, nodding. "We are ever in King Olaf's debt for the land on which the abbey stands and the timber he gave us to build. And now he encourages us to build anew in stone and grants us more land."

"I would dread having to leave my father to marry a man tied to Norway. I have no wish to live far away on those dreary islands with their harsh cliffs surrounded by sea. And I refuse to marry a murderer."

The abbot's forehead furrowed as if he were unaware of the rumors that had dogged Earl Rognvald. Surely the priest had heard of Earl Paul's demise.

"Come, child, let us share some ale and we will speak more of it."

As well as raising cattle and growing herbs and vegetables, the monks of the abbey produced excellent ale. Ragnhild was not averse to raising a goblet with her dear friend. "Very well," she said, following him inside. "I am in sore need of your advice."

In the monks' dining hall, Abbot Bernard called for ale and, soon, Ragnhild was sipping the warm golden liquid and pouring out her heart.

His goblet held between his sure and steady hands, the priest stared into his ale. "It is common for lords to barter their daughters for alliances, Princess."

Wishing he would raise his kind brown eyes to her where she hoped to see sympathy, she asked, "Is the situation so dire that King Olaf needs this alliance?"

"Aye, there is a need," he said raising his head. "The Norse pirates are ranging farther south. Earl Rognvald could stop them if he chose." Meeting her gaze, he said, "If it is you the earl desires, mayhap the sea-raiders serve his purpose to pressure your father into meeting his demand for your hand."

"Oh." She sat back, twisting her goblet in her hands, her fingers running over the raised carving. "I had not thought of that." Nothing would bring her father to the negotiating table sooner than if his kingdom and the people of Man were threatened. "But what of his alliances with King Henry and King David, not to mention Lord Fergus of Galloway? Are they not protection enough?"

"They have served King Olaf well these many years. Like your father, David was raised in Henry's court, a hostage really. Yet now Henry and David squabble over Cumbria. Their eyes are diverted from what is happening in the west. If there were another way to keep the Norse pirates from our shores, it is possible your father might delay an alliance with Earl Rognvald."

"*Is* there another way?" she asked, looking into his wise face with anxious eyes.

He nodded sagely. "Aye, there might be. News spreads of a strong warrior driving the Norse menace from the shores of Argyll."

Her heart raced to think of such a possibility. She looked at the abbot with hope in her eyes.

He rested his hand on hers. "Worry not. I will speak to the king."

CHAPTER 3

The Village of Drimnin, Morvern, Argyll, late summer 1136 A.D.

SOMERLED SMELLED THE SMOKE before he reached the village.

A small community nestled around a crescent bay on the western shore of Morvern, everyone who lived in Drimnin was related either by blood or marriage. In the past, the villagers had made a good life raising cattle and reaping the bounty of the sea. Somerled had passed this way only once, and then he had approached from the Sound of Mull in his galley. He remembered the villagers' humble but generous hospitality.

Today, he and his men had traveled on foot along the coast, wending their way through the pine woods in search of the Norse rumored to be raiding the shores of Morvern, hoping to catch them before they could strike. His ships were still too few to take them on the water.

He stepped out of the trees, lush with ferns at their base, his hand on his sword hilt, prepared to fight.

A ghastly sight met his eyes, sickening his stomach.

Too late.

Bodies were sprawled upon the grass between the shore and the woods, struck down while trying to flee. Dreadful wounds revealed some had fallen to axes.

Acrid smoke rose from the cottages still burning, the flames leaping from the dry thatched roofs. He could see no longships pulled up on shore but the raiders could not have been gone long.

Aghast at what he saw, he was suddenly aware there were no birds to be heard, save the hooded crows pecking at the blood-soaked bodies. "See if any live," he said to Domnall and started forward.

"Aye," said his cousin and swung his arm in silent command, pointing to the fallen. The men hastened to obey.

Both old and young had been killed by the merciless Norse. Seeing the women who had been violated, Somerled ground his teeth. Their tunics had been ripped from their bruised bodies before they were killed. "Cover them," he said to one of his men. "Cover them all with whatever you can." The men closest to him hurried to accomplish the task.

He walked through the village, assessing the carnage. The doors of the burning cottages stood open. Goods, taken in haste, had been discarded like so much rubbish. So, too, had the Norse raiders considered the lives of the people. He knew they would see judgment in the next life but Somerled wanted justice in this life. He did not hate the Norse. How could he when his mother was one of them? But these were lesser men, ruthless pirates, some ostracized from their own people to prey on others.

When his men returned with reports that none lived, Somerled faced the woods and, in Gaelic, said in a gentle voice, "If you live, come to us or make a sound. We will help you."

A moment passed and then two boys staggered out of the woods, their fearful expressions and tear-stained cheeks bearing witness to what they had seen. From the look of them, they were brothers, close in age, both with dark brown hair and wide eyes. To them, Somerled's height and sun-gilded fair hair would mark him more Norse than Gael.

Kneeling before them, he said, "I am Somerled, a man of Argyll, and these are my men. You will be safe with us." When he saw relief on their faces, he said, "We will return to bury the dead but now we must go in haste to exact vengeance on those who did this. Do you come with us?"

The boys shared a glance and the older one nodded. "We will come." Somerled gave them into the care of a MacInnes man who stepped forward and offered to raise the boys with his own children.

As they started to go, the older one turned and said, "They took our sister and another girl." It was clear from the boy's haunted eyes he had an idea of the girls' fate. Likely he had already witnessed the rape of the village women, including his own mother.

Somerled's eyes narrowed as his heart hardened within his chest. "We will see them avenged."

A short way down the coast, one of Somerled's men scouting ahead had spotted dragonships offshore.

They approached the top of the rise and Somerled signaled his men to stay low. Yellow wildflowers bloomed where he crouched behind a boulder to observe the Norse longships.

He counted five, three just pulling up at the water's edge, their sails doused, their dragon-carved stems boding ill for the people who lived farther down the coast. Counting shields, they numbered more than two hundred.

The sea was calm, as if nature herself was unaware a massacre had just taken place to the north. Somerled's heart burned within him, a furnace of rage. He wanted the waters to roar, to cry for vengeance on the heathen dogs.

Behind him were the forests in which he had hunted. Gathered around him was his group of one hundred men, MacInneses from Morvern, archers from Argyll and Irish mercenaries from Antrim, who had heard of his plan to retake Argyll and joined the cause. They were stout-hearted men yet still too few to take on so many Norsemen armed with swords, axes and spears, many clad in mail and conical helms.

The Highlanders and Islesmen wore tunics of linen or wool over tight-fitting trews or hosen, their tunics secured at their waists with belts. Their feet were clad in soft leather boots. Around their shoulders, some wore woolen mantles. A few, like Somerled and his brother, wore leather armor. None wore mail. It was costly and rare in these parts. All carried weapons but not all had steel swords at their waists.

No matter the odds against them, Somerled wanted those ships and he wanted justice for the lives cut short at Drimnin.

On either side of him, Angus and Domnall drew close. "What can we do against so many?" inquired Angus, staring at the dragonships.

Somerled considered what to do as he watched the raiders unloading from the dragonships to swarm on the beach like flies. Shorebirds circled above, diving for discarded scraps as the raiders paused to eat. Likely they intended to sort what they had gained in the raid before taking the next village.

"We must make them believe they face a great force," said Somerled. "When they are scattered and running, we will attack, more ruthless than they."

"And how might we do that?" asked Domnall. Somerled knew his cousin did not ask because he doubted it could be done; he only wanted to know how Somerled would do it. His men had learned from the battles won thus far to trust him. His methods might be unusual but, against so many Norse, he had to be clever. Always outnumbered, they had gained the three longships they had now by stealth, not greater numbers. In such a manner, he had stalked the wild boar and the deer in the woods of Morvern. Now he stalked the Norse pirates.

Over his shoulder, he sighted a herd of black long-haired cattle grazing nearby, as yet undisturbed by the Norsemen on the beach below. An idea came to him.

"Take the men and kill enough cows for hides to cover all the warriors except the archers. Be careful not to make noise to cause the raiders to look up. Bring the hides to me and I will tell you what shall be done."

Somerled was a man content with silence, broken only by the sounds of God's woodland creatures and the conversation of a good friend. But he had been their choice of leader and that required voice.

His men returned with the hides, and he told them, "First, you will move around the hill, allowing yourselves to be seen wearing whatever you have on. Then, wearing the skins, the long hair side out, you will march around the hill again. When that is done, turn the hides inside out and march across the hill one last time."

His captains hesitated only a moment before nodding and moving to carry out his order.

From the top of the rise, he watched the Norse. Of the raiders who had already landed, one shouted, pointing up the hill, drawing attention to Somerled's men repeatedly circling. Since the two ships still in the water had not come ashore and of the three that had, only two had fully disgorged their raiders onto the beach, he knew the Norse were rethinking their intended course of action. To them, Somerled's men would appear as three well-armed divisions of warriors.

When his men had completed the last round, Somerled rose and with the sound of shuddering steel, slid his sword from its scabbard and held it high. Gripping his shield tightly in his other hand, he shouted in Gaelic. "Be of good courage, men. Remember your loved ones the Norse have taken from you and those they have slain this day. This is our land we fight for! Our lives we defend!" Then, roaring out his war cry, he leaped from the top of the hill and rushed like a fast-moving gale down to the beach.

A screaming tempest of deadly blades and spears followed in his wake, his men shouting the revenge they would claim that day, the justice they would dispense. In his mind, Somerled saw the faces of the fathers, mothers and children lying dead at Drimnin and the boys whose parents were lost to them forever.

From the rise above, his fifteen archers loosed their arrows, following his orders to pick off the leaders and strongest of the pirates.

With shock still on their faces, the Norse raiders fell dead on the beach.

Somerled slashed his way through shield and skin, ripping wildly into the raiding party, delivering death to the first to face him.

He fought for his slain father and the fallen MacInnes chief; he fought to restore his family's ancestral lands; he fought for the people of Argyll, long subdued under the Norsemen's blades; he fought for the village of Drimnin. And, in the remotest part of his mind, he fought for a red-haired vixen he would never know unless he proved himself worthy against the Norse menace.

Using the edge of his shield, Somerled dashed out a Norseman's teeth and with the might of a madman, he laid low the warrior whose glazed eyes spoke of his death. Then, in front of the enemy fleet and his own men, he tossed aside his sword and shield and yanked his dagger from his waist. With a great show, he carved the dead Norseman's heart from his chest and flung it toward the enemy ships, shouting in Norse, "And so will be all of you if you darken these shores again!"

At his order, his men did the same to the pirates they had killed, flinging their foes' hearts at the floating longships. So wildly did Somerled's grim gift enthrall his warriors, they tore into the raiders with strength beyond their own, bathed in their enemy's blood.

Seeing the hearts of their companions torn from their chests, the Norse raiders who were left standing fled the beach for their ships. Many drowned in their mail coats. Three of the five dragonships made it away from that crimson shore. The rest had not enough crew for the oars and fell under the fury of Somerled and his men.

The Norse warlord who led the pirates stood on the main longship, his hands fisted on his hips. His long sun bleached hair hung in greasy strands, a woven band holding them from his eyes. His face reflected his great anger. On his chest shimmered a large piece of gold jewelry, catching the sun. No matter his harsh demeanor, as the Norseman watched the ruin of his landing party, he must have decided discretion was the wiser choice. He shouted an order in Norse to his warriors to row for the open sea.

Somerled heaved a sigh of relief as the Norse in the remaining longships pulled at the oars with all their might. As they set out to sea, the war song of Somerled and his warriors called to them from the blood-soaked beach.

Angus, wiping the blood from his face, came up to Somerled. "What made you think to rip out their hearts?"

Somerled liked not the grisly gesture but it had been necessary. "They are no Christians. As pagans, they had to believe we were more vicious than they, else they would not have fled as they were more than twice our number."

"The show worked," said Angus, shifting his gaze to the blood running from Somerled's upper arm. "You are wounded, Brother."

Only then did Somerled feel the pain of his wound. "'Tis nothing. Scratches from the pirates; they did not stop me."

Somerled gave his brother a wide smile as he wiped the blood from his face. He had successfully fought back the Norse raiders who had, with greater numbers, defeated his father and killed the MacInnes chief.

He and his men had dispensed justice for Drimnin and added two longships to their growing fleet.

He felt as if destiny had taken him by the hand and was leading him forward.

"Lord," one man said approaching Somerled, "should we roast the dead cattle for the evening meal?"

Surprised at the manner of address, he nodded, "Aye, the men will be hungry. Put the beasts to good purpose, and the men not needed for that task shall return with me to Drimnin to bury the dead." The man and his companions raced up the hill, eager for the meat they would dine on this night. They had not eaten so well in some time.

Somerled and Angus walked among their warriors still on the beach. Only a few of his men had been badly wounded and they were being tended by ones who had a talent for healing. Another half dozen sported wounds that were slight in nature.

"We found the girls," said Domnall coming toward him with two young women in tow, their faces still showing fright but also relief at being rescued. "They were tied in the bow of one of the ships left behind."

Down the hill ran the two boys from Drimnin, shouting their joy. "Deidre!"

The girl, who had the same dark coloring as her brothers, opened her arms and swept the two lads into her embrace. "Thank God you live, little brothers," said Deidre, hugging them tightly. Tears streamed down her cheeks. "I thought never to see you again."

The other girl smiled at the scene before her, but Somerled saw only despair and sadness in her eyes. Did she have a sister or brother lost to the raiders' axes? Likely so. "There are no others?" she asked hopefully.

The older boy shook his head balefully. "Nay, Lucia, only us."

Her expression was pained and her body rigid as if she were making a great effort not to give in to hysteria. When her tears flowed freely and she looked to collapse, the other girl bore her up.

The bittersweet reunion caused Somerled to shake his head in sorrow. "I am sorry we did not arrive sooner."

"You did what you could," said Deidre. Then casting a glance at the blood-soaked bodies on the beach, she said, "You avenged our kin."

"Know this," said Somerled, "you will all have a home with the MacInneses. Good men and their wives."

As the Drimnin youth slowly climbed up the hill, leaving the dead Norse to be piled up and burned by his men, Somerled continued his walk among his warriors still on the beach. On the faces of all were smiles like he had never seen before, the smiles of free men. They had not fought for the kings of Ireland, Scotland or England. They were Highlanders and Islesmen who had fought for their people and the lochs, glens and bens that held their hearts.

His heart swelled in his chest.

They had wanted Somerled to lead them and so he would, not just to free them from the Norse, but to secure for them a kingdom independent of the foreign powers surrounding them. A place where their children and their children's children could thrive.

To his men who were not among the wounded, he said, "We will wash the blood of the defeated from us and then go to Drimnin to bury the slain." A large group broke off from the others and, once they had washed in the waters of the sound, followed him up the coast to see to the somber task.

When the deed was accomplished, he and Domnall led the men south, back to the top of the rise.

As they approached, Somerled's mouth watered at the smell of the cattle being roasted. He had not eaten all day save for the stale bread and smoked fish he'd had that morning. "I am reminded that I must pay the farmer for his cattle. I would not take from our own."

"Aye, Somerled, I will see it done," said Domnall. With a grin, he added, "In addition to the girls, we found gold beneath the boards in the two longships we recovered."

"See if the MacInnes man who took the boys will take the girls. Whoever agrees to raise the Drimnin children should receive some of the gold."

Domnall nodded and went about the task.

When the meat was cooked, Somerled, his cousin and brother sat with him in front of the blazing fire and feasted on thick slices of roast beef.

"The men are calling you the Thane of Argyll," said his brother.

"You have earned the title and, by rights as our father's eldest son, it should be yours."

Somerled wiped the meat's juice from his mouth. That the men had called him "thane" pleased him but there was yet more to reclaim before he would feel comfortable with the title "Lord".

His mouth hitched up as he considered his younger brother. "If I be the Thane of Argyll, then you are surely now Chief of the MacInnes."

Angus smiled sheepishly. "The men have spoken of it."

"Good." Somerled gazed across the Sound of Mull as the sun drifted low in the sky turning a blood red, the ominous hue reflected in the glistening waters of the sound. He hoped it would keep the superstitious Norse from their shores. "Tomorrow, we retrieve our other ships and go to Mull where the rogue Norse still prey upon our people." And then with a smile, he added, "We have need of more of the enemy's longships for our many warriors."

Domnall slapped him on the back. "Aye, Cousin, more ships!"

Somerled now had five longships and two galleys. Enough for his men but, if they were to reclaim all that the Norse had taken from them, they must fight more battles where they would gain more ships. Ships that could defeat the Norse dragonships.

In the back of his mind, he had a thought to build a fleet of galleys and an idea about how to make them turn more quickly. "I've an idea to replace the steering board on the right side of the ships we have with a moveable stern rudder. 'Twould render them more maneuverable. In a close sea battle, our galleys would be faster."

"Aye," said his brother, "'tis a worthy idea."

"It has not been done before," said Domnall, "but I can see how it might work as you conceive."

Sipping ale from his goatskin, Somerled sat back and stared into the fire, seeing the future as he imagined it. Around him, his men ate and drank, speaking in low voices.

His thoughts on the day were mixed. They had not been able to spare Drimnin but they had rescued a remnant and obtained justice for the others. One by one, he would retake the coastal lands and the isles of his forefathers. As the people were being freed of the Norse yoke, he would turn his attention to the isle that had never left his mind—the Isle of Man.

CHAPTER 4

Castle Rushen, Isle of Man, autumn 1137 A.D.

BOISTEROUS CONVERSATION erupted in Olaf's ears. His chieftains
and their wives and his full contingent of warriors packed the hall and
filled the trestles. There were a few guests as well, visitors from Orkney
sent by Earl Rognvald to assure Olaf of the earl's continued interest in
an alliance and his daughter's hand.

Torches flamed in sconces set into the stone walls and candles
burned on the trestles and high table, giving the great hall a warm glow.
The fire flickering in the hearth added heat to the large space though
Olaf suspected it would not be a terribly cold night.

Spirits were high and lighthearted frivolity prevailed as the farmers
congratulated themselves on producing a great crop of barley, oats and
rye. The monks had brought a goodly supply of ale to make hearts
merry and roasted meat from the island's cattle filled hungry bellies.

Minstrels added to the pleasant evening with their flute, lyre and
wooden lurs. Olaf had enjoyed the music in King Henry's court and had
insisted they have similar bards and minstrels at his court on Man.

With his wife on one side, his daughter on the other and Godred, his young heir, asleep above stairs, Olaf was content, at war with no one, save possibly the Norse renegades that preyed on Skye and the Northern Isles under his lordship.

Olaf inclined his head to get a better look at Abbot Bernard, sitting on the other side of the princess. The priest had come at Olaf's invitation to share in the celebration. It made his daughter happy to include him and the man of God was well liked and generally good company.

More than a year ago, Olaf bid Godspeed to Earl Rognvald as he departed, telling him to return the following spring if he was still of a mind to have the princess as his bride. The earl's absence since then had lifted Ragnhild's spirits. Though his wife, Affraic, would have it otherwise, Olaf was in no hurry to marry off his daughter, more especially after Abbot Bernard had told him the Norse pirates were in retreat. Perhaps he might not need the earl's strength to keep the raiders at bay.

When spring came and flowers bloomed across the isle, a messenger arrived from Orkney with Rognvald's missive telling Olaf that he had not lost interest in the princess but the affairs of Orkney would keep him occupied for some time. Olaf smiled to himself. After all, Earl Rognvald had to make good on that promise he'd made to the people of Orkney to erect a great cathedral. His delay in returning to Man was not inopportune.

Ragnhild was an intelligent voice among his advisors, one he did not want to lose. None could argue with the way she kept his household, nor the tapestries she and her late mother had made that graced his hall. More than Affraic, Ragnhild was a gracious hostess to his guests. The queen was content to let the princess manage the servants and attend their guests. As he thought about it, he sighed. One day, he would have to let Ragnhild go yet it did not have to be soon.

"Abbot Bernard," Olaf said, leaning across his daughter to address the priest, "Did you send the message to your fellow priest on Lismore asking about that Gael? The one you told me was chasing away the Norse raiders from the coast and the Isles?"

"I did, Sire. Somerled is the Gael's name and, at your direction, he now has your invitation to come to Man."

"*Sumarliðr*," said Olaf, letting the sound roll off his tongue. "A Norse name."

"He is rumored to have a Norse mother," the priest continued, "but he fights for the Gaels in Argyll as one of them."

"A Norse-Gael?" Olaf asked. He should not be surprised. There were many pairings of Norse and Gaels as the Norse settled in Ireland and the Hebrides. His own ancestors had been some of those.

The abbot nodded. "'Tis said he is wily and bold, a leader of men. And his fame spreads with the number of dragonships he has acquired from the Norse pirates he has vanquished."

Olaf sat back in his chair, twisting his silver chalice in his hand, the rubies flashing red in the candlelight. He considered the abbot's news. He had never been one to encourage close ties to Norway, though he paid King Magnus homage. He preferred his alliances with England, Galloway and Scotland. They were closer and stronger. In precarious times, they had assured none would threaten his rule. Still, there was this Norse pirate menace to deal with. It might be wise to make an ally of this Somerled. "Will he come, do you suppose?" He was curious to meet this warrior who had risen from nothing to be the talk of the night fires and the chatter of priests.

The abbot returned him a knowing smile. "He will come, Sire. How could he refuse an invitation from the powerful King of Man?"

RAGNHILD TRIED NOT TO LOOK at the men in her father's hall who had come from Orkney but she felt their eyes upon her all the same. Sweyn Asleifsson had been among those accompanying Earl Rognvald when he came before and she had not liked him then. One of the guards told her Sweyn's companion called him "the Skullcrusher", a name that, while fitting, made her shiver to think of it. From his belt hung a wicked-looking axe he sharpened each day.

His companion, Holdbodi Hundasson, was like him. Both were only a few years more than a score of summers in age, and yet already they displayed a great talent for drunkenness, consuming much ale from their drinking horns deep into the night. She had listened from the shadows on the circular staircase and learned of their adventures and plundering.

They made free with her father's female servants and, more than once, the castle guards had stepped in to prevent the Orkneymen from taking advantage of a frightened girl.

Sweyn had the harsher mien. Like the other men in her father's hall, he wore a beard and whiskers on his upper lip. Yet the lines in his face were deep for his age and the haunted look in his pale eyes seemed to bear witness of evil deeds. His tunic was fine enough, speaking of wealth. On his chest, he proudly displayed a large gold Thor's hammer, a pagan symbol, yet he served a Christian lord, who, she was reminded, bragged about his skill at casting runes. Worse still, the bold leers Sweyn gave her made her skin crawl. It was as if he were undressing her with his eyes.

Both Sweyn and Holdbodi had the look of pirates, their lank brown hair bleached from the sun hanging in long tendrils. Their eyes were lustful and acquisitive. She wondered how their master, so meticulous with his person, tolerated such a slovenly appearance in his warriors.

She had not liked the vain Earl of Orkney but she liked even less these men who purported to speak for him. She only hoped, having conveyed their master's message of his delay, they would soon be gone.

STANDING IN THE PROW of his longship, Somerled watched the Isle of Man grow larger as they sailed nearer to the coast. All around him, the setting sun had turned the sky the color of orpiment, the flame-colored mineral whose poison archers used to render their arrow tips deadly. Where the sun met the sea, the bright color faded like dying embers.

The ship he sailed was one he had captured from the Norse raiders that had attacked the Isle of Mull, now refitted with a hinged stern rudder and plain stem posts. Larger than his fast-moving galleys that carried sixteen oars and thirty men, the twenty-bench longship carried forty or more.

Word had spread of the successful uprising he was leading in Argyll and the Southern Isles, causing men to flock to him in great numbers. Some had lost all to the Norse and cried for vengeance while others wanted to be a part of what had begun in Morvern. Somerled was pleased to see the spirits of the villagers rise with their victories.

He now had more than thirty longships and galleys under his command and, with each battle fought and won, he gained more. With them, he had taken back much of Argyll, including Kintyre and Lorne, and the people now addressed him as "Lord".

"Are we expected?" asked Angus, staring at the white limestone castle silhouetted against the salmon-colored evening sky.

"Aye and no," said Somerled, amused at the situation. "We are invited but I sent no message as to when we might call upon the king. Nevertheless, I assume we will be welcomed, particularly with Maurice at my side."

Maurice MacNeill, who joined Somerled after Morvern, had been a foster brother to King Olaf while he was still living in Dublin. Somerled hoped Maurice's presence would make the meeting go easier, a gathering of friends, not strangers.

As they entered the crescent harbor, the King of Man's longships closed in behind them, sealing off their exit. It was what Somerled would have done had he commanded Man's fleet. He had expected the move, hence he did not take offense. A dozen of his own longships remained on the coast just outside the harbor as a precaution should a fight ensue as he tried to leave. Invited guest or no, he would be prepared.

At the pebbled shore, they beached the three longships alongside a dragonship already there. The Norse warriors standing on the deck studied Somerled and his men in curious fashion, the unique rudders drawing their attention.

The round shields of Somerled's men carried different designs than those of the Norse and their clothing was Gaelic. Had they met on a distant shore a battle might have ensued but Somerled had come to visit the King of Man.

He turned to Domnall, now a senior captain in charge of ships and men. "Some of the men can bed down on the beach; the others should remain onboard." With a look toward the dragonship, beached nearby, he added, "I trust not the Norse, even invited ones."

Domnall nodded. "Aye, Lord."

Somerled, his brother, Angus, and Maurice headed toward the castle. Beneath Somerled's boots, the dry grass crackled with his footfalls.

The hillsides, once green with summer, now wore the rich brown mantle of autumn.

He and his companions scaled the small hill from the harbor to the wooden palisade that surrounded the tall stone fortress with its crenelated top and numerous arrow loops. The battlements were manned by warriors in helms and hauberks. King Olaf did not leave his peace to chance.

"It has been a long while since Olaf and I were foster brothers in Dublin," said Maurice, "yet, despite the years, I expect he will know me."

Somerled glanced at Maurice, judging him to be in his fourth decade, somewhere between his own age and the King of Man's. "I am hoping Olaf will be pleased by your presence and his welcome all the warmer for it."

"Aye, he will be glad to see me," said Maurice. "We were unruly lads together and said our goodbyes on good terms. I was younger and looked up to him. Which reminds me, best be prepared for his short height. 'Tis the reason he was dubbed 'Bitling' as a youth."

It was difficult for Somerled to think of such a powerful king as a man of small stature. The image he had conjured, particularly after seeing the Princess of Man, was quite different. "His lack of height does not seem to have impaired the respect he has garnered as a king among kings."

Maurice shook his head, the light from the setting sun making his face glow. "Nay, it has not, though he generally leaves the fighting to others. He was trained to use a sword, but he is no warrior. His strength lies in diplomacy."

They crossed the bridge over the moat and approached the gate to the wooden palisade where a guard in hauberk and helm stood, lance to hand.

Uncharacteristically, Somerled was anxious. It had nothing to do with the guard or meeting the king. Two years had passed since he'd first glimpsed the red-haired princess. Did she still remain unwed? The thought that she might now be the possession of another did not sit well. The pleasures of women were not unknown to Somerled but none compared to his memory of the girl tearing across the green hills of Man on a magnificent white horse. He had hoped then their futures might somehow be entwined and that hope still lived.

Somerled had enriched his clothing for the occasion. He wore a crimson tunic embroidered with silver thread and a mantle of fine wool in a deep shade of blue. Clasped at his throat was an intricately carved silver raven brooch with a ruby eye, a gift from his Norse mother. Yet, as he intended, there was much of his attire, including the Celtic embroidery on his tunic, that proclaimed him a Gael. Proud of his heritage, he would not seek to hide it, not even for a Norse king.

At the gate, the sound of merrymaking reached his ears. Beside him, Maurice announced to the guard, "The Lord of Argyll, Kintyre and Lorne would see the King of Man, having received his invitation."

"Wait here," said the guard who carefully perused the three of them before stepping through the gate and closing it behind him.

Moments later, he returned to open wide the gate. "The king bids you and those with you welcome, Somerled."

So, Olaf did not choose to recognize his title. Well, that would soon change.

RAGNHILD LOVED HARVEST time when hearts were merry and food was plentiful. Now that the hard work was done, there was time for celebration and dance. Except for the high table where her father and Affraic still sat observing all, the trestle tables had been taken down and stored against the walls to allow room for dancing. She anticipated this part of the evening with eager delight, for she loved the many forms of dance visitors had brought to Castle Rushen since she was a child.

The music had just changed to the circle dance and Ragnhild was joining hands with the others when the doors to the great hall opened to admit three men. They paused before striding toward the high table. The hounds resting near the hearth raised their heads but showed no alarm.

At her father's signal, the music stopped. "It seems we have a late addition to our celebration."

The tall, fair-haired man in crimson tunic and blue mantle bowed before her father. He was lean and his movements agile. His hair, shining in the light of the torches, was long to his shoulders. His prominent jaw was outlined by a trimmed copper-colored beard. Her first impression named him Norse, yet his clothing spoke of a Gaelic connection.

Rising, he said, "I come at your invitation, good king. I am Somerled, Lord of Argyll, Kintyre and Lorne." There was the hint of a lilt in his accent. His voice was clear and deep, the voice of one who knew his own worth but was neither proud nor boastful. She sensed an underlying strength that belied his humble stance before her father. Could this be the one Abbot Bernard had spoken of?

Somerled continued, "Allow me to introduce my brother, Angus MacGillebride, and my companion, whom you may recognize as your foster brother, Maurice MacNeill."

Her father was already smiling at the Irishman who appeared a Celt in green and brown, his curly dark hair shorter than that of the other two, his skin swarthier. The one called Angus, Somerled's brother, was dressed as a Gael, his hair slightly darker than his fair-haired brother.

Ragnhild was intrigued.

Her father nodded to the one called Maurice. "Many years have passed since we lifted cups of mead together in Ireland. I am glad to see you have gone far and stand before me a fine man."

"You flatter me, my brother, for it is you who has gone far."

Her father's smile was wide. "Who would have thought the King of Dublin's youngest son would have risen to be a king himself?"

"Fate, my lord," suggested the one called Maurice, "and the will of King Henry, God rest his soul."

Her father laughed. "You speak truth." Then, turning to the golden-haired one, he said, "You are welcome in my hall, Somerled. I have heard much about your conquests. There is room at the high table for the three of you. Come, sit beside me and share your tales while the music and dance resume."

As the three men approached the high table, Ragnhild, not wishing to be left out of the introductions, walked to the raised dais and gave her father an expectant look.

Her father chuckled. "I must not forget to introduce my ladies." He gestured to Affraic on his right. "Allow me to present my wife, Queen

Affraic, daughter of the Lord of Galloway." He did not mention that Affraic's mother was one of King Henry of England's many bastards.

The queen smiled but there was no warmth in her greeting.

"And my daughter," said the king with a sweeping gesture, "Princess Ragnhild, the jewel of Man."

Her father did not see the grimace that came and quickly went from Affraic's face but Ragnhild, expecting it, had taken in the expression and knew its source was jealousy. Her father had given her the byname when she was but a small child. Affraic, being close in age to her stepdaughter, chafed at the description.

The visitors, who had paused at her father's words, bowed to Affraic and then to Ragnhild. The eyes of the golden one were clear blue and piercing in their intensity as he faced her. "I have heard much about you, Princess, and have longed to meet you."

She felt the heat of her blush at his words. Studying his face for only a moment, what she saw there was sincere, unclouded interest. "I am happy to welcome you, your brother and your friend to my father's court, my lord." She gave the visitors a brief curtsey before returning to the dancers.

What had he heard about her and from whom?

OLAF HAD NOT EXPECTED Somerled to look the part of a nobleman, his posture erect and his clothing fine. He carried himself as one born to wealth, not a man who hunted pirates. His steps, too, were measured and his voice one of authority. About him was an air of greatness Olaf had observed in few others and it made him wonder what might be the fate of such a one.

So, this foreign Gael was now Lord of Argyll, Kintyre and Lorne, was he? Mayhap it was by his own pronouncement but, nonetheless, if the Gaels in the Highlands and Ireland supported him and he could send the Norse running, Somerled was one step short of being a king.

The three men joined Olaf on the dais. Their goblets were soon filled with the rich red wine Olaf favored. "Might you be interested in some food?" he asked them.

Somerled shook his head. "We have only just dined."

Olaf asked, "Well, perhaps some cheese and bread?"

"Thank you," Somerled said. "Some bread and cheese would suit."

It occurred to Olaf the young lord's request for food to accompany the wine was driven not so much by hunger as by the desire to preserve his wits in the midst of a strange court. For that, Olaf admired him. It was the first lesson learned by a young man destined to rule. Only fools were governed by drink.

Olaf gave the order to bring bowls for washing their hands and then for food and some sweetmeats. "Have you known my foster brother long?" he asked Somerled with a wink at Maurice.

"Since Ireland," offered the young lord, "where I spent my youth."

"Somerled trained with my young warriors," said Maurice, "quickly rising above the others. Once I'd heard of the victory at Morvern, I offered him my sword."

"Morvern in Argyll?" Olaf asked. "Tell me." As the food was delivered and the men began to eat, Olaf leaned forward eager to hear more.

Maurice launched into a description of a battle won by a subterfuge Somerled had conceived that challenged one's belief. But, if it occurred, it had been an ingenious strategy by a brave young man outnumbered by stronger and more numerous Norse raiders.

The tale having ended, Maurice said, "'Tis all the men speak of. And, since then, Somerled has led us to victory in each battle fought. The Norse pirates now fear his strategies as much as his might."

The two men with the young lord went on to describe other battles with the Norse in Argyll and the Isles. Throughout the telling, Somerled remained silent, though occasionally his expression spoke of amusement. Often, the young lord's gaze drifted to the dancers whirling about the hall and to Ragnhild where she danced in a circle with others.

Olaf was not surprised. His daughter's beauty and lively manner attracted many men. The Earl of Orkney was not her only suitor.

Listening to Maurice with one ear, Olaf had heard enough to persuade him. "How many ships do you now have, Somerled?"

Shifting his gaze back to Olaf, he said, "Thirty, my lord. Three are beached at the edge of your harbor and another dozen are anchored without. The rest await me off the coast of Kintyre or remain farther north in Argyll. I do not keep them all in one place."

"A goodly number," said Olaf, impressed. "The least I can do for your men in the harbor is to feed them from the richness of our harvest." Olaf turned to give the order that would see it done.

"They will be most grateful," said Somerled.

"With your success in the north where I have interests," said Olaf, "it seems prudent for us to speak of an alliance."

Somerled's eyes narrowed, the blue growing more intense. "An alliance would be of interest to me."

"Very well," said Olaf. "Be my guest this night. Enjoy the celebration and my hospitality. My daughter will see you have chambers in the castle. On the morrow, as you break your fast, we will speak more of this." Olaf got to his feet and offered his hand to Affraic. "Come, Wife, let us leave the hall to those who would continue the celebration. Just now, I would seek my bed."

Somerled rose and bowed, his companions following his example.

Olaf turned to go. Over his shoulder, he said to Somerled, "You might wish to partner in a dance with my daughter. She is well accomplished."

"It would be an honor," replied Somerled. As the music changed, Olaf paused to watch the young lord set aside his mantle and stride to the middle of the hall to bow before Ragnhild. He did not hear what was said but the princess smiled and nodded.

Olaf ascended the stairs, thinking his daughter would enchant the young lord as she did most men. So much the better for what he had in mind.

"Surely you do not intend to give the princess to an upstart foreign Gael?" asked Affraic in that nagging tone he disliked.

"No, of course not. But, if I can, I would have his ships and his warriors at my beck and call."

CHAPTER 5

RAGNHILD THOUGHT PERHAPS she should not have had that last goblet of her father's best wine. But mayhap her lightheadedness was due more to the company of Lord Somerled, for he was fine to look at, an adroit dancer and courtly in his manner.

As their palms came together, their heads neared. "You spoke of hearing much about me. Tell me, what have you heard?"

He smiled, his white teeth gleaming in the torchlight. "Only that the Princess of Man is a termagant."

Her mouth dropped open and she paused in her dancing at the outrageous description.

"Nay, I but tease, my lady. In truth, I have heard only that you are as beautiful as you are intelligent and wise."

"First you tease," she said, resuming the dance, "now you flatter."

"Nay, not flattery but truth. For I have seen with my own eyes your grace, the spirit in your emerald eyes, like sparks on a dark night, and your laughter that brightens the hall and draws the gazes of your father's men."

She blushed at his words but, being familiar with the compliments of men, she returned him a skeptical look. When they came together again, she said, "It is told you mean to chase the Norse pirates from the Isles. That will be a difficult task. They are a vicious lot."

"Indeed, they are. Yet the tide has turned, my lady. We were once few in number. Now we are many. My men have become bold warriors. Were I not a believer in the one true God, I would say the fates are with us."

Inwardly, Ragnhild smiled. So, he was no pagan. "Is your goal merely to drive the Norse from the Highlands and the Isles? Back to the Orkneys mayhap?"

"Or farther. And, no, I do not merely seek to be rid of them. I imagine a new kingdom in which the sea lanes are protected by castles at strategic places, assuring we live free of invaders and foreign rule."

She studied the determination in his expression, the set of his jaw. He did not appear to be bragging. Rather, he merely stated what he believed to be fact, what he would one day accomplish. "You speak of castles. Are you impressed by my father's stone castle?"

He looked high above them and then around the hall, his gaze taking in the tapestries, shields and weapons adding dignity to the walls. "I am impressed by the fortress, yea, and its location, protected against the king's enemies. But there is more. I see a woman's influence and I doubt it is all Queen Affraic's doing." His blue eyes bored into hers as if he knew the embellishments had been hers. "One day, I would have such for myself."

Was he speaking only of the castle? The possibility of his wanting more—perhaps her—was intriguing. "Mayhap you shall," she replied, trying not to smile.

"There is time, I think, unless the jewel has been committed to a particular setting."

He spoke in veiled terms but Ragnhild well understood his meaning and her heart sped apace. Many men had sought her hand. And while she had no desire to marry anytime soon, when she did, would Somerled be one of her suitors? Yet there was her father's will to consider.

Her dowry would be a rich one with lands and an alliance with her father that would bring ships to make her future husband a wealthy, powerful man. Somerled would know all this yet she detected none of the avarice in this man she had seen in others. Still, she would not let him see her interest. Shrugging, she tossed her braids. "Who can say?"

He laughed and her smile grew into a grin.

"Might you show me more of the castle tomorrow morning after we break our fast?" he asked.

His interest in her home drew a smile. "I would be pleased to do so, my lord."

When the music ended, gesturing to the side table, she invited him to have some wine.

He nodded and they walked together to where the flagons sat. He poured her a goblet of wine.

"I perceive you are both Norse and Gael," she said between sips, "and with courtly manners besides. Why have I never heard of you?"

"You perceive correctly," he said, smiling down at her. "I am Norse by my mother's blood and Gaelic by my father's. I spent my youth in Ireland, where my family was banished from the lands of our forefathers by the Norse invaders. In those days, I was known to no one save my family. I returned to Argyll with my father, engaging in battles with the Norse pirates. When those were lost and my father slain, I lived simply. But, then the clans sought my leadership against the pirates. I could hardly refuse. Now, I seek to take back my forefathers' lands and free my people from the Norse that have long preyed upon them."

She considered this late risen champion. Could he be believed? Would he succeed in so great a venture where others had failed? Still, for all the uncertainty, there was something about him that made her take seriously his words. She wanted him to win. "I believe you will accomplish the task you have set for yourself, Lord Somerled."

He inclined his head to her. "Your endorsement means much, my lady."

"I am curious about your family, Lord Somerled. Is Angus your only sibling?"

He took a sip of his ale. "I have a sister, Bethoc, wed to Malcolm MacHeth."

Her brows rose at the name for she knew of him. "The one in rebellion against King David?"

"Aye," he said sheepishly, looking into his wine. "He is a good man save he was impatient for his lands in Moray to be restored to him. He rebelled and King David captured him to hold as a prisoner these past three years."

"My father is King David's ally and good friend. Mayhap he can help."

"I am glad to know of it as it makes any alliance between us all the more auspicious."

"Has my father spoken of an alliance?" Abbot Bernard had suggested such an alliance could forestall the need for her father to give her hand to the Earl of Orkney.

"He wants to discuss the prospect on the morrow when we break our fast."

"I wish you luck in your pursuit of such an alliance. It could prove helpful to both you and my father."

His only response was a knowing smile.

IF THERE WERE OTHER women in the king's hall that night favored with beauty, Somerled could not have said. For him, there was only one whose brilliance shone as the morning star the Norse called *Aurvandil*. Her mother must have been tall for the flame-haired, green-eyed lass garbed in emerald silk, whose smile made his heart race, was not short like her father. She was all he had envisioned that day he had observed her on her white horse.

King Olaf had not misspoken. Ragnhild was the true jewel of Man and, if God were with him, Somerled meant to one day have her by his side.

As she was beginning to speak further, a Norseman approached, his walk more a swagger. The first thing Somerled noticed about him was the large gold Thor's hammer hanging from a cord around his neck. Somerled had seen the same item of jewelry on the Norse warlord who led the attack on Drimnin, the one Somerled drove away.

Grinning broadly at the princess, the Norseman said, "Would you favor me with a dance, Princess? Surely, you cannot mean to allow this foreign Gael to dominate your evening."

The princess frowned at the Norseman and turned to Somerled. "Forgive Sweyn's rudeness and allow me to introduce you." Then to the Norseman, she said, "This is Somerled, Lord of Argyll, Kintyre and Lorne, my father's invited guest."

The Norseman called Sweyn stared at Somerled as if he were seeing a ghost, his eyes growing large. "Ah, the Norse-Gael from Morvern. I have heard much of you."

Somerled imagined Sweyn had not only heard of him but had personally witnessed Somerled rip out the heart of one of the raiders manning Sweyn's longships on a distant shore nearly two years prior. Had he not been a guest in Olaf's court, Somerled would have considered killing Sweyn in retribution for the innocent lives he had taken. But courtesy restrained him and, because he was interested to know where the man dwelled when not pillaging Argyll, he asked, "Where do you call home?"

The Norseman hesitated, mayhap reluctant to divulge his hiding place to his enemy. The princess answered for him. "Sweyn Asleifsson is an Orkneyman in service to Earl Rognvald."

"So that is *your* longship in the harbor?" Somerled asked, though he already knew the answer.

"Aye. I come on business for the Earl of Orkney who has every hope of becoming betrothed to Princess Ragnhild. While I am here, I guard his interests."

Somerled's heart sank to hear this news yet he reminded himself there was no betrothal as yet. He liked not that Sweyn referred to Ragnhild as if she were another longship, one of Rognvald's "interests", and he felt her bristle at his side as Sweyn spoke.

Without a word more, Sweyn reached for Ragnhild's hand. Somerled took a step forward, thinking to thwart him but she waved Somerled away. "'Tis all right. As hostess, it is my duty to dance with those guests in my father's hall who bid me do so."

Somerled did not like the way the man looked at Ragnhild as he led her to the dance just beginning as if she were his possession and not the sought-after bride of his master.

With Olaf retired to his bed, Somerled joined his two companions and told them all that had occurred.

"Olaf's guards watch her," said Maurice, "but it might be wise for us to do so as well."

"That is the man we fought in Morvern?" asked Angus.

"And defeated," Somerled reminded them. "Get word to Domnall and our crew in the harbor to be wary of treachery this night. Sweyn knows who we are."

"As you wish," replied Angus, as he turned to leave.

SOMERLED ROSE WITH the dawn the next day and dispatched Angus to check on his ships and Maurice to survey their surroundings from the ramparts where he could also see their ships outside the harbor. Then he went to the hall.

Olaf's warriors who had drunk too much ale and wine the night before still lay asleep in the rushes or on pallets next to the walls. The servants were stirring them to wake so the trestles could be set up.

Somerled strode past them to the castle door open to the morning light. "Is the king about?" he asked the guard stationed there.

"'Tis Lauds, sir, when the monks say their morning prayers. Oft-times, the king joins them. But he should be returning now."

Somerled thanked the guard and stepped into the light of the rising sun that had turned the blue waters of the harbor and the sea golden. In the distance, he caught sight of the king and one of his guards ascending the hill toward the castle.

"Good day," said King Olaf, reaching Somerled. "I trust you slept well?"

"I did and thank you for your hospitality."

They walked together toward the castle door, the guard dropping back allowing Somerled and Olaf to talk.

"Will you and your companions join me at the high table to break the fast?"

"Aye, we will. And the princess has promised to show me more of Castle Rushen. Then we must sail."

When they arrived at the castle, the king was met by his daughter, who greeted Somerled with a smile. She wore a blue wool bliaut, its waist, long sleeves and hem decorated with a Norse-patterned braid.

Around her head was a circlet of silver from which cascaded a veil falling down her back. Her long red braids, shining in the morning light, reached past her waist to her hips. In the sun, she was more fetching than even the night before when he had seen her by candlelight.

As he waited for her father to finish what he had to say to her, Angus and Maurice approached and he excused himself to speak to them.

"Our ships in the harbor were undisturbed through the night," began Angus, "possibly because Domnall had more men stationed on deck so as to discourage whatever the Norse pirates might have planned."

"From the battlements," said Maurice, "I viewed your ships resting outside the harbor. I imagine, after lingering so long in one place, the men will be glad to depart."

"We won't be long," said Somerled. "We are to join the king to break our fast when I would speak with him further about an alliance. After that, the princess has offered to show me more of the castle ere we leave."

"You have obviously captured the attention of the king's daughter," said Maurice.

Somerled darted a look in her direction, taking in her fair skin and rosy cheeks as she spoke to her father. "For certes, she has captured mine." By Somerled's reckoning, Ragnhild was eighteen or nineteen. If Olaf valued her advice, as was told, then he might delay her marriage for another year or two. Somerled prayed there would be time.

When Ragnhild left her father, Somerled excused himself and crossed the hall to join her. "My lady, you are a vision this morn."

Her eyes sparkled as she smiled. "Thank you, my lord."

"I look forward to seeing more of the castle with you but, first, I have business with your father." He hoped she saw in his gaze his intent to make her among the topics they would discuss. He bowed. "I beg your leave to join him."

She acknowledged his words with a nod of her head and hastened off to address the servants bringing platters of food to the tables. The men who had been sleeping had now risen to take their places at the trestles. Other men and their wives descended the castle stairs to join the king's morning meal. Among them was Sweyn Asleifsson who gave Somerled a surly look as he took his place at a trestle table.

45

At the high table, Somerled and his two companions took the places Olaf indicated.

"Does the princess not join you?" Somerled asked the king.

"Most often but, today, with so many guests, she will likely stay busy directing the servants until all have food. Ragnhild enjoys being my chatelaine. There is a place for her next to the queen when she is ready to join us."

On Olaf's right sat his wife. Somerled remembered the queen, a plain woman, from the night before. Maurice had told him Affraic's mother was one of King Henry's bastards. Affraic's appearance recalled to mind what he had once heard, that the Conqueror's line bred no beauties.

Affraic remained aloof as she surveyed the hall. As the mother of Olaf's heir, she would have a place of honor but Somerled doubted she would ever replace her stepdaughter in the hearts of the people.

He cut off a piece of the warm barley bread and added cheese and salted herring in mustard sauce to his wooden trencher. Servants poured ale into the goblets. "'Tis a hearty fare you serve your guests to break their fast, King Olaf."

The king gave him a satisfied look. "We have long fished the waters of the Irish Sea and we are blessed with a rich abundance of food grown on the isle."

Somerled's gaze shifted to Ragnhild, who was moving about the hall, instructing the servants and greeting the guests, seeing to their comforts. "Your daughter is very capable and unselfish, attending to the needs of your guests before her own."

"Indeed, she is." Then, setting down his goblet, the king changed the subject. "What is your destination when you leave Man?"

"I had thought to sail to Irvine where I'm told King David holds court. At some point, I must discuss with him the matter of my brother-in-law Malcolm MacHeth."

Olaf laughed. "Ah, MacHeth. I know of him. A rebel many times over. But then every family has its troublesome members. Doubtless, David will appreciate your efforts to chase away the pirates from his western shores and may help you with your brother-in-law. I think he will like you, for you two are of a similar nature. Both of you weigh strategy before committing to war. But beware any alliance he offers you; it will come with a cost."

"As I expect, though it is in the interest of my people to be at peace with the Scots and to have David's blessing for all I would do. As it would be for me to be at peace with you, Your Grace."

"Well said. An understanding between us would suit," said Olaf, spearing a piece of herring on his eating knife. "As you provide a benefit to David, so you provide one to me."

Somerled's eyes had followed Ragnhild as she attended to the king's guests. Once she was finished, she took her place at the high table on the other side of her stepmother. The last to break her fast, Somerled noticed she did not take long in partaking of her small meal. Her slender but well curved form attested to the fact she did not eat overmuch. When she caught him looking at her, she met his gaze for a brief moment and smiled before returning her attention to her trencher.

He took a draw on his ale and spoke in a low tone to the king. "I would agree to an alliance that would have my ships and warriors come to the aid of Man whenever there is need, but I have a condition."

"Only one?" the king asked, his expression one of amusement.

Somerled faced the king and, in a hushed tone, said, "I would have the hand of your daughter in marriage."

The king sputtered into his ale, then whispered to Somerled. "Ragnhild? You would have *my daughter* to wife?"

Somerled was glad for the noise in the hall that kept their conversation to the two of them. "Aye, I would. It has long been my dream and meeting her has only cemented that desire."

The king seemed to ponder the possibility as he stared at the food before him. "Mayhap 'tis her dowry you seek, a rich one to aid your cause."

"I am not so foolish as to refuse her dowry," said Somerled, "but I would take the princess if she came to me naked with none."

Olaf smiled and then launched into another objection. "She was raised in a castle, the daughter of a king. Where would you have her live?" In a sarcastic tone, he added, "On one of your ships?"

Somerled had known it would not be enough to retake his lands. He must secure the harbors and sea lanes with fortifications. "Nay, she will have her choice of many abodes for I will build castles along the sea lanes I control."

Olaf gave him an incredulous look.

Undaunted, Somerled shared his vision. "One of the men who has sworn allegiance to me, Ewan MacSuibhne, possesses a stone castle in Knapdale, a square tower built in the Norman fashion, much like Castle Rushen. Surely you know of the imposing structure for it is very old. He will have a hand in the construction of my castles built in like manner."

"Hmm…" The king ran his fingers over his red beard, seeming to ponder Somerled's words. "An ambitious undertaking for one so young."

"You were young when you became King of Man, were you not?"

"Aye, but I had help from King Henry. Your plan will take time…years, if it happens at all. You might let me know when one of your castles actually rises from the earth. Then, I may again consider your request."

Somerled clenched his teeth, holding in his anger and disappointment, certain Olaf never expected that day to come. "Do not doubt I will do this, King Olaf. I may be young but I am a man of my word. I can call upon thousands of men who, freed from the Norse, have joined my cause. In time, there will be more men and more ships. They share my vision of a kingdom of Argyll and the Isles not tied to any country save by bonds of honor and friendship."

The king abruptly got to his feet. "Mayhap we will speak more of this in time. But, for now, I encourage you to go about your business with my blessing."

Knowing he had been dismissed, Somerled watched the king stride across the hall, disappointed at the reaction to his offer. But since the hand of the princess had not yet been given, he refused to lose hope. There would come a time when King Olaf would need Somerled's might and he would be there.

The princess cast him a hopeful glance, her brows raised in inquiry.

He shook his head, whereupon she rose and excused herself, an ethereal vision in blue gliding into the hall. A dream yet to be realized.

Reluctantly, Somerled turned to see his brother and Maurice had gotten to their feet and were waiting for him at the other end of the dais.

"How went the conversation with the king concerning an alliance?" asked Angus. "Your words were too whispered to be heard."

Somerled frowned. "Not as I'd hoped. He is unwilling to give me what I want in exchange for my pledge. We will speak more of it at another time. Ready the ships. We sail in an hour."

Acknowledging his command, Angus and Maurice stepped down from the dais and departed.

The princess hurriedly finished with the servants and came to stand before the dais, looking up at him. In a formal but gracious manner, she said, "Are you ready, my lord?"

"Eager, my lady." He stepped down and offered his arm.

There was no more talk of alliances. She placed her hand upon his arm and began to speak of her home. "You might have noticed as you arrived yesterday that the castle is a large square tower and the walls of the keep very thick. On the west side is the Silverburn River, which forms part of the moat."

"A natural moat is always an advantage," he remarked. "Did your father construct the castle?"

"Nay, his forefathers. It is Norman in design. But he has improved it." Somerled had recognized the square tower as Norman. He'd seen others like it and determined he would build the same kind of fortresses.

She swept her hand in a wide gesture, taking in the hall. "There are chambers above and you probably saw the guardhouse attached to the wall facing the gate. Between the wooden palisade and the castle is the outer bailey where the men train. But inside the square tower is another bailey. You may not have seen it as your rooms were on the outer wall. Come, I will show you."

She led him through a door and down a corridor into the inner bailey open to the sky above. Sunlight shone down on the well-ordered space.

"Here we have the kitchens, the kitchen garden and the stables," she said, gesturing around her.

"You supervise all of this?" he asked, willing to believe she did.

She laughed, a musical sound. "All but the stables and we have a cook who keeps a tight rein over the kitchens."

He took in her words but felt sure she was being modest about her role. In one corner of the open space he glimpsed a swath of green. "Is that the garden?"

"Yea, 'tis the cook's garden where she grows all manner of herbs, even a few vegetables. It will not be flourishing again until spring. And, of course, the monks in the abbey have a much larger garden."

He had met Abbot Bernard the evening before so he was not surprised to learn there was a religious house on the isle. "I wish I had time to see the abbey."

"It is timber now but my father means to rebuild it in stone like the castle." Her green eyes sparkled as she spoke of her home and all her father had accomplished. It was clear she took great pride in both the castle and her role in assuring it remained a comfortable place for all.

Somerled envisioned her caring for his castles, his people. His heart swelled at the thought. She would be his lady, the Lady of Argyll and the Isles. "It seems to me you have had a large part in what I see around me, Princess."

She smiled up at him. "The castle is only one of my interests, my lord."

Returning her smile, he said, "I doubt not you are skilled at many things." She was a beautiful flower just beginning to bloom, yet it was not hard to imagine the rose unfurled.

They returned to the great hall and he bowed to her. "Thank you for showing me your home, Princess. I will miss seeing your face when we sail." Having now seen the one whose memory had lived long in his mind, he did not wish to relinquish the contact though he knew he must.

She looked up, concern on her lovely face. "Do you leave so soon?"

It gladdened his heart to know she did not want him to go. "Aye, this morning."

"Very well," she said with a sigh. Then she curtseyed. "I bid you Godspeed and good sailing, my lord. I go to the stables as I always greet my horse after breaking my fast before we ride."

He watched her as she took an apple from a table and gracefully walked toward the corridor that led to the inner bailey, her head held high like the queen she might one day be.

RAGNHILD WAS NEARLY to the corridor leading to the inner bailey when Sweyn and his companion rose from their trestle table and stepped into her path. She tolerated them for a long minute ere begging off. "I was on the way to greet my horse when you stopped me," she said. "I hope you will excuse me as my time is now short. I bid you both a good day."

"As you wish, my lady," Sweyn said, bowing as he returned her a treacherous smile. She felt his eyes follow her as she left the hall. It made her skin crawl. 'Twas nothing like the warm feeling she had when Lord Somerled looked at her.

The sunlight from the inner bailey fell on the clean straw where Fairhair stood in his stall, waiting for her. It was a ritual between them that after she broke her fast if no other tasks required her attention, she came to take him for a ride.

Already she was late for having shown Lord Somerled around but she did not regret the time spent with him. There was something about Somerled beyond the ordinary.

"There you are, my handsome one," she said to her horse, running her fingers down his white forelock.

Fairhair nickered softly and raised his head over the stall door.

She touched her forehead to his. "Did you hear the sounds of revelry in the hall last night? I brought you an apple as your part of the feast." She held out the prized fruit she had kept behind her and the horse took a large bite.

Behind her, she heard footfalls. Thinking it might be the groom, she turned to greet him but encountered instead the surly smile of Sweyn Asleifsson.

Turning back to her horse, she offered the rest of the apple to Fairhair. "Did you think it necessary to follow me, Sweyn?"

"I thought you might want company and could think of none better than myself."

She whipped around. "You are overbold for a guest in my father's hall. Worse, you do not honor your lord in seeking me out when you knew I would be alone."

"Rognvald and I have often shared women," he said coming closer, his presence like an evil omen.

"You speak lies. The Earl of Orkney would never sanction such a thing and I do not want you." She backed away only to encounter the stall door. Fairhair must have sensed her alarm for he raised his head and gave off a loud whinny.

Ragnhild's eyes darted to the pitchfork set against the stable wall and knew it to be out of reach. But she still had her eating knife secured at her waist. She pulled the knife free and held it in front of her. "Come no closer!"

With a swipe of his hand, he knocked the knife to the ground. "Your smile would invite the coldest of men, Princess, and I am not cold to you."

"Leave now, Sweyn, else my father will kill you!"

He reached out to grab her and she yanked her arm back. "Do not touch me!"

He closed the distance between them and pressed her against the stall, his breath hot against her neck. "I can make you want me."

Behind Sweyn, there was the flash of a sword and the edge of a blade suddenly rested against his throat. "Do as the lady says or I will remove your head from your shoulders."

"Lord Somerled!" she exclaimed, relieved and happy to see him.

Sweyn slowly backed away from the blade at his throat. "No need to get riled, lordling. I merely came to join the princess in greeting her horse."

"You lie!" Ragnhild and Somerled spit out at the same time.

"Leave while you have all your members, Sweyn," said Somerled. "There is a score to settle between us and I would be happy to see it done this day."

The Orkneyman turned and, tossing a mean look at Somerled, fled out the stable door.

Somerled gave Ragnhild a look of concern. "Are you unhurt, my lady?"

Flushed but unharmed, she said, "I am well but I thank you for intervening. You spared me an ugly scene or worse."

"I saw him follow you from the hall, and knew he intended mischief. That snake is not to be trusted."

"A vile man," she agreed, wrapping her arms around her. "I like him not."

"It would be well to stay clear of him. Come," he said, offering his arm, "I will see you safely to the hall and then I must meet my men at the shore."

As they walked back to the hall, she said, "Say nothing of this, my lord. Some would not think kindly of me. They would say it was my fault."

He gave her an enigmatic look. "Aye, some might but I never would."

The blue of his eyes was clear, his demeanor sincere. Had she gained a champion, a protector? Or mayhap more?

Once they entered the hall, he faced her and, taking her hand, pressed a warm kiss to her knuckles. "I will see you again, Princess. Once I have set my mind to something, I never falter."

She did not know how to respond. Should she be flattered? Insulted at the possessive gleam she glimpsed in his eyes? In truth, she felt none of those things, only an inner warmth at his words. She very much wanted to see him again.

His companions approached and, after greeting her, they walked with Somerled and her to the castle door where she bid them "Godspeed". From the top of the rise, she raised a parting hand to Somerled as he looked back at her one last time.

CHAPTER 6

BY THE TIME Somerled returned to the shore, Sweyn's dragonship had gone. "Did he leave in haste?" he asked Domnall as he stepped on deck.

"Aye, and very angry."

"He was shouting at his men," said Angus, raking a hand through his windblown hair.

"He would have been angry," Somerled muttered under his breath, looking into the harbor. "The King of Man is well rid of him."

"A menacing character," said Maurice, who had been listening to their conversation. "One day, you will have to kill him."

Somerled recognized the truth of the Irishman's words. "Indeed, but not today."

"To where do we sail?" inquired Domnall, as the men readied the ships.

Somerled stared out to sea. "I had thought to go to Irvine on the shores of the Firth of Clyde where King David holds court. There are many things I would discuss with him."

"You might want to alter your plans," said Domnall. At Somerled's raised brow, his cousin added, "One of our men heard Sweyn speak of

Islay, no doubt with pillaging in mind for they have no base there."

Somerled frowned at this news. Irvine could wait but Islay could not. "Aye, Sweyn would be one to inflict his anger on the people. We sail to Islay."

As they left the harbor, they met the rest of the longships and galleys Somerled had brought to the isle. Those captains, too, had watched Sweyn sail away from Man. "They were joined by two other dragonships as they entered the Irish Sea," Ruairi MacInnes, now one of his captains, shouted from the deck of the galley he commanded.

Somerled decided to take four of his longships with him to Islay and send the rest of those here with Ruairi to Kintyre to check on the settlement there. "We'll meet you at Dunaverty Bay ere we sail to Irvine."

The winds from the southwest were with them as Somerled sailed north, arriving at Islay late that afternoon. Covered by a gray sky filled with dark clouds and spitting rain, Islay lay due west of Kintyre and contained both sea and freshwater lochs. The isle was essential to Somerled's strategy, for, along with Argyll, Kintyre and Lorne, it had been part of the ancient kingdom of *Dál Riata*, his family's royal lands. It must remain free.

The island's coast had always been plagued by winds and Somerled knew the approach from the south to be difficult. There were many places from which Sweyn could launch an attack but there were settlements on the east coast, bordering the narrow straight between Islay and the Isle of Jura that was the main route to the rest of the Isles. Though the tides ran fast and had to be carefully navigated, Somerled believed the pirates would set their course for Askaig, a secure haven, for a mile inland lay the settlement of Keills. It was there Somerled directed his four ships.

They came upon Sweyn's dragonships beached in a cove set into the wooded coast just south of Askaig. They could not have been there long as the afterguard was taking down the sails, their shields still hanging from the rails.

Seeing Somerled's four longships rowing hard toward them, filled with two hundred warriors, Sweyn's men shouted to each other and scurried about, readying a longship to sail. Before Somerled's lead ship reached them, the Orkneymen jumped into that dragonship and hastily rowed north with the tide, abandoning their fellow pirates to their fate.

"Let the cowards go!" Somerled shouted to his captains who were about to pursue. "We have their two ships. Sweyn and the bulk of his warriors may already be attacking Keills. We must aid the people. I'll take most of our warriors and the archers and go after them. The rest of you stand guard and deal with any of Sweyn's men fleeing this way." To Maurice, he said, "You are in command here."

"As you wish," said the Irishman, though Somerled could see he relished the thought of engaging the pirates.

"Sweyn is a wily one, Maurice, and I trust you to manage him should he get away."

Maurice nodded and Somerled grabbed his shield, hurrying inland with Angus and Domnall and their well-armed men.

Screams rent the air as they neared Keills and the pungent odor of smoke drifted to Somerled's nostrils. It was always the same with these Norse invaders. Some might come for slaves but Sweyn was not one of those. Mayhap unwilling for his master to know of his pursuits, Sweyn came only for plunder and mayhem, leaving cinders and corpses behind. Still holding to pagan beliefs, he would burn all in his wake to make sure the spirits of the dead did not follow him home.

Somerled was glad to see only one building had been set afire. He motioned his warriors from the path into the woods. "Surround the village," he ordered. "When I give the war cry, attack from all sides. They will have no time to think of strategy. Protect the chapel where innocents may be sheltering. Save as many as you can." To his archers, standing nearby, he said, "Get to high ground and mark your targets well for time to save the innocents will be short." He looked into the eager faces of his men. "Show the courage I know you have."

His warriors hurried into place. Somerled sounded his war cry, a shout above the fray heard by all. It must have sent chills through the pirates, for they turned with shocked expressions to see who was descending upon them. Clearly, they expected no one to come to the aid of Keills for they wore no mail, only helms and light armor.

Somerled plunged into the battle, his men behind him a screaming tempest come to harvest pirate blood. With sword, spears and wooden shields, they attacked the Norse raiders with a vengeance.

Taken by surprise, the pirates turned from seeking plunder to defending their own skins.

As he had once hunted wild boar in the forests of Morvern, Somerled now hunted the Norse who preyed upon his people. He slashed his sword right and left, cutting a swath through the stunned invaders. His shield gathered more than one enemy arrow but he took comfort in seeing his own archers claiming the lives of Sweyn's men. Some of the pirates were just drawing their swords when they were cut asunder.

Hard Norsemen screamed, grabbing gashed faces and severed limbs, as they dropped to the ground, vomiting gulps of blood.

The violent clash of fierce Gaels and raiding Norse lasted more than an hour for there were more than two hundred Norsemen pillaging the village. When he had a moment's respite, Somerled gazed down the length of the village, pleased to see his men were gaining the victory.

At the far end of the village in front of the chapel, he spotted a young villager swinging his sword with practiced skill in a magnificent fight against a taller, more powerful Norseman. The lad was holding his own, but Somerled knew the boy lacked the power in his arms to continue the fight against so fierce a foe.

Such courage had to be aided. Somerled rushed to the fight, hacking away at the Norse raiders who stood between him and his goal. Arriving at the lad holding back the pirate's attacks, Somerled drew the Norseman's attention with a shout. "You will die this day!"

Equally met, their swords clashed, once, twice. Somerled hammered him with his solid round shield then turned in a circle, his sword flashing silver around him. Stooping low, he swept his blade over the Norseman's legs.

The pirate screamed, stumbled and fell. Somerled seized the opportunity, piercing the pirate's flesh above his leather jerkin and thrusting his sword deep.

Withdrawing his blade, Somerled wiped it on the Norseman's tunic. Then he turned to the boy, who still held his sword ready. "Who are you, lad, and where did you learn to fight so well?

The boy, tall for his age, ripped off his hat. Long tendrils of auburn hair fell nearly to her waist. Falling to her knees, the young woman said,

"I am no lad, Lord, but your servant, Liadan MacGilleain."

For once in his life, Somerled was speechless. She was a beauty by any man's standard. And she had fought like a man, never wavering.

"It was my eldest brother who taught me to use the sword. Diarmad took our galley north to join your ships. My younger brother, Brian, fights here this day."

Her eyes were a vivid gray, a likely source of her name, which meant gray lady. "You did well," he told her. "If your brother, Diarmad, is half so skilled, I am glad he is one of my men."

He started to walk toward the others when she called him back. "I would go with you when you sail, my lord. Because few believe a woman can be skilled with a sword, I could guard your back."

"What is your age, Liadan?"

"Seven and ten summers, my lord."

It was the age Somerled's father had arranged his own brief marriage. Old enough to sire a son but too young to command men as he did now. He was tempted to put her off. She'd be safer on Islay once the pirates were gone. But she lifted his spirits, standing there proud and undaunted, her shoulders back, meaning every word. Doubtless, she would guard his back, but she would create problems among the men. "We will see," he said, sheathing his sword.

Around him, he saw mostly dead or captured Norsemen. A few of his own had fallen along with a dozen brave villagers who had died defending their holdings and families. Women cried over their loss but the men still standing seemed pleased their village had been saved.

Some distance away, he saw Domnall standing over a cowed enemy—Sweyn Asleifsson on his knees.

As Somerled approached, the Norseman yelled, "Mercy!" Next to Sweyn lay his bloodied companion, Holdbodi Hundasson, still alive but badly wounded.

Somerled narrowed his eyes on his defeated foe. "Why should I show you what you did not show the people of Keills or Drimnin?"

"Give me my life and I will be gone from these shores never to return. You would not kill the right arm of the Earl of Orkney, would you?"

"I might." Somerled did not trust the pirate but, for his word never to return, he would consider allowing him his life. Too, Sweyn could tell his master that pirates, if he had sent them, would no longer be allowed to prey upon Argyll and the Isles. "Order your men to drop their weapons and I'll allow you to leave—on one ship. You must vow to never return to Argyll or the shores of Islay."

Blood flowing from one of his arms, a beleaguered Sweyn said, "You have my word." He then gave the order that saw the pirates' weapons dropping to the ground, the sound of metal hitting metal echoing in Somerled's ears.

Domnall arched a brow but did not question Somerled's decision. Instead, he prodded the Norseman up. "Get moving!"

Sweyn helped his friend, Holdbodi, up and the two limped back toward shore. Somerled wondered if Holdbodi would live to see Orkney.

The rest of the wounded and captured Norsemen, now weaponless, were herded by Somerled's men back to the ships.

When they arrived, Sweyn stared open-mouthed at his two remaining dragonships, a look of shock on his dirt-smudged face. He spit out an oath. "My warriors?"

"The pirates on one of your ships, unwilling to confront my men, sailed without you," said Somerled. "Your third ship is now mine, along with your weapons and shields. You may leave on the remaining ship. Be certain to tell the Earl of Orkney that no invaders will be allowed in the lands of the Lord of Argyll, Kintyre and Lorne. Islay, too, is under my protection and will forever be a stronghold of our clans."

Sweyn, his face twisted in a grimace, nodded once.

The Norse pirates climbed aboard their remaining longship. To Domnall, Somerled said, "Mark the ship so we will know if ever it appears again."

Guarded by Somerled's men, Domnall and Maurice lifted the carved dragon head free from the stem post and pitched it off the side of the ship. Then Domnall raised an axe and struck the bow keel post, chopping it off, so as to render the longship without a soul in the eyes of the Norsemen.

Sweyn glared at Somerled from the deck of his longship, his men pulling the wounded aboard while casting fearful glances at the maimed keel post.

Somerled returned the pirate's harsh glare. "You should not have come, Sweyn. I have not forgotten Drimnin, nor do I forgive you the lives you have taken. I showed you mercy where you rendered none. But I say this, if you return to these shores, your life will be forfeit."

Without another word, the bedraggled pirates took to the oars, rowing south toward Ireland. "He does not return to Orkney?" asked Angus, joining him to watch the departing ship's sail rise.

"Oh, he may go to Ireland for a short while, licking his wounds, but I doubt not he will return to his den in Orkney to whine to his master."

"Ireland will be none too glad to see him," offered Maurice.

"Do we sail for Kintyre?" asked Liadan, coming out of nowhere to stand beside Somerled.

Amused, he asked her, "And how do you know that is our destination, lass?"

"I listened to your men talking," she said, raising her head proudly. "If you allow it, I would be your spy, my lord. I am very good at listening behind doors."

Somerled chuckled, doubting not she spoke truth. He looked around, seeing no man near her. "Did your brother give his permission for you to sail with us?"

She clutched a small bundle to her chest and averted her gaze, wiping away the tears that began to flow down her cheeks. In a small voice, she said, "My brother Brian died this day."

Somerled was truly sorry for her loss. "Your brother is a hero then and will be celebrated as such. And what of your parents?"

"Gone to Heaven, my lord," she said, looking up at him, her gray eyes pleading.

"Well then," said Somerled, "there is nothing for it but to take you with us." To Angus, he said, "What think you of our new crew?"

Liadan's eyes grew bright at his acceptance of her wish to accompany him.

"Why not?" said Angus. "It is clear she will serve no other. But you will have to keep her close, else the men will compete for her attention. She is a bonny lass."

"If they try anything with her," said Somerled, giving Liadan a smile, "they will get a knife in the gut. And it will not be mine. I have seen her fight."

"Do we depart for Kintyre?" asked Domnall, his expression one of concern.

Aware of his men's fatigue and the waning day, Somerled said, "Nay, the tide will soon change and not in our favor. Besides, we may be able to offer aid to the people of Keills. Tomorrow morning will be soon enough and the tide will be running south through the sound."

Somerled left a small contingent of his men with the ships and set off on the short return trip through the woods to Keills, his warriors and Liadan falling into step behind him.

They arrived on the fertile plain that was home to the village to see the men piling the bodies of the Norse pirates at the far end to be burned. "We have come to help where we may," Somerled told a man who approached them.

"Aye, we could use some."

"Shall we send some of the men off to hunt deer for the evening meal?" asked Maurice.

Somerled nodded. "For certes, the villagers would appreciate it. The herds would be culled by this time."

Maurice gathered a group of his archers and headed off to the hills.

Somerled dispatched the rest of his men to help where they could while he and Angus went to the chapel. "I want to see what damage the Norse raiders have done."

With Liadan at his back, where she seemed most content, Somerled and Angus headed toward the old stone chapel. A graveyard with stone slabs stood off to one side. He glanced at Liadan. "Are your parents buried here?"

She nodded, silent and somber.

He patted her shoulder, much as he would one of his men. "We'll see your brother laid to rest beside them ere we leave."

Liadan looked up at him with grateful eyes, the color matching the brooding sky. "Thank you, Lord."

In the chapel, the altar remained intact but the pirates had taken whatever had stood upon it. "Likely, we'll find the vessels scattered where they dropped them."

"I can find them," Liadan volunteered.

"A holy task, lass. See it is done and then find us when we stop to eat."

Somerled watched the girl hurry toward the center of the village, still wearing the attire of warrior. "It is best she be about some task without time to agonize over her loss," he said to Angus. "There will be time to mourn when we say the words over her brother's grave."

"Aye, and a sad day it will be."

Somerled heaved a sigh. "'Twould be sadder if we'd not come." In the distance, he heard the bellowing of the red deer harts, reminding him the rutting season was upon them. At least the Norse invaders had not stopped the cycle of life on the island.

A few hours later, what work they could do was done. The light was beginning to fade as fires were lit and the deer taken in his archers' hunt had been set to roasting over the flames. Both the villagers and Somerled's men, including those guarding the ships, would soon feast on venison.

They sat around the fires, warming themselves against the chill. Somerled drew his woolen mantle around him as the flames sent sparks rising into the night air. His mind drifted to the scene at the chapel where the pirates had shown little respect for the center of the villagers' worship.

Islay had been a place of faith in the tradition of Columba for centuries and Somerled revered its past. "It occurs to me," he said to himself as much as to his men gathered around him, "Islay would be a worthy place to base our Kingdom of the Isles."

Liadan scooted closer. "Lord, there is a long loch in the moorlands not far from here, named for St. Findlugan, the Irish monk. Near the shore is an island that St. Columba is said to have visited."

"An island within an island," Somerled muttered, liking the sound of it. "But so far from the sea?"

"Nay, not far," she said. "'Tis a few hours' walk from there to the great sea loch Indaal where you could beach more than a hundred longships and galleys."

Somerled ran his hand over his well-trimmed beard. The idea of a hundred galleys and longships bringing the clan chiefs to a safe place where they could deliberate matters of importance greatly appealed. He would need such a place if the kingdom he envisioned drew chiefs from all the Isles and the coast. "At dawn, I would see this loch you speak of."

"Aye, Lord, I can take you there," said Liadan.

The Isle of Man

RAGNHILD'S EYES LIT WITH PLEASURE at the small emerald leaves embroidered at her wrists and on the hem of her gold silk gown. "The embroidery is exquisite, Cecily." The fabric had been a gift from a visiting noble, the bliaut the one she would wear when she was presented to David, the King of Scots.

Cecily, Ragnhild's handmaiden, smiled, her dark hair making her blue eyes more striking. "I thought the small green leaves would be a reflection of your eyes, my lady." Only a few years older than her mistress, Cecily was skilled with a needle and thread. More than her skill, Ragnhild valued her friendship. There were few women on the isle who could be a close companion to Olaf's daughter. Affraic had her women who came of an afternoon to stitch with her but their gossip left Ragnhild wishing for more interesting conversation. Cecily provided a worthy friend but not always the conversation Ragnhild longed for. Mayhap she would find it at King David's court.

The shimmering gown hugged her curves until it flared out at her hips to form the full skirt. The long sleeves were tightly fitted to the wrist where they joined graceful folds of silk reaching nearly to the floor. Her long red hair hung loose beneath the circlet of gold on her head from which hung a transparent silk veil flowing down her back. "I have never been to King David's court. I do hope my appearance will bring honor to my father. I wouldn't want him to be seen as less by the Scots."

"Worry not, Mistress. You are a king's daughter and will outshine their women."

Just then, the king appeared at her door. "I have something for you, my beautiful daughter." For a moment he looked sad, as if remembering a time past. "It was prized by your mother. Ingibiorg asked me to give it to you when you were a woman full grown, which you are."

Her father handed Ragnhild a small velvet bag, embroidered with silver thread in a scrolling Norse design. She turned it over letting its contents spill into her hand. She inhaled sharply at the singular beauty of the necklace she had not thought about in years. "I remember my mother wore this once when I was a child." In the center of the necklace of onyx beads hung a gilded cross, its arms equal. At the center of the cross was an onyx stone.

She met her father's thoughtful gaze. Though a daughter of a king, Ragnhild rarely wore jewelry, but she would proudly display this beautiful reminder of her mother. "I will treasure it always."

Cecily came alongside her to admire the necklace. "'Tis a rare piece of fine workmanship."

Ragnhild was glad her mother had left her no pagan symbol but an emblem of the true faith. "Thank you, Father."

"'Tis an unusual cross," he said. "Likely acquired by your grandfather Earl Hakon from a Byzantine merchant." As he made to leave, he turned. "Attend to your packing, Daughter. We leave two days' hence."

When he had gone, Cecily said, "The onyx will look wonderful around your neck when you wear this gown. 'Tis said King David, though he be your father's age, is handsome of face and now widowed yet still young enough to sire more children. You will not go unnoticed by him."

"I don't want to marry a man my father's age, Cecily, not even the King of Scots. Besides, they also say that he loved his wife, Matilda, and like his mother, Queen Margaret, David is pious. Perhaps he does not wish to wed again. He already has his heir."

"Well, you need not consider the Scots king. At his court there will be other men who would gladly seek the hand of the beautiful and wealthy Princess of Man."

Ragnhild gazed out the arrow slit in her chamber to the blue sea beyond, pondering her handmaiden's words. Her mind filled with questions. If many nobles flocked to King David's court at Irvine, might her father seek to barter her hand anew or was he set on the Earl of Orkney? Her own mother had been the daughter of one of Orkney's earls so Olaf had before sought their alliance through marriage.

Into Ragnhild's mind came the face of Lord Somerled, the golden warrior who had never been far from her thoughts since the day he left Man. Could a man desire more than her physical appearance and her father's wealth? Was Somerled such a man?

CHAPTER 7

Dunaverty Bay on the Mull of Kintyre

SOMERLED SIGHED his relief as the wide beach at Dunaverty Bay on the southern tip of Kintyre came into view. The setting sun cast streaks of gold and copper onto the land and the sea. Where the waters receded from the shore, the wet sand appeared like sparkling gemstones. After the gray clouds and mists of Islay, the azure sky streaked with gold lifted his mood from the somber leave-taking following the burials at Keills.

The only bright spot had been his dawn walk to the hidden loch named for St. Findlugan. There, autumn had painted the bracken on the deer-covered hills brown but there were vast areas of greensward at the base of the gently sloping hills that circled the loch.

Wild geese and ducks inhabited the shores, including sheldrakes with their striking black and white plumage and red bills. Golden eagles soared above the loch's silver waters causing him to raise his eyes to the cloud-filled sky.

As he had gazed at the loch, he imagined a great hall rising from the island nestled close to shore. There, the clan chiefs could gather to deliberate great matters. He had walked along the shore of the loch that morning, experiencing a great peace. In the distance, he had seen the mountains on the neighboring Isle of Jura called the Paps, so named because of their shape like a woman's breasts. At the northern end of the loch, there were two ancient standing stones, reminding him that centuries ago, the ancients had lived there.

His stronghold on Loch Findlugan would not require a stone castle, for it would be easily defended. And its purpose would not be to protect the sea lanes but to shelter the center of his lordship. It would be a fine spot for a redheaded princess to race her horse without concern for invaders. A lump formed in his throat as he considered the future that might be. A future he very much wanted.

Somerled's musing came to an end as his crew's singing ceased and they rowed hard for the Dunaverty shore. He glanced up at the familiar cliffs rising on the left side of the bay now reflecting the golden sun. He did not look long at those cliffs for the other side of the bay held more interest for him. There, a large headland jutted out from shore ending in the huge Dunaverty Rock.

The craggy outcropping would serve well as the foundation for the castle he would build that would guard the sea lanes in this part of his kingdom.

Somerled's warriors, who had remained on Kintyre, had beached their galleys and longships in the wide crescent of sand, their colorful shields decorating the rails.

As his longships met the sand, men came running to meet him with shouts of welcome. Gaels, Scots and Irishmen still formed the ranks of his warbands. At the sound of the men rushing forward, shorebirds scurried out of the way and seals, resting on the rocks nearby, raised their heads in inquiry.

When they first came to Dunaverty Bay, his men had camped on-shore but now they lived in a settlement of thatched cottages they built for their families who would join them. The castle would be the eventual home for many.

A cheer rose up as his longship came to rest. "Somerled!"

"The men are glad to see you," said Domnall, standing at his side.

"And I them." He waved his hand to the men gathering to welcome him.

Those onshore stared at the longship that had no stern rudder but only a steering board and carved dragons on the stem posts.

Ruairi MacInnes stepped from the crowd. "I see you have gained another ship!"

Somerled swung down from the deck to the sand. "Aye, from Sweyn Asleifsson at Islay."

"Did you kill the thieving bastard?" asked Ruairi, running a hand through his long brown hair. His face, tanned from the sun, had only a few wrinkles and most of those around his eyes.

"Nay," said Somerled. "He has a purpose yet to serve."

"And the lass?" Ruairi asked, glancing behind Somerled to Liadan standing in the stern.

"Liadan!" Somerled shouted to the young woman. "Join me." To Ruairi, he said, "She is the sister of Brian MacGilleain, a hero who died fighting the Norse pirates at Keills."

"The lass insists on guarding our lord's back," said Angus with a wry smile as he came to stand beside them.

Somerled nodded his agreement, still amused at his new guard. Facing Ruairi, he said, "She has another brother who yet lives, Diarmad MacGilleain, one of our galley captains. Know him?"

"I do," said Ruairi. "Diarmad is a good man and a worthy captain of his own galley. He is among those I sent north to fortify Ardtornish Point in Morvern."

Somerled introduced Liadan to his small group. The men onshore sent her curious gazes, taking in her warrior's garb, before returning to their tasks. He would have to do something about her clothing if she were to accompany him to King David's court at Irvine. Meanwhile, he must see to his men.

He looked back over his shoulder. His warriors, who had done some hard rowing to Kintyre, climbed down from the beached ships. Somerled turned back to Ruairi. "The men are tired. Do you have shelter for them and an evening meal you can share?"

"Aye, Lord. We have built many new cottages and made use of the stone houses the Norse left. As for food, there will be both fish and venison for tonight's dinner. Liadan, you can lodge with my wife and me."

Somerled nodded. Glancing at Liadan's male attire, he said, "She'll be coming with me to Irvine to meet with King David so she'll need a lady's gown."

Ruairi smiled at the lass. "My wife will see to it."

"Though I have never been to a king's court, I have a gown that might be suitable," offered Liadan.

Somerled thought she likely brought the best one she possessed. "I leave it to you and Ruairi's wife."

Somerled dined with some of his men in the house that Ruairi had built for him and his wife and their two children, Bran and Ceana, eight and ten. He asked Liadan to join them so he could keep an eye on her.

Ruairi's wife, an attractive woman in her late twenties, had always impressed Somerled with her kindness.

"I will take one longship to Irvine," he told the small group. "I would ask Angus, Domnall and Maurice to accompany me." He looked at the three men named. "The rest of the men and ships I leave with you, Ruairi. Should David permit it, I hope to return with a stone mason who can supervise the building of the castle."

The next morning, shortly after sunrise, Somerled took the winding path to the top of Dunaverty Rock. He went alone, conscious of the fact his feet trod the same ground as Columba centuries before. Somerled felt a kinship to the Irish monk who founded the abbey on Iona, for they had a common ancestor, however distant, the great *Ard Ri*, the High King of Ireland. And both cared deeply for those they served.

With so much at stake, Somerled felt the need to meet with his God before going on to meet the Scots king.

At the summit, he gazed south, beyond the stone curtain wall that formed the remains of an ancient fortification, to the deep blue waters reflecting the golden rays of the sun rising in the east. Above him, gilded white clouds drifted across the azure sky. On three sides of the headland were the waters of *Sruth na Maoile*, the narrow expanse connecting the Irish Sea with the Atlantic Ocean. Twelve miles south of where he stood lay Ireland, the land of his birth, just visible on the horizon.

These sea lanes were critical to his kingdom, for any ship had to pass through this channel to sail from the Isle of Man north to Argyll and the Southern Isles.

Somerled took a deep breath, inhaling the familiar salted air that was his lifeblood. He spoke to God as his liege Lord. "Father, you have given me this great task to set the people free. Grant me wisdom to lead them and give me favor with King David. May I honor you in all things."

He did not linger overlong but, by the time he turned to retrace his steps, he had peace about his meeting with the King of Scots and his intention to build castles, not just here in Kintyre, but at all points necessary to keep the sea lanes free.

He descended the headland to find his brother Angus waiting with his cousin, Domnall, and Maurice. "Well, was it worth the climb?" asked Angus.

"Aye, it was," he said, experiencing again the peace he had gained atop the great rock. "I believe it is right to build a castle here. But, for that, and the others I see in my dreams, I must gain David's agreement. I would have no challenge from that quarter."

"It sounds like our trip to Irvine is timely," said Maurice.

"We have only to bid Ruairi good day and we can depart," said Angus.

"His wife is eager to show you what she has done with your guard," put in Domnall.

Maurice smiled, shaking his head.

Somerled raised a brow but his companions declined to say more. "Very well, lead the way. I am anxious to reach Scotland's coast in time to secure lodgings for the night."

Aileas, Ruairi's wife, appeared in the doorway as they neared the cottage where they had dined the night before. Her hair was a lighter brown than her husband's and her eyes were blue, whereas Ruairi's were hazel. For all that, they made a handsome pair. More importantly, the men respected Ruairi.

Aileas stepped forward to greet them and Liadan came out from behind her.

"What think you, Somerled?" asked Ruairi's wife, casting a glance at the young woman. "Will this do for her to greet the Scots king?"

No longer dressed in a warrior's clothing, Liadan now wore a close-fitting bliaut of fine blue wool. Her hair hung long behind her in rippling auburn waves, the sides had been braided and confined at the back of her head. She looked the part of a noble lass, though he was well aware her eating knife, secured at her waist, could be deadly given her skills. "Aye, she'll do," he said.

Domnall stared open-mouthed at the girl's altered appearance.

"I know I must change before we leave to cross the firth," said Liadan. "I just wanted your approval."

Somerled nodded. "You have it. And my thanks, Aileas, for what you have done for the lass."

"I was happy to do it," said Ruairi's wife. Except for those who had lived in Kintyre before the Norsemen were driven away, there were few wives yet among his men. That she had been willing to leave Morvern told him much about her character. And her smile told him she had enjoyed taking the younger woman under her wing.

Ruairi joined them, stepping out of his cottage and wiping his mouth with a cloth. "Will you three break your fast with us?"

Somerled was anxious to leave but his men would row harder and without complaint if they were fed more than the meager fare available on his ship. "Aye, and thank you. Have my men been fed?"

"They are eating now," Ruairi said, gesturing to a group of men sitting around a fire some distance away. "Come. Aileas has made porridge and there are eggs from our chickens as well as berries and bread. She has set aside smoked fish and apples for you to take with you."

Somerled had not thought much about his stomach until now but the offer of a hearty meal before sailing appealed. "As you wish. We are grateful for your hospitality." He followed Ruairi and the others into the cottage where Ruairi's two children sat eating.

An hour later, Somerled stood in the bow of his longship as his men rowed them past the waves to the open water, singing a Gaelic tune as they often did. Liadan, once again attired as a lad, stood in the stern, a picture of confidence as she spoke to the steersman.

Once the sail was raised, they aimed for the Isle of Arran. They would pass its southern end on their way to the coast of Scotland.

Somerled was delighted to see the *deilf*, dolphin, swimming alongside his ship, leaping from the water, providing escort, as if urging them on.

Destiny's path lay just ahead.

CHAPTER 8

Irvine on the west coast of Scotland

AS THEY REACHED the Firth of Clyde, the wind billowed the sail and blew Somerled's long hair behind him as he stared resolutely ahead. The deep firth formed a wide sea lane of great importance, sheltered from the Atlantic by Kintyre and Arran.

A few hours later, his men took to the oars as they entered the wide mouth of the River Irvine that would take them to where the King of Scots was holding court. The river made a great loop ere it reached the town's center. Once there, they beached the longship inside the harbor.

With the shortened days of October, the sun was now low in the sky, putting on a glorious display, its golden shafts reflected in the scattered clouds, turning the water in the river a brilliant amber.

Leaving a half-dozen men to guard the ship, Somerled and the others set off for town, which was not far.

Domnall knew well the royal burgh, for he'd been there before, so he agreed to find them lodgings. "Since the king is here with his retinue, rooms will be in short supply but I know of an inn off Seagate that might have something available. Go on ahead. I will find you."

As his cousin turned to go, Somerled said to Maurice, "Once we have secured lodgings, I would ask you to act as messenger to the king's constable to advise him that I have come to see David."

"Aye, I can do that. I once met Edward Siwardsson, the old Anglo-Saxon noble who is the Lord High Constable of Scotland. He will dwell here. Mayhap he can help us gain an audience with the king. I do not know the Deputy Constable, Hugh de Morville, but he is one you should meet. A Norman and the king's good friend."

They walked up to Seagate where a timber castle stood, its tall tower looking toward the harbor. Somerled stared up at it, surprised it was not stone.

"This is just one of the many places the Scots king visits in his travels across Scotland," said Maurice, "so no stone castle here."

"'Tis not so large as I would have expected either," said Somerled. "Still, I imagine there is a great hall."

"Yea, there will be that and tonight you will see it," Maurice said with a grin.

The people on the street, some Scots, some Normans, cast them curious glances. Somerled supposed he looked more Norseman than Gael and his men, all day on the sea, were wind-tossed and dressed in all manner of clothing. As well, he carried a sword at his side and a nasty-looking dirk with a carved handle at his belt. It was the latter that drew the gazes of the clean-shaven Normans.

"I expect King David will be glad to greet the one who has sent the Norse raiders fleeing from Argyll and the Isles," said Maurice. "He has no time to worry over them with his troubles in England. Now that Stephen of Blois has usurped the throne, David is bound by oath to support his niece, the Empress Maud, who vies for England's crown promised to her by her father."

That encouraged Somerled. Mayhap, given the king's other distractions, Somerled could offer him something he needed—thousands of Islesmen to guard his back door, the western border of Scotland.

"His court will be more English than that of the Scots kings before him," put in Angus, gazing up at the timber castle. "'Tis said he brought many Normans with him when he left Henry's court to take the Scots crown at his brother's death."

Having been raised as one with noble parentage tutored by monks in Ireland, Somerled could speak Latin, English and French, as David must also. They would have no trouble understanding each other. But would the king see the Lord of Argyll, Kintyre and Lorne as a threat or an ally?

Domnall returned just as they were beginning to take in more of the town with its narrow streets and buildings standing close together. "We are in luck," he said cheerfully. "They've a large room where the men can bed down and two smaller chambers, one for us and one for Liadan."

"Aye," said Somerled, "the lass needs her own chamber. I am glad you thought of it," Domnall. Somerled dispatched some of the men to gather the things from the ship they had brought with them while he, Angus, Maurice and Liadan followed Domnall with the rest of the men to the inn.

Sometime later, Somerled was bathed and dressed for his visit with the king. His long flaxen hair was plaited on the sides and tied back from his face.

Maurice returned to advise they would be welcomed this eve. "We are invited to dine as the king's guests," said Maurice, "surely a good sign."

They arrived at the castle at the hour stated in the king's invitation and were allowed inside. Hundreds of candles lit the large hall giving the air the scent of honey. Though the walls were wooden, the floor was stone, covered in herbed rushes. The sounds of lute, lyre and pipe provided a pleasing background against which many voices rose in conversation.

Silence descended upon the crowd as Somerled and his four companions entered. The crowd parted and, before him, some ten feet away, stood an older man with a handsome bearded face, dark hair with gray at his temples and a welcoming smile. He wore no crown but, from his rich attire, including purple mantle and green silk tunic, and the deference paid him, Somerled knew this was the King of Scots.

He walked forward and bowed. Rising, he said, "Your Grace, I am Somerled, Lord of Argyll, Kintyre and Lorne."

David's gaze roved over Somerled's clothing, the same he had worn to meet King Olaf, not quite Norse, not quite Gaelic, but a mixture of both, yet most adequate to meet a king. "I have heard much about you, Lord Somerled. They say you are King of Argyll. I am glad you are here." Looking at those with Somerled, the king said, "Introduce me to your friends."

Somerled gestured to the young woman who guarded his back. "This is Liadan of Islay, whose brother serves in Argyll as one of my warriors. I am returning her to him." This Somerled had said so that the king did not think Liadan was his woman. "And this man," he said, gesturing to his brother, "is Angus MacGillebride, my brother and chief of Clan MacInnes. And this Irishman is Maurice MacNeill, foster brother to King Olaf of Man when he still lived in Ireland."

David seemed pleased. "Welcome. We were just about to dine. Come meet my son and sit by my side. Your companions will be the guests of the Lord High Constable, Edward Siwardsson, at his table."

The Anglo-Saxon that Maurice had described earlier, a tall man whose fair hair was laced with silver, stepped forward. "It will be my pleasure, Sire." He indicated one of the long trestle tables sitting at right angles to the head table. Somerled's friends thanked him and followed.

Somerled fell into step behind the king as he walked to the dais and indicated Somerled should sit on his left. There was no queen to sit on the king's right, for his much-loved English wife had died years before. But taking the place on the king's right was a young man in his twenties, thin of body and handsome of face with a gentle demeanor. "My son and heir, Henry," said David.

Somerled inclined his head to the prince who was only a few years younger than him.

On Somerled's other side stood a Norman of an age with him, clean-shaven with dark hair and strong features, who the king introduced as Hugh de Morville. "My friend since we were lads at King Henry's court. And his wife, Lady Beatrice."

Somerled bowed to de Morville's young wife, whose dark brown plaits hung long beneath her veil.

"I am delighted to be invited to sit with you and your guests," he said. "I hope I shall always be considered one of those you accept at your table."

Just then, King Olaf of Man appeared out of the crowd with Queen Affraic and Princess Ragnhild. Somerled drew a steadying breath, his eyes fixed on the princess, hungrily taking in the sight of her. She looked more like a queen than a princess with her golden bliaut and circlet. Her red-gold hair, falling free of her veil, reflected the light of the many candles.

King David must have detected his keen interest. "Do you know my guests from the Isle of Man?"

"Aye," said Somerled. "I accepted Olaf's invitation to visit him not long ago."

The King of Man and his two ladies climbed onto the dais.

Somerled said, "Good day to you, King Olaf, and to your queen and daughter."

"'Tis good to see you again, Lord Somerled," replied Olaf. "And so soon."

His queen sagely nodded but said nothing.

The princess cast him a quick glance and then averted her eyes as if suddenly shy.

With an amused look, King David said to Somerled, "So you have met Olaf's daughter, the lovely Princess Ragnhild."

She looked up then and, meeting Somerled's gaze, blushed.

"Aye," he said, "I have had that pleasure." And then to her, "Princess, I did not realize you were here and it warms my heart to know of it."

"I think we should have the princess sit between you and de Morville," said David. "Olaf and his queen can sit on the other side of my son."

Somerled was pleased with the arrangement that put Ragnhild at his side.

There was one seat left. David looked up as a Norseman approached the dais.

"Rognvald, Earl of Orkney," said King David, "the last of my guests. Have you met?" he asked Somerled.

"We have not met, but I know Sweyn Asleifsson, one of his men."

"So, you are Somerled," said Rognvald, eyeing him with interest. "I must apologize for Sweyn's behavior on Islay. It will not be repeated."

David and his son appeared bemused, unaware of the earl's part—or that of his men—in pillaging the isle.

"So, he returned to Orkney?" Somerled asked the earl. He had no doubt Sweyn would again act the pirate given the chance but he would not mention it to Rognvald.

"Aye, with his tail between his legs. You may keep the ship he left behind with my compliments."

Somerled was amused that Rognvald should think he needed permission to claim a ship he'd won fairly in battle. "Forgive us," he said to King David, "for speaking of a matter that you may know little of."

"There is much to discuss," said the king. "You can explain all to me later. Meantime, Rognvald, take the seat on the other side of Queen Affraic and let us partake of our meal afore it grows cold." As they claimed their seats, platters of food were immediately placed before them and wine was poured into silver goblets.

Somerled turned to Ragnhild. "Your appearance dazzles, my lady."

She beamed her pleasure at his words.

"I can only say I am more than glad to see you."

She returned him a sweet smile. "As am I to see you. I would have thought you off chasing Norse pirates."

His mouth twitched up at one end. "One does not exclude the other. And, even when I am not with them, my men monitor the isles to discourage pirates."

The king drew his attention with his words. "My trip to Irvine has brought many here who might not call upon me at my castles in Carlisle and Roxburgh. At Irvine, those who travel by ship can sail nearly to my door."

"'Tis true," said Somerled. "We who travel the sea lanes are more comfortable on water than land."

"Tell me of this ship the Earl of Orkney has allowed you to keep."

"That ship was one fairly claimed as spoils, Your Grace. Rognvald's man, Sweyn, attacked the people of Islay and I defended them."

"Ah, said the king. I have wondered, though Rognvald assures me he is no threat."

Somerled was disinclined to believe the earl's motives were pure but he would not slander the man to the King of Scots. "Let us hope that is true."

David looked across Somerled to Ragnhild, now conversing with de Morville and his wife. "I noticed you have an interest in the Princess of Man. Many other men here do as well."

"Aye, she is beautiful and intelligent and would make any man proud to have her by his side."

The king acknowledged the truth of it and expressed his deep felt loss of his queen. "Her presence is missed every day."

Encouraged by Somerled, David spoke in gracious manner of the years since his wife had died and his plans for Scotland, including the abbeys he had yet to build and how he had changed the administration of his country, patterned after all he had learned in his long sojourn in England.

Somerled thought here is a man who does not put on airs or act in arrogance, demanding his due, but, rather, a man content to be in service to his God and his people. Here was a man Somerled could like.

The music resumed as they partook of the varied dishes set before them. Venison stewed in red wine and spices and roast fowl stuffed with spiced bread were offered them along with vegetables simmered in herbs. Bread, butter and cheese were also placed on the high table.

Though Somerled was fervently aware that Ragnhild was barely inches from him, so close he could smell her rose perfume and feel the heat of her body, he managed to attend to his food. He had not eaten so well since dining with her father.

RAGNHILD'S HEART POUNDED in her chest as she had watched Lord Somerled stride into King David's hall, unaware she stood among the gathered crowd. Her heart leaped within her to think he was here. Eyeing him pensively, she had noticed a new air of confidence about him in the way he held his head, only hinted at before. She wondered at the battles he had fought in the short time since she had last seen him yet there were no signs of wounds, none visible at least. He walked without hesitation or limp. Ragnhild chided herself for examining his person as might a concerned wife. She had never had such thoughts for another man.

Who was that lovely creature who had followed on his heels, gazing at him with adoration in her beautiful eyes? Even now, she kept watch on him from where she sat at one of the trestles. She could not be a wife as she was not by his side at the king's table. Who then? A mistress? The possibility grieved Ragnhild.

She had come with her father to King David's court several days ago, her father now considering King David's invitation to stay longer. She enjoyed Irvine with its markets where there were goods aplenty. All manner of merchants had come to serve the king and his entourage. And there was hunting in the forests nearby, which she dearly loved.

While Fairhair was not with her, King David and his retinue had brought many horses to Irvine and the castle's stables were available to his guests. Too, there were interesting women to converse with. She and de Morville's wife, Beatrice, had become fast friends.

Now that Somerled was here, her spirits rose even higher.

Ragnhild gazed down the table to her right to Rognvald who had come the day before to pay homage to the king and assure him that Orkney had no designs on Scotland. Thankfully, he had left Sweyn behind.

Having reminded her father she did not favor the earl, she hoped Olaf and Affraic discussed no betrothal with him. But her father was ever the statesman, bargaining whatever he had to gain security for his kingdom. And Affraic would see Ragnhild gone if she could.

She stole a glance toward Somerled. He bent his head to speak to King David, one fair and one dark but seemingly of a like mind as they laughed easily together. Her heart had fluttered and her palms grew moist when he looked at her with admiration. One glance from Somerled's piercing blue eyes could stop her heart.

Perhaps he had not forgotten her. For certes, she had not forgotten him.

THE KING SET DOWN his wine and glanced in Somerled's direction. "How did you come to the position you now hold as leader of the Gaels?"

"I did not seek to be their chief or their king, if that is what you are asking, Your Grace. When the MacInnes Clan lost their chief to the Norse pirates, they came to me to lead them."

"Ah. We have that in common, for never did I, the youngest son, believe I would wear Scotland's crown."

Somerled nodded, glad that David and he shared a similar beginning—both of royal linage but without expectations of rising to lead a kingdom. "The people of Argyll and the Isles were suffering under the Norse yoke," he went on. "I accepted their request to help them throw it off."

"For that, you have my gratitude," said David. "I have been concerned about the continued attacks of the pirates on the Isles and Scotland's coast but with little time to attend to it. Only recently did we send the Norse invaders fleeing from the Firth of Clyde's Isles of Arran and Bute."

"I, too, have worried over those isles," Somerled said. "In the hands of the Norse, they would present a threat to the whole of southern Argyll, especially Kintyre."

"For protecting Scotland's western coast, I am inclined to grant you a boon," said the king. "Is there something you would have of me?"

Somerled took a deep breath, praying his plans wouldn't offend the Scots king. "Aye, there is. To hold the sea lanes free, I must build fortifications in strategic places. Not just timber castles," he said, looking up at the rafters, his hand raised, "though this is a fine one. I wish to construct stone towers like the Normans built, and as you are building in other parts of Scotland. For that, I would seek your approval and, were you willing to part with skilled masons, I have need of them. My people can quarry stone, crush shells for mortar and cut timber for scaffolding, but they have not the skills to design and construct a stone edifice."

David smiled, his ringed fingers gripping his goblet. "I have some thoughts on the matter, but I need to make inquiries. Let us speak again tomorrow. There may be things I would ask of you as well." Turning the goblet in his hand, he said, "A hunt is planned for the morning. Perhaps you and your companions might like to participate? My constable's stables are at your disposal. I suppose I should ask if you ride as well as sail?"

Somerled chuckled. "I do. The coming of the Norse exiled my family to Ireland where I lived as a boy. I learned letters and Latin from the Culdee monks and the ways of a horse from the great horse lords in my mother's family."

The king nodded. "I know well the good teaching of the Culdees. They were the priests who taught my father King Malcolm. But my lady mother wanted the church in Scotland to be tied to Rome."

"I would have Argyll and the Isles free," said Somerled. "I fear the yoke of Rome could be as oppressive as that of the Norse."

David gave him a measured look.

Somerled met his gaze and did not look away.

"Very well," said the king. "Tomorrow it is. Meantime, enjoy the pleasures of my court." He turned to converse with his son, leaving Somerled free to speak again with Ragnhild.

"I know you can ride," he said to her, "but do you hunt?"

The green of her eyes, deeper in color in the evening, glimmered in the candlelight. "Of course. I learned the way of the bow as a young child, taught to me by my father's men."

"Then I shall look forward to joining you on the hunt tomorrow. The king has invited me and my companions to take part."

"I was hoping he would," she said, her smile brilliant.

AS THE MUSICIANS BEGAN to play, Ragnhild accepted Somerled's invitation, thrilled he had been the first to ask, for she had hoped to dance with him. There were other men with whom she would dance but none like Somerled. She liked Prince Henry's gentle ways and would have happily partnered with him but Earl Rognvald she would try to avoid.

Once the trestles were taken down and the musicians readied their instruments for more lively tunes, the dancers took to the floor. With each touch of Somerled's strong hands, each smile he gave her, she felt a contentment she had not previously known, a joy in his presence.

"Will you stay long at Irvine?" she asked.

"I cannot say. It depends upon the king." Somerled's blue eyes alighted with mischief. "And you."

"Me?"

"Aye. I have business with King David but had I known you were here, I would have come even without that purpose."

When the music stopped. Earl Rognvald came to stand in front of her. As always, his long chestnut hair was in perfect order and his clothing fine, his tunic crimson silk, embroidered in golden thread, his trousers blue. Around his shoulders, he wore an ermine-trimmed woolen mantle in the deepest shade of woad blue.

"I have written you a poem, Princess. A tribute."

Inwardly, she groaned. Glancing at Somerled, who had stepped back and lifted a brow at the earl, she said, "Say on."

"The verses came upon me as you entered King David's hall this eve," said the earl, and he began to recite.

Golden one, tall one
Moving in perfume and onyx
Witty one, you with the shoulders
Lapped in long silken hair
Listen: because of me the eagle has a red claw

Behind Rognvald, Somerled covered his mouth and looked at his feet.

She considered the poem a bit outlandish and the last line, a reference, she presumed, to Rognvald's warlike ways, served little purpose as a tribute to a lady. Rather, it reminded her of the rumors he was responsible for the disappearance of Earl Paul.

Fingering the onyx beads at her neck, she said, "You do have a way with words, Lord Rognvald."

The Norseman returned her a possessive grin. "I would have you know of my fondness for you, Princess." With a glower in Somerled's direction, he added, "That last verse assures you I am strong and will guard my own even drawing blood if I must."

Before she could reply, Rognvald asked her to partner for the next dance. With reluctance she placed her hand on his offered arm and allowed him to lead her to the new circles just forming.

Glancing over her shoulder, she met Somerled's intense gaze. He was not pleased.

INWARDLY, SOMERLED FUMED as he watched the Norseman dancing with Ragnhild, sending her frequent lust-filled glances. It was time for Somerled to speak to Olaf again concerning his daughter.

"How fares the Princess of Man?" Angus asked as he, Domnall and Maurice came to join him.

"Well enough by the look of her," replied Somerled. "Still, there are too many suitors here for my liking."

"Would you compete with them for her?" asked Domnall. "It does seem time for you to consider marrying again, and where you once had nothing to commend you, now you have a growing kingdom. She would be a fine bride with an unmatched dowry."

"Aye, he would be her suitor," interjected the older Maurice, his curly dark hair grown longer since their first voyages. "An alliance with the King of Man would gain our lord much more than he has now."

Angus ran his hand through his hair, as long as Somerled's but darker. "I sense it is the lady herself my brother wants as much as Olaf's gold or his lands."

"Enough!" Somerled scolded. "At the moment, I have no castle to offer and gold enough only for my ships and my men. Though, now that I think on it, when we leave here, after stopping at Kintyre, I would like to return to Islay and begin work on a timbered lodge on the island in Loch Findlugan. We need no mason for that. And, lest you worry that all my thoughts are for the princess, I do not forget the Norse menace."

"Which reminds me," said Domnall, "what is the Earl of Orkney doing here?"

"Since he has no daughter to offer David's son, I suspect he came to assure the king he poses no threat to Scotland," replied Somerled, continuing to watch Ragnhild dancing with the earl. "And, since Olaf is conveniently here, Rognvald is likely to again take up his quest for the princess' hand."

"By the look on her face," said Angus, "'twould seem she is not warm to that prospect."

THE NEXT MORNING Somerled and his brother, after having a

word with the stable master, took up their bows and quivers of arrows and headed to the streambank where David and his company were breaking their fast as was the custom before a hunt if the weather was fair. Domnall and Maurice had not wished to participate in the hunt but offered to stay behind and secure the provisions they needed.

The day presented all they could hope for in weather, the sky nearly cloudless and the leaves on the trees that had changed with autumn were ablaze with red, yellow and gold. The air, too, spoke of autumn, being dry and crisp.

Somerled was nearly to the gathering of hunters when Liadan rushed up to him, breathless. A look of concern shadowed her face. "I am glad I found you, Lord. I have heard something that concerns me."

"What is it?"

Angus furrowed his brow, intent upon the news she carried.

"I heard the Norseman, Rognvald, tell one of his men that he would deal with 'that bastard Gael' afore the hunt was done."

Somerled cast a glance toward those who sat in the clearing just ahead. The Earl of Orkney was nowhere to be seen. "He does not hunt this morning."

"Might he not set a trap somewhere along the route?" offered Liadan.

"The woods in which we hunt are dense," said Angus. "Best be on your guard, Brother."

Somerled gripped his bow tighter and turned to Liadan. "You have my thanks, lass."

Her dark eyes conveyed anxiety as she wished him well.

He and Angus joined the gathered assembly seated at tables arrayed on the streambank.

The men were richly attired. All carried weapons—spears, swords, bows and daggers of one sort or another.

Spotting Ragnhild sitting with her father, he went to join them, while Angus bid him a good hunt and ventured on to another group.

The princess had foregone a veil and confined her hair to one long plait. Her green bliaut was simple with a wide skirt for riding. At her side was a bow and a quiver of arrows. "We are waiting for the huntsmen to return with news of the harts. Join us." She swept her hand toward an empty bench.

"Happily." He greeted King Olaf and accepted the open seat.

As they partook of the meal of bread, bacon, smoked fish and apples, Somerled asked Olaf, "Will you participate in the hunt?"

"Nay and neither will David," he said, glancing at King David speaking with his men at a nearby table. "We have agreed to wait for you young ones to return."

"We did not see you at Mass," remarked Ragnhild, her delicate fingers holding a piece of bacon before her lovely mouth.

"I first had to see to my ship and my men, else I would have attended." Though that was truth, Somerled preferred the Culdee services. Still, he would have made an effort to attend just to be with her had he known she would be there.

The huntsmen in their green garb and hats returned, telling the Master of the Hunt they had spotted several harts, at least one of which possessed ten tines on his antlers.

The deerhounds, waiting with their keeper and sensing the hunt was about to begin, whined and strained at their leashes. At the instructions from the Master of the Hunt, the huntsmen took the hounds forward to be stationed along the expected route the hart would take.

Somerled quickly finished his meal and rose with Ragnhild and the other hunters, who were heading to their horses. One of the grooms brought a chestnut courser to him. "He's swift and sure, my lord. A good horse for the hunt."

"My thanks," said Somerled. He checked the cinch and stirrups, then mounted and walked the horse to join Ragnhild, who was stowing her bow and arrows in a leather bag tied to the saddle of a black palfrey. "You ride another horse today."

"I do. Fairhair stayed on the isle. I miss him, but King David's constable has been most gracious to offer the use of his stables."

The hunting horn sounded a double note to signal that the hunt had begun. In the distance, the braying of the hounds echoed through the woods.

They set off, Somerled keeping just behind Ragnhild as she urged her horse into a gallop. As they entered the forest, the hair on the back of Somerled's neck prickled.

He would not have needed Liadan's warning to know danger was near.

RAGNHILD GALLOPED BEHIND the other hunters in pursuit of the hart, the sound of pounding hooves echoing through the woods. Around her, dappled light filtered through the trees. Behind her, she heard the sound of Somerled following. She hoped the hunt would give her a chance to show him she was capable and quick with her bow.

A hart could be cunning, dashing into a burn to hide his trail or doubling back to confuse the hounds. Thus, she was careful to listen for the horn's signals indicating such might be happening. Ahead, she heard the hounds baying loudly. They must have encountered a hart, perhaps more than one since the harts ran in packs this time of year.

The huntsman sound a quick series of doubled notes, indicating the hart being pursued was running in the open. As her horse galloped ahead, she looked around, listening for a creature crashing through the woods.

He could be anywhere.

"I see him!" Somerled shouted. "He has doubled back and is coming this way. Quick, watch the clearing on your right."

Ragnhild reined in her horse, reached for her bow and nocked an arrow, its point sharpened only this morning.

The large deer bounded into the clearing and she focused, then loosed her arrow. It hurtled though the air toward the hart, catching him in the chest, bringing him down.

Before she could turn to see Somerled's reaction, the sound of another arrow whizzing past her caught her attention. Behind her, she heard a grunt.

Turning in the saddle, she saw Somerled slide from his agitated horse, a splash of red turning his sleeve scarlet. An arrow was lodged in the flesh of his arm.

"Somerled!" she shouted, getting down from her horse and running to where he stood among the leaves strewn about the forest floor. "You're hit!"

SOMERLED HAD WITNESSED the princess' well-aimed shot and had seen the hart drop to his knees in the clearing bathed in sunlight. The successful kill had distracted him. By the time he had heard the release of another arrow, it was too close to avoid altogether. He pressed himself to the courser's neck but that did not spare him.

He grunted as the arrow struck, tearing through his sleeve and ripping into the muscle of his left arm. His horse reared and a stab of pain made him grimace with the movement.

Sliding to the ground, his left arm throbbing, he soothed the courser with soft words. Carefully, he scanned the trees, searching for the one who had loosed the arrow. A movement in the undergrowth some distance off drew his gaze but he saw no one. Mayhap 'twas only a forest creature frightened by the sounds.

Ragnhild rushed to his side, eyes wide at the arrow protruding from his arm. "You are bleeding!"

"Aye, but I do not think the arrow hit the bone, thank God."

She looked around and then back to his arm. "What a clumsy hunter to not see you in the way of his shot."

He didn't want her to know the shot had been intentional, a near miss of his vital organs. "Aye, a shot gone awry. Help me remove the arrow."

She swallowed, pressing her lips together, and nodded. "What shall I do?"

"Break the shaft that is behind me and give me the fletching." He clenched his jaw and waited as she snapped the shaft and handed him the part of the shaft that contained the fletching. He tucked it into his sword belt. "Do you have any ale? Wine?" he asked her.

"I do," she said, quickly going to her horse and leading him back to Somerled. She held up a drinking flask. "'Tis wine."

"Pour it over what's left of the shaft."

Her brows drew together as she moved to take a stance behind him. "All right but 'twill sting like a wasp."

He was tempted to laugh. "I expect it will." He winced as the liquor met his raw flesh. Once done, he gripped the arrow tip and, with clenched teeth, yanked the shaft from his arm.

The blood ran free from the wound and she covered it with a wine-soaked cloth, a worried look on her face. "You are pale but at least you are free of the wretched barb." She pulled a cream-colored scarf from inside her sleeve. "Hold still while I try and stop the bleeding." With her forehead furrowed in concentration, Ragnhild tied the scarf around his arm above the wound, cinching it tight.

Aware her face was mere inches from his own and her faint scent of rose wafting to his nostrils, he lifted her chin with his right hand and looked long into her eyes that were the green of the hills of Morvern in spring. Loose tendrils of her red-gold hair had come free to frame her beguiling face. "Princess, do you care so much I shed a little blood?"

She met his gaze and her mouth opened as if in surprise, or mayhap in sudden realization. Averting her eyes, she said, "Why, yes…I do."

"That being the case, I would show my affection for you." He brought her face to his and pressed a kiss on her sweet lips. He wanted more but since she was an innocent and this their first kiss, he refrained. Meeting her wide-eyed gaze, he said, "I write no poetry, Princess and, as yet, have no castle, but my intentions are honorable and I am ever constant once my heart is given."

Her gaze lingered on him, her mouth slightly open, as if begging for another kiss.

The sound of the other hunters riding toward them and the hounds baying intruded into their private moment. Somerled stepped back, leaving a blushing Ragnhild to take up the reins of her horse.

Moments later, the hunters entered the clearing and the huntsman sounded a wavering note on his horn, signaling the kill had been made. Though they could not see him and Ragnhild where they stood among the trees, he thought it time for him to leave.

"Best claim your kill," said Somerled.

"But your arm—"

"Do not worry. I am fine." Wincing against the pain, he swung into the saddle and smiled down at her. "We will take up this meeting again soon. Meanwhile, tonight we dine on venison, thanks to you, Princess."

Not wishing the hunters to see his bloodied person, he led his horse from the woods in another direction, still experiencing the taste of her lips.

CHAPTER 9

RAGNHILD WONDERED at Somerled's seeming indifference to being shot through with an arrow. He sat straight in the saddle as he turned to go, his head up, as if nothing had happened. He was an altogether fine-looking man with the sides of his hair taken up for the hunt, emphasizing his strong jaw.

The wound from the arrow had stopped bleeding but he would still be hurting. She wanted to follow him and tend his arm but she knew he would not want her to. He would hide the wound and his pain from all.

"Will I see you this eve?" she had asked to his back. It was a bold question for a maiden, but his kiss, the touch of his lips on hers and his words had changed everything. What she would have resisted from any other man she had encouraged from him. And, had they not been interrupted, she would have welcomed another of his kisses.

She could no longer hide her desire for him.

At her question, he had turned in the saddle. "Aye, or before. I am to meet with King David this afternoon so I must change my clothing." He glanced at his blood-spattered sleeve and then at her. "I thank you for your ministrations."

When he had gone from her sight, she rode to where the hunters had dismounted and were now standing around the dead hart. One of the huntsmen was cutting the entrails from the deer to offer to the hounds now leashed but whining, eager for their prize.

"Was this your kill?" asked Hugh de Morville. "I have asked and it was none of ours."

"It was," said Ragnhild from where she sat on her horse. "He doubled back or I would not have had a clean shot."

"I congratulate you on your good fortune," said de Morville. "He's a grand specimen and will feed us all." Then with a bow and a grin, "The honor of the hunt goes to the Isle of Man and to its princess."

As the hunters nodded their agreement, she inclined her head. "Thank you." Wishing to change from her hunting attire, Ragnhild bid the men good day and returned to the stables where the king's constable kept his horses. Placing the reins in the hands of a groom, she sought her chamber where Cecily waited.

"How went the hunt?" asked her handmaiden as she began to help Ragnhild undress.

She hesitated. There was so much she could have said but did not. Instead, she treasured in her heart the moment in the woods with Somerled and would share it with no one. The memory of it still made her pulse speed and brought a smile to her face. "It went well," she finally said. "'Twas my arrow that brought down the hart but, as I think on it, I believe Lord Somerled allowed me to take a shot that should have been his."

Brows raised above her blue eyes, Cecily said, "A gracious man. Still, however you came by it, my lady, you did well. And how did the hunters react?"

"They were generous, expressing congratulations."

Having unlaced her tunic, Cecily helped her shed the garment and the chemise underneath. "That is to the good, though they had to be jealous."

"Possibly. Hugh de Morville was kind. I think he was even pleased it was my arrow that felled the deer."

Cecily gestured to the large wooden tub with steam rising from the water. "I had a bath drawn for you in anticipation of your return. I have added your rosewater to it."

"Bless you," said Ragnhild, walking to the tub. "I wouldn't want to smell of horse and sweat in the king's presence."

Ragnhild allowed her handmaiden to scrub her back, then accepted the sponge from her to see to the rest.

"While you were at the hunt," said Cecily, standing before her, "I spent some time in the kitchen, inquiring about herbs. The servants were chattering away like magpies."

"Really, about what?" she asked with fleeting interest.

"'Twas all of Lord Somerled. He seems to be a man about which there is much speculation, especially by the young maids."

"And?" Ragnhild tried not to show her interest yet she waited with great anticipation.

"I learned something I thought would interest you."

Ragnhild raised a brow, impatient for Cecily's news.

"He was married young in Ireland and his wife died giving him a son."

He is a widower? "He cannot be thirty now. How old might the son be?"

"The women guessed eight or nine."

"I have never seen such a child with Lord Somerled. Where is he?"

"One of the kitchen servants heard the lad is in Ireland with his grandmother, a Norsewoman."

Ragnhild rose from the water and Cecily handed her a drying cloth. As she wiped the water from her body, she thought of what her handmaiden had told her. She was unsurprised that Somerled's mother was Norse; he had the height, fair hair and blue eyes that would name him such.

The news of an earlier marriage did not trouble her. A man who loved once could love again. Marriages between the young were often arranged, the two individuals knowing little of each other. Surely Somerled's marriage had been one of those, for he might not have been twenty when he was wed. Too, women often died in childbirth, leaving their babes to be raised by others. Ragnhild was not opposed to raising another woman's child, especially a boy in need of a mother's love.

Cecily helped her into her chemise and the gown of copper-colored samite threaded with gold, fitting the fabric belt around her hips.

Accepting her knife from her handmaiden, Ragnhild tucked it into her waist. "If I must be hailed as the one who brought down the hart, I would have them know I am a woman of royal blood and not an ill-bred hoyden who prefers to ride with men. My father would want me to be dressed as befits a princess." What she did not say was that the pains she took with her appearance were not just for her father, but for the golden warrior who now occupied her thoughts and filled her heart with longing.

"Aye, Mistress, he will be most proud of you this eve."

Cecily combed Ragnhild's long hair until it was shining.

She asked her handmaiden to form it into two plaits. "I'll not have the Earl of Orkney spouting poems about my hair falling around my shoulders tonight."

Cecily laughed as she wrapped the braids with copper-colored ribands and set a circlet of gold on Ragnhild's head from which her silk veil flowed down her back like a pale waterfall.

"The earl makes quite an appearance when he recites in loud voice for all to hear," said Cecily. "The younger servant girls giggle behind their hands."

Ragnhild let out a sigh. "I had to hold my tongue not to do the same. He meant well, I'm sure, but humility is not in his nature. And I cannot forget he may have murdered a good man."

AFTER HE BATHED and managed to clean the wound which was beginning to bruise, Somerled wrapped a new bandage around his arm before donning clean clothes. Just as he was leaving his chamber, Angus returned.

"I was wondering where you were," said Somerled.

"After the hunt, I shared a few tankards of ale with the other hunters," said his brother. "You should have joined us. The men were in good spirits even though a woman brought down the hart."

"I might have done had my arm not been covered in blood." He glanced at the bloodied tunic he had tossed on the floor. A shaft of light from the small window made the blood appear a dark red.

Angus shifted his gaze to the torn tunic. "What happened?"

"Do you recall Liadan's warning this morning? It seems someone decided an arrow would suffice to remove the troublesome Gael who would court the princess."

Angus looked over the tunic Somerled now wore. "I see no bandage. Is it a bad wound? Your sword arm?"

"Nay, my left. The bandage is beneath my sleeve. It aches like the devil but at least the wound is confined to my arm and the bleeding has stopped. The arrow would have hit my chest had I not moved just before it struck."

"Fortunate that," said Angus.

"I would have no one know I was hit. Even the princess thinks it was a stray arrow from a hunter with a bad aim."

"Who did it, do you think?"

Somerled handed the fletching to his brother. "Mayhap whoever owns this. See if you can find out to whom it belongs."

Angus accepted the broken arrow shaft and studied the fletching. "Not one of ours. After Liadan's comment this morning, I would have thought the Orkney earl was your only enemy but I am certain Sweyn still hates you and one of his men may have come with the earl. I will see what I can learn, but first, let us eat. They have set out a table of victuals in the hall."

"Aye, I am hungry," said Somerled. "And then I need to meet with the king. Much depends on it."

After he and Domnall had eaten some bread and cheese, quaffing it down with ale, he inquired where he might find the king. A servant led him to a small solar up a narrow set of stairs. "You are expected, my lord."

David sat at a table with another man, a shaft of light falling behind them. The king waved his hand, welcoming Somerled into the private chamber. "Come in, Lord Somerled. Allow me to introduce you to my steward, Walter Fitz Alan."

Somerled offered his hand to the man, glad the arrow had not hit him in his right arm. Fitz Alan, of an age with Somerled, rose to shake his hand. The steward wore his light brown hair short and his beard close-cropped like the Normans who sported beards. "Welcome to

Scotland," he said before resuming his seat.

"Thank you," said Somerled.

David indicated with his hand that Somerled should take the open chair at the table. "Join us. We were just discussing the Isles of Arran and Bute in anticipation of my meeting with you."

Somerled sat down and leaned forward, anxious to hear more.

"Arran, as you likely know," began Fitz Alan, "is largely unproductive."

It was not the isle's productivity that occupied Somerled's thinking but, not wishing to appear disagreeable, he said nothing.

"Since Arran and Bute are of no particular interest to my steward," interjected the king, "but doubtless of some importance to you, I propose to make them a gift to you. We have done little to aid the Gaels there in the face of Norse raids, save for recent attempts to send the pirates fleeing."

A feeling of excitement built in Somerled's chest. He had not expected so great a boon. "Arran and Bute are part of my heritage, the ancient Dalriada. Guarded by my longships and galleys, they will provide no haven for the Norse, nor will they pose a threat to Argyll or to Scotland."

"Then 'tis done," said David. "I will have the charter drawn up. To your request, I will send you back to your isles with two of my French stonemasons. They use the idle days of winter to lay their designs and cut the stones, so the timing is right. By spring, you will be ready to build."

Somerled was pleased. "You have assisted me greatly, Your Grace."

David sat back in his chair and fixed Somerled with a pointed look. "And what will you do for the Scots and their king in return?"

He did not have to think long before replying. "You will have Somerled, Lord of Argyll, Kintyre and Lorne as a friend, which is no mean thing."

The king nodded. "Would you swear fealty to me as your overlord?"

Somerled shook his head. "Homage and respect I freely give you, for it is well deserved. Fealty, nay. As you have said, I am a king. Thus, I am bound to other kings only by my bond of friendship and my word of honor. Instead, I would propose an alliance. Should you have need of my thousands of warriors and my hundred galleys and longships, we would come at your call. And should I have need, you would do the same for me."

The king leaned forward, his forearm on the table. "If what I am told is truth, you are a leader loved by your people, even the Irish, and honest and fair to all. Believing this, I can accept your word and will hold you to it." The king narrowed his eyes on Somerled. "It did give me pause when I heard you ripped out the pirates' hearts in Morvern."

Somerled looked down. "A necessity in the beginning." Raising his gaze to meet the king's, he said, "I had but few warriors then and winning that battle was crucial. I have since killed many a Norse pirate, but I've not again repeated that display."

David laughed, shooting a glance at Fitz Alan. "For a time, I thought you as savage as the Norse pirates you chased from our shores but then I heard more. And what I heard, I liked. Moreover, I do not hold it against you for not offering an oath of fealty to me for lands you consider yours. In truth, I am busy in England and cannot be concerned with Argyll and the Isles. Too, when I became King of Scots, I denied King Henry his demand for my oath of fealty. My people would not have understood. But I gave him my word to support the claim of his daughter, my niece, the Empress Maud to the English crown. And I do to this day."

His jaw set in firm determination, Somerled offered his hand to David. "You have my word, Your Grace, as long as we both live."

The king accepted Somerled's hand and then poured wine for the three of them.

Somerled quaffed the wine and spoke again. "There is another matter I would discuss with you if you are willing."

The king looked up, his dark brows arched. "Yes?"

"'Tis my brother-in-law, Malcolm MacHeth."

"A troublesome oaf," put in Fitz Alan, frowning.

"Aye, probably," replied Somerled, "but for the sake of his wife, who is my sister, and my nephew, I must inquire of his welfare."

"He remains my prisoner," said David, "yet he is treated as a guest at my castle at Roxburgh. Your sister and nephew may join him if they choose. You do understand why I cannot free the rebel from the house of Moray?"

"I do and I thank you for your leniency." Somerled well knew another, less merciful king, would have taken Malcolm's life for he had rebelled more than once in pursuit of his lands and title. As David's guest, Malcolm would be treated well. Somerled would assure his sister she had no cause to worry.

Satisfied he could do no more, Somerled lifted his drink in toast and three goblets came together.

His business done, Somerled set down his wine and rose. Bowing, he thanked the king and inclined his head to Fitz Alan before taking his leave.

SOMERLED CELEBRATED that night, first with his men, and then in the king's hall with Angus, Domnall, Maurice and Liadan. All were delighted they had added Arran and Bute to the isles over which he reigned and lifted many cups of ale in toast.

"With Arran so close to Kintyre, Ruairi and those at Dunaverty will sleep more soundly," said Domnall.

"Aye," agreed Somerled, "and so will I."

"What did you give to gain so much?" asked his brother, his expression skeptical.

"Only my word that my ships and my warriors would come should King David have need of us." When his companions looked at him with questioning eyes, he said, "I could not have done less. 'Tis an alliance we sought."

"I suppose it a fair bargain to have David as friend," put in Maurice, "though, with his troubles in England, a call to arms might not be far away."

"Aye," Liadan agreed, "even so, there is no doubt you did well, my lord."

Somerled dined on the haunch of venison provided by the Princess of Man, all those attending the king praising her winning shot. She had emerged into the hall as an elegant lady, making it hard to imagine one so winsome had, but a few hours earlier, galloped in the hunt.

She took her place beside her father and stepmother at the high table, her smile wide when she glimpsed Somerled sitting at the trestles with his companions. For a moment, he could not look away.

"I found the fletching's owner," said Domnall, drawing his attention, "or at least the men who have the same fletchings on their arrows."

Somerled turned his eyes on his cousin. "And?"

"One of the grooms remembered seeing that fletching on the arrows in the quivers of Earl Rognvald's men. He said they were unique to the Norsemen, the arrowheads, too."

"So, the earl greets me warmly and asks forgiveness for Sweyn's treachery yet he would send one of his men to kill me."

"'Tis how the Norsemen from Orkney take revenge," said Maurice. "They do not openly speak of it until accomplished. Once they have killed and burned without mercy, they claim victory. But I believe Rognvald is too concerned with how he is perceived to be directly involved in treachery."

"Remember, Brother," said Angus, "he knows of your interest in Princess Ragnhild and likely resents what he deems interference in his plans for a bride with a large dowry."

Somerled acknowledged the truth of it. "I must speak to Olaf and see if I can delay his acceptance of the earl's suit. There is no need for such an alliance now that we protect the Isles and, besides that, have the favor of King David."

As the dinner drew near its end and the trestles were taken down to allow for entertainment and dancing, Somerled watched for King Olaf to descend from the dais. Once he did, Somerled bowed to Queen Affraic and to the princess and asked if he could speak privately to Olaf.

Ragnhild returned him an anxious expression went with Affraic to join the other women.

Olaf suggested he and Somerled take some evening air.

Outside the hall, the air was cold and brisk. The street was empty. Somerled drew his mantle around him, glad his men had lodgings, for the night would be colder still. The smell of sea and salt brought a welcome change from the heat and pervasive smell of wood smoke in the hall. He had posted a guard for his longship that changed every four hours so none of his crew would face the entire night on the ship.

He paused to admire the evening sky and Olaf stopped beside him.

The sun was nearly set behind the mountains of Arran. The sky was the color of the bitter oranges from Seville they sold in Dublin's markets. Clouds had gathered since the morning, their edges now gilded with the golden light. Somerled smelled rain in the air as a man used to travel by sea senses such things. "Winter approaches."

"As November descends," began Olaf, "I want to be home on Man, in my own bed and dining in my own hall. Where will you winter?"

"I have stops to make when I leave here but I am hoping to spend the winter on Islay where I will build a new timber lodge on Findlugan's Loch. Do you know it?"

Olaf nodded. "Once, I sought shelter from a storm in the waters of Loch Indaal. My travel was delayed for a week and the loch you speak of was merely a good walk away."

"It was the large bay of Loch Indaal that I had in mind when I picked Findlugan's Loch as the ideal place for the clan chieftains to gather. It will be one of my first strongholds, one that will not require stone to be secure."

"And do you still plan to build stone castles?"

"Aye. King David has given me his blessing—and more importantly, two of his French stonemasons—for construction of castles at strategic points in my growing kingdom of the Isles."

Somerled would not have sounded so boastful but he wanted Olaf to know he was a man of his word and had already begun to build his chain of strongholds. Castles fit for a princess.

"Ah, I can see where you are taking me. Now that you are building, you think to again ask for my daughter's hand."

"I do. I believe she would welcome my suit and, within a year, I can offer her a home like she has on the Isle of Man. Think, King Olaf, if you gave her to me, Ragnhild would not be as far as she would be in Orkney or some other place. You could see your grandchildren often. And I would give my word to you, as I have to David, to come when you have need of my many ships and my thousands of warriors."

"You make it sound attractive," said Olaf, rubbing his hand over his beard.

Somerled considered the aging but still healthy king. With no height to compensate, Olaf had grown rounder. Surely, he desired grandchildren, and Somerled would need heirs for the kingdom he was building. "Give her to me, King Olaf, and you will not regret it. Neither will she, for I love her."

The king turned from the setting sun to face Somerled, as if surprised at his bold declaration.

Somerled felt the sun's dying rays on his face and wondered what Olaf saw. Did he see a man in love, a man committed to one woman no matter the cost?

"Mayhap one day I will give her to you, but not, I think, this day."

Somerled's heart sank. He had hoped for a betrothal even if the marriage took place a year hence. Disappointed once again, he asked, "What of Rognvald's suit? Will you give her to him?"

"That is a question I have pondered since we arrived here and I discovered the earl had come to call on King David. Rognvald informed me his next stop would have been the Isle of Man. I cannot dismiss him, for he is a noble of royal descent. He continues to want Ragnhild for his countess, and my queen urges me to give the princess to him. But my daughter does not favor the man. Though he is wealthy with strong connections to Norway's king, he is also a braggart, which does not wear well."

"You must know that I am now stronger than Rognvald."

"I know your fleet of ships has grown and you can call upon more of your Highlanders."

"Aye, all that is true." Somerled pressed his case, deciding to share with Olaf what he would not even tell the Scots king. "And there is something more I would tell you. It concerns the earl."

Olaf's bushy red brows lifted. "Yes?"

Somerled rolled up the sleeve of his tunic to show the bandage, the linen still bearing a small smear of dried blood. "This day, he had one of his men try to kill me on the hunt but when I bent to my saddle, the arrow hit my arm instead of my heart."

Olaf stared at the bloodstained bandage. "Rognvald has admitted this?"

"Not yet, but I have proof and will soon confront him."

"Why should he do this?"

"Do you not know?" At Olaf's blank look, Somerled added, "He is aware of my feelings for Ragnhild and, I suspect, of hers for me. He would have no competition for your daughter's hand. And murder is not above him."

Olaf let out a sigh of resignation. "A wise man guards what he considers his."

"And that is how I see Ragnhild, Dear King...my own."

Olaf shrugged. "There is no reason for haste or violence in this matter, for nothing has been committed. In the meantime, I am selfishly inclined to give her to no one."

Somerled frowned his frustration. Lacking the prize he had hoped for, he took the crumbs Olaf offered. "Very well, I accept your decision—for the meantime. Still, I will not forsake my quest to claim Ragnhild as mine."

On Olaf's face appeared the merest of smiles.

RAGNHILD WONDERED what Somerled had in mind when he asked her father for a private conversation. Might they speak of her? Would Somerled ask for her hand? Or, was she just hoping? They might only discuss an alliance, the kind men who commanded warships and territories might desire.

The two were not gone long. When they returned, her father went to speak to some of his friends and she turned her attention to Somerled. His mood appeared somber. What could have caused so serious an expression?

She watched as Somerled looked around him, his gaze coming to rest upon Earl Rognvald, who had just finished a game of chess with Hugh de Morville. Then he strode to where Rognvald sat before the empty board replacing the chess pieces. He must have asked the earl if he wanted to play another game for Rognvald gestured to the empty seat. They exchanged a few words and began to play.

From where Ragnhild stood next to Beatrice, Hugh de Morville's wife, she could see well the chess game as it proceeded. Not far away, the pretty girl Somerled had brought to David's court stood, her eyes always on her lord. Who was she?

Ragnhild had observed no whispered words between the girl and

Somerled, no touches or looks like a man would give his mistress. But did that signify? Mayhap he was just being discreet.

The women's gossip around Ragnhild did not require her attention but she did not hesitate to respond to the question Beatrice asked. "Have you enjoyed Irvine?"

Between sips of her wine and furtive looks at the chess game, Ragnhild said, "Oh, yes. There is so much more to occupy one's time here than at home."

Beatrice smiled, her dark eyes glinting in the fire light. "I forget you live on an island."

Ragnhild nodded. "The Isle of Man does have its limitations. We've not the many shops, but I often sail with my father to Ireland and Galloway and the isles that are his."

"My travels are mostly on land," replied Beatrice, "and the distances across Scotland are far. Riding for long days can be wearisome."

Ragnhild stole a surreptitious glance at the ongoing chess game. Judging by the pieces piled up next to Somerled, he was winning. The scowl on Rognvald's face, made harsher by the candle casting him in shadows, gave proof to her assumption.

"I do love to ride," Ragnhild said, "though perhaps not for days on end."

"You do not mind the cold and wet weather of the Irish Sea?" asked Beatrice, seeming to shudder.

"My father takes pains to see I am comfortable, giving me the warmest of fur-lined mantles. Aside from that, I was raised as much on his longship as on land. I love the sea and the sight of the isles rising from it."

Ragnhild diverted her gaze for a moment to the chess game where a smile suddenly appeared on Somerled's face.

"CHECKMATE," said Somerled, fixing his eyes on the shocked earl. For one who had touted his prowess at the game, this must not have happened often.

With an indifferent grimace, Rognvald tipped over his king, one of the carved pieces of walrus ivory Somerled had been admiring. "What would you have of me for your miraculous win?" A boon had been promised to the winner but it was clear to Somerled that the earl never expected to lose.

Somerled pulled from his tunic the broken arrow shaft, the feathers still intact. He had learned more about it since Angus had told him it belonged to one of the earl's men. "I would know which of your men thought to slay the King of Argyll with this arrow." Though King David had called Somerled a king, it was only with a man as self-important as Rognvald that Somerled would use the title "king" for himself. Somerled was pleased to see it had the desired effect.

If it were possible for the Earl of Orkney to be embarrassed, he was. His cheeks flamed. "I know nothing of such a plot! And my quiver is missing no arrows."

"Is that so?" Somerled flicked his fingers over the feathers. His left arm still ached like perdition and he had used only his right hand in the game, a fact apparently unremarked by the earl. "Mayhap 'tis not yours. Yet this is one of your Orkney arrows. The feathers may be common goose but different than ours in the way they are affixed to the shaft, a shaft made of Norway pine, a wood only Orkneymen use."

Rognvald abruptly rose and glared down at Somerled. "You slander me and mine!"

Somerled relaxed in his chair, confident he had hooked the salmon. He had only to land it. He leaned forward and spoke in a low voice. "The next time you try something like that, I will show no mercy. If I must kill all to get one, I will."

The earl's dark eyes, full of menace, narrowed on Somerled. "The next time, I will not fail." Abruptly, he turned and stalked off.

Somerled sat back and crossed his arms over his chest. *Well, well, well.*

OLAF STROLLED THROUGH THE HALL, greeting the men he had come to know over the many years he had been allied with the King of Scots. Raised together in the court of Henry I, he and David had learned the ways of the powerful King of England together, both his treachery and his harsh demands. Henry was a sovereign who considered his subjects playthings. For certes, the women Henry took to his bed, even the wives of his barons, fell into that category. Olaf had lost count of Henry's bastards.

Though he did not lament Henry's passing, Olaf regretted the current state of affairs that pitted Henry's daughter, Maud, against his nephew, Stephen, who had seized England's throne on the old king's death. A civil war was threatening to ensue that would surely entangle David. Olaf might be David's friend but he had no intention of becoming involved in England's affairs.

Seeing Ragnhild talking with the women of the court, Olaf let out a measured sigh. She was his jewel and not only his but that of his kingdom. His people loved her and since her mother, Ingibiorg, had died, they treated the young princess as their own. He must arrange a marriage that would serve his kingdom yet assure his daughter would be well treated and given a worthy home. After all, if anything untoward happened to his young heir, Godred, it would be Ragnhild's sons who would inherit the Kingdom of Man and the Isles.

His daughter did not lack for suitors but which one would be best?

The Earl of Orkney admired the princess though, at times, it seemed his fondness for her was the same as his fondness for his dragonships. Rognvald would give her a title, jewels and poems. But would he care for her as Olaf had? Did his great view of himself leave room for a wife to dominate his heart? Mayhap not. And now that Olaf no longer needed Rognvald to keep the sea pirates from the Kingdom of Man, could there be a better choice?

In contrast to Rognvald, Prince Henry, King David's son, was humble as well as handsome, beloved by all. Undoubtedly, he was a young man who would treat Ragnhild well, as his father, the King of Scots, had treated his own wife, loving her even after her death. But was David inclined to have a Norse daughter-in-law when his ties had always been to England? And did Olaf want a Scot to inherit his kingdom? Besides that, while Olaf had observed the two young people dancing together and could see they had become friends, the twinkle in her eyes and the smile that lit up her face she reserved only for Somerled.

The Lord of Argyll, Kintyre and Lorne had risen like a comet to outshine all the young lords who would pay suit to Ragnhild. Olaf was coming to see that, one day, Somerled could be lord, not just of Argyll and a few isles, but lord of far more. With King David's blessing, and rents from the lands he controlled, Somerled could now construct the castles that would secure such a kingdom. But the Gaels were a troublesome lot, often fighting among themselves. And if not killed by a fellow Gael, Somerled could be slain on one of his many voyages attacking the Norse pirates, for he engaged in warfare on a near daily basis. No, if Somerled were to be considered for Ragnhild's hand, Olaf must wait to see if the young lord could deliver on his many promises and survive to tell of them. After all, the princess was only nineteen summers. There was time.

Affraic crossed the hall to his side. "Lord, might we retire soon? It has been a long day."

He considered his young bride, glad his stamina had not flagged as the years had passed. "Aye, my love, and perhaps 'tis time we return to Man."

CHAPTER 10

"LORD SOMERLED," whispered Liadan, coming to stand over the chess table abandoned by the earl, "I heard that scum's words. Shall I kill him now?" Her gray eyes, together with her frown, gave the impression of an impending storm.

Amused, but realizing the lass was serious, he said, "Nay, Liadan. God willing, Rognvald will yet serve my purpose. Only consider how rude it would be for us to slay one of King David's guests in his royal court."

She dropped her gaze, contrite. "Aye, Lord."

"But, if you wish to aid me, you can let my brother, cousin and Maurice know I would see them outside."

Her face lit up, pleased to be given a task. "Gladly," she said and turned to go.

Somerled rose. Wending his way through King David's guests, he stepped outside, into darkness broken only by torches lighting the front of the castle. Clouds marched slowly across the night sky. Between them the full moon appeared with scattered stars. The temperature had dropped; the air was now like that on the open sea.

In the distance lay the harbor where lanterns would be glowing from the decks of beached longships, casting their light onto the waters of the River Irvine. Though the buildings in front of him prevented his witnessing the sight, he would soon be there, for he was intent on visiting his ship.

"You asked to see us," said Angus, coming through the door of the timber castle, followed by Domnall, Maurice and Liadan.

"I did," said Somerled. "I thought to visit the ship and speak to the men standing guard. Tomorrow morning, I will meet with the others. Unless you advise otherwise, we will sail mid-morning."

"I expect the men not on the ship will be in the taverns enjoying their ale," offered Angus.

"True," said Somerled, "and I would not take them from their last night of pleasure. But let them know that they should be sober tomorrow morning and in their lodgings tonight. I don't want us searching for them at dawn in some lass' bed."

Angus chuckled. "Aye, I will find them and deliver your message."

"What did you learn from your game of chess?" asked Maurice.

"I confirmed the arrow that pierced my arm belonged to one of the earl's men, so much so that my words drew a threat from Rognvald."

"I liked him not at all," said Liadan, who had been listening to them speak, "but Lord Somerled would not let me take the villain's life."

His cousin gave the girl a reproachful glance. "Just as well," said Domnall, "or you might have lost yours."

"Well then," began Somerled, "Angus, you check the taverns." Glancing at Liadan, he added, "I think 'tis best one of you escorts the lass back to her chamber ere you join me at the ship."

The flickering light from the torches made clear the girl was unhappy at being left behind but she said nothing.

Domnall quickly volunteered. "I'll do it."

"Very well," said Somerled, giving his cousin an assessing gaze. "Maurice and I will meet you at the ship."

As he and Maurice began to walk down to the harbor, Somerled said, "It appears Domnall has developed a tendre for the lass."

"Aye, he has."

"Need I worry?" Somerled considered the girl like a younger sister, to be protected.

"There is no cause for concern," said Maurice, his dark Irish looks blending with the night. "He treats the lass as a precious flower to be coddled. However, a wedding might be in her future if the lass is willing and her brother, Diarmad, consents."

"She could do worse," said Somerled. "Domnall is an honorable man."

"And he fights like the devil," added Maurice with a grin. "Recall he was the one who brought down Sweyn."

"Aye, he did." Then, changing the subject, Somerled said, "Before we sail, 'twould be good to procure all we need to aid our building on Islay. Timber we can cut but, unless the Islay smith has many on hand, we will need nails and tools."

"I'll see to it," said Maurice.

"You will have the morning. And here are two more things to acquire," he said, handing Maurice a paper on which he had written the items.

They arrived at the harbor and Somerled climbed aboard his ship. Immediately, he felt at home, even though the deck was not moving. Leaning against the gunwale, he crossed his arms and addressed the men he had left there as guards. "Our trip to Irvine has been successful. We sail tomorrow mid-morning. There will be time for you to patronize the shops in Irvine before then." Trinkets, fabric and spices for their wives and lovers were in abundance here whereas they would not be available on Kintyre or many other places they would sail.

"Lord," said one of his men, "did you make an alliance with King David?"

"Aye," said Somerled, "we have his favor and his permission for our stone castles. He has granted us the services of two stonemasons, as well. They will sail with us. And I've a boon. He has granted me the Isles of Arran and Bute for chasing the Norse pirates from Scotland's shores."

A cheer went up from the half-dozen men sitting on their sea chests.

"Do the Norse still plague those isles?" asked one.

"Nay, they do not," said Maurice. "David swept them free of the scoundrels a short while ago."

"One less task for us," said another.

"In exchange," began Somerled, "I have pledged my honor that we will come should the King of Scots have need of us."

The men nodded soberly.

"I could do no less."

EARLY THE NEXT MORNING Somerled addressed his men in their lodgings. He describing all that had been achieved by his meeting with the King of Scots. He did not mention Rognvald attending King David's court, nor the Orkney arrow that had wounded him, for he did not want his men seeking revenge ere they sailed.

"Once we are free of Scotland's coast, my intention is to visit our new Isles of Arran and Bute and speak to the people there before returning to Kintyre. And then we will see to the building of our strongholds."

The men nodded as he spoke, enthusiastically agreeing with his plans.

"Will we build castles of timber or stone?" asked one.

"Undoubtedly, some will be timber. But eventually, all save the one on Loch Findlugan will have castles of stone. King David has lent us two of his stonemasons. I intend to send one stonemason north from Kintyre to assess the sites where we will build. While he is away, the other mason will begin the castle on Dunaverty Rock. I will go to Islay to build the timber castle there. You can choose to come with me, go north with the other ships or spend the winter on Kintyre."

More questions were asked but none expressed opposition to what Somerled proposed. He knew them to be loyal men who shared his vision for an independent kingdom.

After the meeting, he left Liadan with Domnall. Maurice went off to his errands and Angus promised to see to the final details before they sailed. Somerled strode back to the castle to bid farewell to the princess and collect the stonemasons. He had already paid his respects to King David.

In the hall, he spotted some of the ladies engaged in stitchery sitting next to the hearth where a fire steadily burned. Ragnhild was not among them.

"Good day to you, my ladies," he said, striding toward them. "Might you know where I can find Princess Ragnhild?"

"She is above stairs packing, my lord," said Beatrice, de Morville's wife. "I will send a servant to fetch her."

The servant was dispatched and a short while later, the princess descended the stairs. She looked very much as she had the night before, her long red-gold hair in plaits, only her garment this morn was of rich brown wool. He tried to memorize every detail of her face for he knew from the ache in his heart he would not see her for some time.

"Princess, I come to bid you farewell. I sail within the hour for Arran and Bute, the isles King David has given me."

"I did not know. Such a gift from the king is a godsend. You have my congratulations. And, after that, to where do you go?"

"To Islay to construct a timber castle and a chieftains' lodge. I expect to dwell on that isle much of the time." He hoped she understood that she could be a part of those plans if, God willing, her father relented. "It grieves me to say I do not know when I will see you again but I will send letters to you as I am able."

"You can write?"

He smiled. He was not offended by her question. Many could not write, even the high-ranking, who might consider it a scribe's task. "Aye and in more than one language." Then with a chuckle, he added, "My teachers were Irish monks."

"Oh," she said. "I am glad of it. For any letters you send me, I will reply."

He smiled, pleased to hear it.

"We return tomorrow to Man." As she spoke, her voice faltered and her green eyes sparkled with unshed tears. "You will be much missed, my lord." She offered her hand and he placed a kiss on her knuckles, her fragrance of roses forever imprinted in his mind.

He turned to go, for if he said more he might declare himself and he had no permission from Olaf to do so.

At the door, the two French stonemasons were waiting for him.

"I am Goubert d'Harcourt, Master Mason," said the one with the gray beard and ermine-trimmed mantle. His accent was decidedly

French. "And this is Aubri de Mares another of the king's masons. King David has bid us work for you to help raise the stone towers you plan, and we are willing. We have a servant, too, who awaits us outside with our things. He will be coming with us."

"I am most grateful," said Somerled. "We cannot provide you the accommodations you may be used to but know that your work will provide security for the Isles and for our people, which will also serve King David's interests."

As they conversed, one of the king's men approached and bowed before Somerled, handing him a scroll. "Your charters, my lord, signed by the king and stamped with his seal this day."

"Thank you and please tell King David I'll take care of the isles he has generously bestowed upon me. If he has need of me, I expect to be on Islay for some while. 'Twill be summer ere I sail north to Morvern."

RAGNHILD SLOWLY ASCENDED the stairs, pausing to look back at Somerled as he stood near the door speaking to two men she knew to be part of King David's retinue. One of the king's servants crossed the hall to Somerled and handed him a scroll. He took it and slipped through the door with the two men following.

A sudden ache filled her heart, a desire she harbored that was not yet fulfilled, a longing for an impossible thing.

He had said nothing of his intentions concerning her, nothing of the future, save that he would send letters as he could. The Isle of Man was not on his way to anywhere in his kingdom of Argyll and the Isles. If she were to receive a missive by messenger, Somerled would have to send one of his ships to bring it.

Might he care enough to do that?

In the meantime, she would try not to think of what might be. She resolved to busy herself serving the people of Man and her father.

Life on the isle had a rhythm driven by the changing seasons. Harvest had passed and soon the seasons of Advent and Christmas would be upon them.

There were many tasks to be accomplished to prepare for winter. While her father's tenants would be gathering wood for the cold months, planting vegetables that could survive winter in their gardens and repairing their roofs, farmers would be pruning apple and pear trees, butchering animals to provide meat and smoking what they could not eat. Abbot Bernard and his monks would be tending their herb garden and brewing ale for the celebrations to come.

Ragnhild would occupy herself with candle and soap making and embroidering winter mantles with Cecily. On sun-filled days, they might gather berries still left in the woods. On colder, rainy days, she might apply her skills to a new tapestry if there was time with her duties of overseeing the decorating of the hall and the planning the feasts that followed Advent. In all this, she vowed to be content now that her father had ceased speaking about a marriage to Earl Rognvald.

SOMERLED AND HIS COMPANIONS arrived in the harbor to find they were not the only ones leaving. Many longships that had been beached there were gone.

His men were taking out the oars as he stepped on deck. All looked to be sober and pleased to be sailing. He invited the masons and their servant to join him onboard and introduced them to his crew, who made room for them to sit.

"You might want to wear another mantle on our voyage," Somerled told the Master Mason. "The one you have is very fine and it may well get wet." The stonemason's servant had brought two bags onboard. One appeared to be very heavy by the way it sagged when he picked up, producing the sound of metal clanging. It was the other bag the servant reached into, pulling out a different cloak and offering it to d'Harcourt.

"Une bonne idée," said the mason, exchanging the mantle he wore for the simpler one the servant handed him. "It has been some years since I crossed to England and I have forgotten the weather on the water." Somerled had another reason for suggesting the man remove the fine garment that marked him a master of his craft. Though they had taken gold from the Norse pirates and would use it to build fortresses, he did not want the villagers they were to encounter to think Somerled and his men possessed great wealth. In truth, they did not.

Angus and Domnall came up to him and, speaking in a low voice,

Angus said, "I observed the Earl of Orkney talking to King Olaf before he sailed earlier this morn. He was scowling when he left the hall." The information pleased Somerled for it confirmed Rognvald's suit had not been accepted and he would not have the Princess of Man to wife, at least not yet.

"I wonder if his anger will cause him to pillage his way north," said Domnall.

"I doubt it," replied Somerled. "He will want to be home for the winter months and has farther to sail than most. Too, if he succeeded in convincing the King of Scots he poses no threat to Scotland, he will not want stories of his raiding as he sails north to come back to David. I have long suspected he leaves the pirating to Sweyn and his friends."

Somerled was glad the earl had failed in his goal to destroy his rival for the hand of the princess, for his arrow aimed did not bring down his prey. Somerled's arm still pained him, but Liadan had applied salve to his arm and said prayers for his recovery. The wound was beginning to heal with no sign of festering.

Somerled gazed into the harbor. The dark blue waters were calm this morning beneath a bright blue sky. The clouds that had threatened rain were gone.

Moments later, they set off, the men pulling at the oars as they followed the River Irvine back to the Firth of Clyde. Once the ship entered the firth, the wind picked up and they raised the sail.

They sailed northwest to the Isle of Bute, beaching the longship in Scalpsie Bay on the east coast where they were welcomed by seals sunning themselves on rocks jutting out of the water.

A short walk took them to the village set on the narrow strip of ground that hugged the coast. Behind the village were low hills of green interspersed with patches of bracken.

At first shy, or mayhap suspicious, the village men eventually came to meet them. Like Somerled's men, they were dressed as Gaels with tunics belted at the waist over trews or leggings, except that Somerled's men carried more weapons, marking them warriors.

He introduced himself and explained that he had come to see the isle and meet the people for King David had granted him both Bute and Arran. "The Scots king and I have formed an alliance," he explained, "each agreeing to come to the call of the other if there is need."

"We have heard of ye," said the grizzled old man with wiry gray hair who appeared to be their leader. "Aye and we are well pleased ye are here. We are simple folk and life was hard beneath the heel of the Northmen who lingered long on our shores. 'Tis glad we are they have gone."

"You need have no worry of the Norse pirates returning," Somerled assured him and the others who had gathered to hear him. "These two men," he said, pointing to the masons, "will be helping us to build castles to keep the sea lanes free. I ask only for the name of your chieftain, so that we can send word when there is news. The rents will not change except to be lower."

That brought a smile to their faces. It was clear to Somerled these were poor people who scratched out a living from the land and the sea. Any treasure they or their monks might have had was taken long ago by the pirates.

The name of the grizzled old man was given as their chief and recorded by Maurice. After that, Somerled and his men stayed to meet all the villagers before sailing for Arran. "Will you spread the news to the other villages?"

"Aye," said the grizzled old chief with a smile. "You could not stop us."

The Isle of Arran lay only five miles southwest of Bute so it did not take them long for its shores to come into view. Where Bute was mostly low and green, Arran was lofty and brown with heath-clad mountains surrounding deep ravines and glens. Its shores were rocky and the coast covered with brushwood.

As they sailed farther down Arran's coast, the brown mountains turned into green rolling hills, broken only by stands of whitebeam trees. The weather on Arran being mild, patches of wildflowers still dotted the hills.

They put in at Lamlash because of its good harbor and its long beach with both shingle and sand. Small boats were pulled up onshore, the kind used by local fishermen, though no men were in evidence.

"The bay must be full of fish, Lord," said Liadan, pointing to a flock of birds floating on the water. "The diver birds are reaping a rich harvest."

Somerled's eyes were drawn to the flock of the great black and white birds repeatedly diving beneath the water to bring up their dinner of what looked to be cod and whiting. In the air above, gannets dove from great heights to compete for the same fish. He was reminded that those were the birds he was admiring on the Isle of Man the first time he had glimpsed Ragnhild riding her white horse.

Heaving a sigh, he turned his attention to the isle before him.

Arrayed along the shore was a village with smoke rising from hearth fires. Facing the village, across the bay, was the small Holy Isle, so named for the seventh century Irish monk who had once dwelled there.

Behind the village rose cultivated slopes. Large stands of trees stood like guards on either side. Despite David's steward, Fitz Alan, having pronounced the isle "unproductive", Somerled did not find it so. While it was possibly true that much of the isle might be best left as pasture for cattle, by the look of it, the farmers here grew flax.

The villagers came to meet them, their expressions curious. Aware he was often taken for a Norseman, Somerled introduced himself and told them a little of his background. As on Bute, they had heard of him. A few asked sharp questions. He had expected they would. He explained his purpose in landing on Arran. "We'll not be a burden to you," he told the men, "unless King David calls upon us to aid him. And you will not see the Norse returning."

"Aye, all know of the great Somerled who has given the Gaels their freedom," said a man of middle years. "We are not unhappy to be under your protection. King David's steward paid us little mind and we feared the Norse would return."

Women crept out to see the visitors, children hiding behind their skirts. Liadan was a subject of much interest as she was the only woman with them, so Somerled explained her presence as he had at Irvine. "Liadan is from Islay and we are taking her to her brother, who serves me in Morvern." While that was Somerled's intention, she would likely not see her brother until summer.

Soon thereafter, the sun set behind the distant hills, making the day seem shorter than it ought to even in October. That night, the villagers cooked fish and roasted geese over an open fire, inviting Somerled and his men to partake. "'Tis very generous of you," he said, accepting their invitation.

"The fish are always abundant and the geese are plentiful this time of year," one woman said. "We are happy to share."

After they ate, Somerled's men shared stories with the villagers of their battles while the local people told him of life under the harsh rule of the Norse.

"They despoiled our most comely daughters and killed any man who challenged them. We were treated like slaves to do their bidding and deprived of all our weapons, save for those we needed to clean fish." The faces of the men were glum as they recited instances of abuse.

"Aye," said Somerled, "it was the same in Argyll. But now you are free to forge weapons to defend yourselves should you have need. All the men of the isles should be warriors as well as farmers and men who raise cattle. They must train to fight."

That night, they took shelter with the villagers who welcomed them into their homes. Liadan was the guest of one family with a daughter her age while the men slept in other cottages on the floor wrapped in their woolen mantles.

Somerled was offered the bed of the village leader and declined. "I have slept in caves in Morvern, on my ship and on the forest floor in many other places. I will not take a good man's bed from him. Grant me a space on your floor and I am content."

The leader nodded. "Aye, Lord. It shall be as you wish."

The next morning, he and his men rose with the dawn. Somerled walked to the shore and gazed east. The sun rising behind Holy Isle rendered the small island a dark silhouette. Visiting his new isles had been necessary but now he was eager to build.

They broke their fast with bread the villagers offered them and shared the herring they had brought from the Isle of Bute.

Somerled asked them to let the other villages know that the isle was now under his protection, which they gladly agreed to do. "Aye, we'll spread the word," said an older man among them.

Their leave-taking was warm, all things considered. Once strangers, they were now friends. The men and women, even the children, gathered on the shore to shout "Godspeed!" and wave to Somerled as his men rowed his ship away.

THE RETURN TO DUNAVERTY BAY on Kintyre was a short one, owing to the wind from the south which allowed them good time. They arrived just before noon. Those coming to greet them were a smaller number than the last time.

"Most of the men are in the woods cutting timber," said Ruairi, coming to greet him. "Some are fishing. We did not expect you so soon."

"'Tis no matter," he told Ruairi, "I will not be here long. I have much to tell you but, for now, come meet the stonemasons whose services King David has given us to help with our castle building."

Before they could move toward the masons, Ruairi's children ran to greet Somerled. "Did you bring us anything, Uncle Somerled?" asked Ceana.

He laughed. "Aye, a pretty riband for you to match your blue eyes." The ten-year-old girl's wide smile told him he had chosen well when he'd asked Maurice to fetch it while they were still in Irvine. "And for you, young master," he said to Bran, "a wooden sword to practice with."

The boy grinned. "Really?" He looked around. "Where is it?"

"Have no worry, Maurice will bring both your sister's riband and your sword from the ship."

That said, Somerled was forgotten as the children ran toward his longship.

The masons were introduced to Ruairi, who invited all into his home. Over a midday meal of trout and salmon, Somerled shared all that had happened. Everyone had something to say.

"I liked David," Somerled interposed between the comments of the others, "and I believe we shall do well together." To Somerled, this had been the great success of the voyage to Irvine. He now had the respect of two kings, David and Olaf. He had only to secure his bride.

"You gained much," said Ruairi's wife, Aileas, her light brown hair confined to one plait. "Two of King David's fine masons and two isles!"

The Master Mason, d'Harcourt, smiled. "As Lord Somerled has explained to me, there are many castles and much work for us."

"Aye," said Somerled, "there is. This afternoon, I'll take our two guests to Dunaverty Rock to see what they think of it. And tomorrow, when I sail to Islay, I want the Master Mason to travel north to the places we have in mind for other castles." Turning to d'Harcourt, he said, "What say you to your partner remaining behind to design the castle here and help cut the stone?"

"*C'est acceptable*, provided I have time to instruct Aubri in what is to be done."

Somerled nodded his agreement. "We will make sure you have the time." To Ruairi, he said, "Since you are a MacInnes, I thought you might be the one to take d'Harcourt to Morvern."

Ruairi glanced at his wife. "Aye, I would like that if I can take my family."

Aileas' face brightened at the prospect. "It would be good to see my family in Morvern and the children their grandparents."

The young ones looked from their parents to Somerled. "An adventure!" exclaimed Bran.

"Then 'tis done," said Somerled with a chuckle. "Will you stay here for the winter, Angus, to oversee whatever work our masons require?"

"Aye, Brother. I'll stay. A few months on land might be a welcome change."

"Domnall," Somerled addressed his cousin, "I've a mission for you as well. I want you to take one of the galleys and sail north to check on the settlements in Argyll, and to ask if any Norse have been pillaging their shores."

His cousin shot a look at Liadan before replying. "As you wish."

"You might consider spending Christmas in Morvern," Somerled added. "And then join me on Islay in the spring." Later, he would remind his cousin that Liadan's brother, Diarmad, had taken his galley to Ardtornish in Morvern. Should the lass be amenable, Domnall could seek her brother's approval to court her. He would also have to carry the story of the battle on Islay and the sad news that Diarmad's brother, Brian, had been slain by the raiding Norse.

"Then you can look for me in early spring," Domnall replied, his eyes on Liadan.

Somerled nodded. "Good. Maurice and Liadan will sail with me to Islay." He had no intention of having her sail to Morvern with his cousin, however noble Domnall might be. He was still a man in love.

When the meal was finished, Somerled thanked Aileas and took the trail that led to the top of the great rock jutting into the sea, the two masons and their servant following in his wake.

"The foundation will be sure," said d'Harcourt, "but getting the stones up here will take much effort. I will think on the design before we depart tomorrow."

The next morning, Somerled sailed for Islay with two longships and seventy men. He had recruited all those willing to winter on Islay and construct the timber hall and lodge. A few were good carpenters, even galley builders.

Ruairi wanted another day to prepare to sail north with the stone-mason.

Somerled's instructions were that, when Ruairi finally sailed, he was to begin with Ardtornish. "Mayhap it will be a timber castle for now, built on the remains of the old hill fort, but a stone castle will follow. You and the Master Mason will be the judge." The wind-swept point that overlooked the Sound of Mull was strategically important to Somerled's plans. From there, he could control the sea lanes giving access to Morvern and Moidart as well as the main routes to the Hebrides. "And make sure the mason sees Ewan MacSuibhne's castle in Knapdale. For certes, Ewan will want to meet d'Harcourt."

"Are you certain you do not wish to take the mason to Ardtornish yourself?" asked Ruairi with a skeptical look.

"Nay, I must go to Islay. I want to see the timber hall and outbuildings standing by winter." In truth, he wanted to do both but the timber castle on Islay could be completed long before the other castles. Should he win Ragnhild's hand, he would need a place to bring his bride.

CHAPTER 11

Loch Indaal, Isle of Islay, late October 1137 A.D.

THE AFTERNOON SUN broke through the clouds above Islay, turning the waters of Loch Indaal silver as the southerly winds drove Somerled's longship toward the northern shore of the great sea loch.

Thousands of white-faced, black-throated Barnacle geese that, a moment before, had been resting on the water took to the air. So great were their numbers, they darkened the sky as their loud clamor of calls sounded over the loch.

A short while later, Somerled and his men reached the sand and beached their longships.

Maurice, who had commanded the second ship, waved to Somerled as he climbed down to the sand, the wind blowing his ebony hair across his face.

Somerled's men took in the sail and he jumped down from his ship, excited for what lay ahead.

"Between fish, geese and deer, feeding the men will present no problem!" shouted Maurice above the raucous cries of the geese flocking above.

"Aye," Somerled shouted back, "we will work hard but eat well."

Once the men had gathered onshore, some of the geese resettled themselves onto the water and Somerled addressed the men. "We will camp at Findlugan's Loch tonight and, at first light tomorrow, we'll begin cutting timber, enough oak for the buildings we need. I am hoping the villagers in Keills will lend us carts and their garron ponies to haul the wood. I want to see the first buildings standing by December so we will have shelter for the winter months." On Islay, it was not likely to freeze at night, even in the coldest months, but the air would be chilled as they entered November and colder still in the months that followed.

"I can speak to the villagers," Liadan offered. "After what you did for them, they will be most willing to help and some have good carpentry skills."

"Aye," said Maurice, "'tis a good plan, lass."

They followed the ancient path leading inland to Findlugan's Loch, the bright yellow gorse on either side lighting their way.

They arrived at the secluded loch, its serenity disturbed only by curlews, geese and a golden eagle soaring overhead. The rays of the sun, shining through breaks in the cloud-filled sky, were reflected in the rippling waters. At the edge of the loch, reeds swayed with the breeze. To Somerled, the place felt ancient, as if Findlugan himself still walked the grass-covered earth.

While the men set up camp, Somerled walked with Maurice and Liadan to the loch's northern shore where he had first glimpsed the two islands. Beneath his boots, the soil was soft and loamy. "See the large island?" he asked them, pointing to the swath of green jutting out of the water close to shore. "The one with the remains of a hill fort on it?"

"Aye," said Maurice, "and a smaller island not far from it."

Liadan's auburn hair, freed from her plait, blew about her face as she spoke. "The people of Islay say the larger island once was home to Findlugan and his monks."

"All the more reason I would build a great hall here and places for the chieftains to lodge." Then he thought of Ragnhild and her love for the abbey on the Isle of Man. "And we'll be needing a chapel."

"We will need a timber path over the reed beds," said Maurice.

"Aye," Somerled said, agreeing. "We can lay it on the muddy ground between the island and the shore where the water is at its most shallow depth." From the first time he had sighted the islands in the loch, he had begun to form pictures in his mind of what his headquarters would look like. And, one day, he would bring horses to the isle. If he gained Ragnhild as his bride, she would want her proud Fairhair to accompany her here.

That evening, when the men finished setting up camp, Somerled took advantage of the abundant geese, sending some of them off to hunt in the grassy areas around the lake where the birds fed incessantly.

The sun was beginning to set, casting brilliant streaks of amber across the sky. Somerled used the remaining light to study the drawings he had made for the buildings they would construct. The hall and its kitchen would come first, then other lodgings and finally a chapel.

An hour later, between the loch's shore and their camp, a dozen fires sprang up to fill the air with the smell of roasting fowl.

Somerled sat on a rock, staring into the flickering flames as the dripping meat juices caused the fire to hiss. Behind him lay the chill of the oncoming night and their tents. In the distance, he could hear the cries of the roosting geese.

Islay soothed his soul, for he was a creature of the Highlands and the Isles as much as the golden eagle. This was home. His spirits soared as he thought of the grand task ahead, the passion that consumed him. Surely God was leading him, for he'd oft been protected from his enemies and gifted with wisdom not his own.

The dawn saw a gray sky though Somerled was thankful no rain fell. Before breaking their fast, his men had already felled several trees. He left Maurice in charge of the effort and, with Liadan and a few of his men, headed east for the village of Keills.

When they arrived, Somerled looked around, pleased with what he saw. All had been put to rights; no sign remained of the pirate attack. The villagers rushed up to greet them. It was obvious Liadan had been missed as the women embraced her and inquired of her wellbeing.

Smiling effusively, she told them, "I have been to Kintyre and to Irvine in Scotland to meet King David!"

Duly impressed, the women chatted away as Somerled turned to greet the men who approached him. "Welcome, Lord Somerled," said a powerfully built Gael dressed, like many of the others, in belted tunic and leggings. His long hair and beard were black, making him look formidable. "I am Duncan MacEachern, the smith."

Shaking the smith's hand, he said, "I come to ask for your help, for I would build a headquarters for the clans at Findlugan's Loch."

"Aye, that is to the good," said MacEachern, "and we can help see it done."

By the time they set off for the loch, Somerled had with him several village men, including those skilled in carpentry. The blacksmith insisted on coming along, giving Somerled some story about making sure his men had sufficient arrowheads. Somerled thought the smith was intrigued by the prospect of construction on the island in Findlugan's loch.

"Has there been any news of raiders on Islay since we left?" he asked MacEachern as they walked along.

"Nay, none here and the word from the other parts of Islay is that they have gone."

That night around the fires, they discussed all they would do on the islands in Findlugan's Loch as well as things to come. When the wind picked up, they damped down the fires with peat and Somerled, drawing his cloak more tightly around him, talked of the future. "The battles are not over and we must remain vigilant lest the pirates return with a vengeance. Until our strongholds rise from the land, our galleys and longships must keep the sea lanes safe from the pirates."

"Aye," said one of the villagers. "We have heard tales of the pirates attacking to the north of Morvern."

Somerled had heard the Norse pirates built dragonships on Skye but, despite their presence, he believed the Gaels were winning. "One day," he said, staring into the fire, "the descendants of the ancient Dalriada warriors will again have a home that is their own, a place where they will forever be free and seas on which to sail our hundreds of galleys."

Castle Rushen, the Isle of Man

RAGNHILD WAS RESTLESS. All Saints' Day was approaching and Advent just behind it and she had much to do. Besides that, they were expecting a visit from Queen Affraic's father, Fergus, Lord of Galloway.

Fergus always arrived with a great show. On his head of limp brown hair would be a golden crown, despite that he was a liege man of King David. Fergus' face, like his beard, drooped in a weary way. Yet his apparel would be so rich as to rival an English king's. His wife, Elizabeth, likewise would glide into the castle with her nose in the air, reminding all she was the daughter, albeit illegitimate, of Henry I, England's dead king.

Ragnhild considered Fergus' son, Uchtred, in a better light, for he had been her childhood friend. But Fergus' kerns, his foot soldiers, were unruly and coarse, rivaling even Sweyn Asleifsson for outrageous behavior. Not a man among them did she trust. It was with good reason they were called the Picts of Galloway.

Her father's guards, when hearing of their coming, had exchanged speaking glances. Nevertheless, the Wolf of Galloway would be entertained in grand style, for he was her father's ally as well as King David's and possessed a great fleet of longships. Hence, Ragnhild had many tasks awaiting her this day.

"You have seen to my father's chamber?" asked Affraic in a disdainful manner.

"Of course," replied Ragnhild. "The same one he occupied the last time he and your lady mother visited. I have asked the kitchen to prepare your father's favorite dishes as well." She had to wonder what Affraic would do when, one day, Ragnhild would leave the isle. She had never before looked upon such a fate as one to be desired but all that had changed with Somerled.

What would it be like to be wed to such a warrior? She suspected 'twould not be an easy life but then she did not desire a life without challenges. She would take the man no matter there would be arduous days.

"You might think to have a new bliaut made," said the queen, giving Ragnhild's simple green dress an appraising glance.

"The gowns I have are more than adequate," said Ragnhild. "In one of them, you will recall, I greeted King David."

"Very well," said Affraic, "do as you wish." She turned in a haughty manner and walked away, reminding Ragnhild of Affraic's mother, the Lady of Galloway.

Several days later, two longships from Galloway entered the harbor. Watching Fergus' men descend from the ships, Ragnhild was glad she had thought to clear one of the buildings that housed her father's unmarried warriors across the moat and outside the palisade so that Galloway's kerns could be housed beyond the castle. She would ask her father to build additional soldiers' quarters so there would always be a place for the troublesome warriors of visiting nobles to lodge.

She asked the garrison commander to dispatch two of Man's most trustworthy guards to Fergus' ships to escort Galloway's warriors—all save Fergus' personal guard—to the quarters prepared for them.

With her father and stepmother, Ragnhild waited at the castle door in the mist-shrouded morning as Fergus and his retinue arrived. Above, dark clouds threatened rain, an inauspicious beginning.

Although Fergus, in his fourth decade, was younger than her father, he was Olaf's father-in-law and addressed the King of Man as such. "Greetings to my son-in-law and to your queen and daughter," said Fergus.

"And to you, your queen and your son," returned Ragnhild's father. Fergus' son said nothing but winked at her. Uchtred had grown since she had last seen him, now taller than she, though his face, thankfully, was still more a reflection of his mother than his father. Whoever had been Elizabeth's mother, one of King Henry's many women, must have been a beauty.

"I hope to soon lay eyes on my grandchild, Godred," remarked Fergus as he strolled beside Olaf into the castle.

"He is a lovely child," Affraic remarked to Elizabeth as they trailed behind Olaf and Fergus. "The king is very proud of his heir."

Ragnhild and Uchtred followed the two women with Fergus' three guardsmen behind them.

"Was it very cold on the sea this morn?" she asked Uchtred.

"'Twas wretched damp and gloomy," and then with a smile, "but the voyage was mercifully short."

She laughed. "Then you will be happy for the fire and hot wine."

"I will, indeed," he said, his hazel eyes twinkling. "'Tis good to see you, Hilde."

They had known each other since they were youths and "Hilde" had been his name for her when they played games, their favorite being hoodman-blind. While Ragnhild was not overly fond of the nickname, she liked Uchtred and knew it was spoken with affection for she was like a sister to him.

One summer, they had learned archery and chess together. Affraic, then only Lord Fergus' daughter, had been a few years older than they were but she never participated in their childhood games and cared not for archery. Even then, she looked nothing like her beautiful mother.

Refreshments awaited them in the hall. As the others accepted mugs of hot spiced wine and platters of bread, cheese and apples, Ragnhild spoke to the servants to assure herself the guests' chambers were ready. When that was done, she spoke to Fergus' chief guard. "I have a chamber reserved for you and the two men with you. It is close to Lord Fergus' rooms."

The guard, more reserved than Galloway's kerns, inclined his head. "Thank you, my lady."

The rain fell in torrents that night, so loud she could hear it beating against the castle from her chamber where she huddled under the furs. Worse, it continued for days thereafter. As a result, there were no long walks along the cliffs, no riding across the hills. Instead, during the day, while Affraic and Elizabeth embroidered and Ragnhild's father and Fergus sat drinking and talking, she and Uchtred kept each other company with games of chess and reading aloud by the fire.

On this afternoon, with the deerhounds at her feet, she read *The Song of Roland*. The story told of Charlemagne's honorable nephew, who died a martyr's death through the treachery of his stepfather. Assigned the rear guard in a march to battle, Roland died when the enemy was told how he could be ambushed. The slaughter of Roland and his men made Ragnhild worry for another valiant warrior who might be fighting the Norse pirates this very moment.

Somerled said he was going to Islay but she had received no letters from him and desperately wanted to know if he was well.

"I have no interest in becoming like one of my father's men," Uchtred said, commenting on the final scene of the story. "Always lusting for battle. My inclinations go the other way. Did you know that my father intends to build an abbey at Dundrennan?"

When she shook her head, he said, "I would oversee not only the abbey's building but become the abbot, should that be possible."

"But Uchtred, you are your father's heir. He will expect you to become Lord of Galloway when he dies."

"Alas, I know it," said Uchtred, his expression downcast. "I fear I shall have to content myself with building abbeys."

"That is not a bad thing," she encouraged. Silently, she thought if Galloway built more abbeys and brought more abbots like Abbot Bernard to its shores, perhaps its men would not have the reputation as violent Picts.

Rising from her seat, she listened and, hearing no sound of rain, said, "Come, I believe we have been favored with a break in the weather. I will take you to meet Abbot Bernard. The monks are busy making ale just now and I'm sure he would be happy to share some."

OLAF DOWNED THE LAST of his second goblet of wine and watched his daughter leave the castle with Fergus' son. "It seems our children have found each other most companionable."

"Aye, I have observed that they often seek each other's company." Running his hand over his scant1 beard, Fergus appeared to contemplate. "As I recall, the princess is of marriageable age. Some might say well past it."

"She is not yet twenty," replied Olaf, defensively. "I know maidens are often wed at a younger age, but I have been loath to give her to one of her many suitors, though I know, one day, I must."

"What say you to adding Uchtred to that list of suitors? He is young, aye. But one day, he will be Lord of Galloway. Only think, Olaf! He could provide support for your young heir, an ally he can trust close to hand."

"As I trust he will be in any event." Olaf was already allied with

Galloway through Affraic. He hoped to gain more than that from the marriage of the princess. In any event, Uchtred would likely be available for some years. "We will see."

Fergus said, "Word has it that David's troubles in England grow with his niece, Empress Maud's defeats and Stephen's rising power. I expect he may call upon us should he venture into England again on her behalf."

Olaf heaved a sigh. "That treaty David agreed to at Durham will not hold. But I have told him I will have no part in any battle in England."

"I would like to have told him the same, but I am sworn. Ah well, the warriors of Galloway love a good fight."

Olaf gave no reply but he wondered what havoc the men of Galloway could wreak on England based upon the stories his garrison commander had told him of the lengths to which he had gone to keep order among Fergus' soldiers.

Loch Findlugan, The Isle of Islay, November 1137 A.D.

THWACK! SOMERLED POUNDED another nail into the beam, satisfied he had hit the mark. The sound of other hammers and the sawing of boards could be heard all around him.

Three weeks had passed and, notwithstanding the occasional rain, the causeway had been constructed from the loch's shore to the large island where a great hall was rising.

The villagers, who brought them bread, gruel and ale to add to their stores of fresh meat and fish, seemed to take great pride in their lord's having selected Islay as the site for his headquarters.

Maurice wiped his brow with his sleeve, dipping a cup into the water barrel next to where Somerled worked. "The building goes well."

Taking the nails from his mouth, Somerled looked around at the work that had been accomplished thus far and nodded. Work had begun on the building that would be the lord's house and, beyond it, lodgings for others were under construction. On the banks of the loch a stockpile of wood and supplies had accumulated. "Aye, it does."

"The men should have no trouble meeting your goal. So, I have been thinking. What say you to letting me take a galley to Ireland? 'Tis only a half day's sail. I would see my family ere we leave on our next voyage."

Somerled thought for a moment. "Would you take a message for me to the Isle of Man on your way back? It would mean sailing farther south before turning north but I'd be most grateful."

Maurice smiled. "A message for the princess?"

There was no sense in denying what was obvious to all. "Aye."

"Of course, I'll carry the message."

An idea came to Somerled that afternoon as he continued to work and he realized that he had his own need to sail to Ireland. In Ulaid, not far from Maurice's family, Somerled's mother cared for his son, Gillecolum, still a boy but of an age to be with his father.

Over dinner that night, he spoke of his idea to Maurice. "I have been thinking that since the smith, MacEachern, has shown great leadership over the construction and will soon see it accomplished, I would sail to Ireland with you to retrieve my son."

Maurice smiled. "I would welcome your company. And then you could deliver your own message to the Isle of Man."

The Isle of Man

RAGNHILD LED FAIRHAIR from the stables into a rare day of sun. Lord Fergus had remained on the isle for a fortnight and, in that time, the rain had been unrelenting. She was glad when he sailed back to Galloway, taking his unruly warriors with him. Fortunately, she had not been forced to deal with them but her father's men complained bitterly of their fighting and harrying the isle's young women.

Now that they were gone and the sky was clear, she wanted to ride to her favorite spot, the cliffs above Niarbyl Bay, where she could think without the incessant duties that dogged her in the castle.

Confined to the inner bailey and the stables for some time, Fairhair was eager to run. So, they galloped over the hills, Ragnhild's mantle blowing behind her, whipped by the wind. Exhilarated, she felt more alive than she had in days.

Arriving at the bay, she reined in Fairhair and looked down from the cliff. The rain of the past few weeks had painted much of the landscape green. Against the blue-gray waters of the bay and the white-topped waves breaking on the shore, it was breathtaking.

She slid from the saddle to walk Fairhair forward where they stood looking out to sea. Stroking his broad neck, she listened to the waves and watched the fulmars as they wheeled effortlessly in front of the cliffs, taking advantage of the onshore winds.

She inhaled deeply the smell of ocean and salt, an elixir to her soul after so many days confined to the castle.

Ragnhild had believed she would be content to stay on the Isle of Man for the rest of her life. Yet, sometime in the last year, she had begun to think otherwise. Now, a longing had grown within her to stand by the side of a golden warrior.

CHAPTER 12

Ulaid (Ulster), the northeast coast of Ireland, November 1137 A.D.

SOMERLED AND HIS two companions trudged up the hill, past tall stands of pine, keeping their hoods over their heads against the light fall of rain. Reminded it rained nearly every day in Ulaid, he began to think of Islay's weather as passably fair. A bit windy, mayhap, but even the short days of November had brought sun.

As they approached the crest, the place he had once called home appeared through the falling rain.

Years had passed since he had visited the house in which he had spent his youth. The two-story white sandstone manor with its gray slate roof brought back memories of a time when his father still lived and his siblings, Angus and Bethoc, played with him on the rocky shores where blustery showers often soaked them to the skin.

The oaken front door, darkened with age, opened to reveal his mother. Her golden hair, now laced with silver, was confined to two long plaits hanging down the front of her sapphire gown. On her head, over her veil, rested a simple circlet of silver.

For a moment, she stared as if trying to determine if she knew him.

Then, with sudden burst of recognition, she cried out, "Sumarliðr!"

"Aye, Mother, 'tis me," he said, taking a step toward her and holding out his arms.

He accepted his mother's embrace and then took her hands in his, gazing into her much-loved face, noting the wrinkles that were new. Looking into her sky blue eyes, he said, "You must forgive my long absence. I have been occupied—"

"So I hear tell." With a smile, she added, "'Tis said you forge a kingdom."

"Aye, one that Father envisioned long ago."

She looked behind him. "Introduce me to your friends and then let us leave this dampness to sit by the fire." Inwardly, he chuckled. Only his mother would call rain "dampness".

Quickly, he introduced the dark-haired Maurice MacNeill and auburn-tressed Liadan MacGilleain, explaining how they had come to join him. He finished with, "We were just on Islay where my men are building a place for the clans to meet."

His mother, ever gracious, welcomed them into her home and ordered a servant to take their wet mantles. "I will ask the servants to see to your crew. They can stay in one of the outbuildings and will be well fed."

"Thank you. I was just about to ask."

She tossed him the knowing smile of a mother. "Recall I did the same for your father's crews."

"Aye, and they loved you for it."

A servant stoked the hearth fire and, at his mother's instruction, went off to heat the wine. It occurred to him then that Ragnhild was not unlike his mother. Both were noble Norsewomen of faith who did their duty with love and affection for those they served.

Somerled smiled at the few servants he recognized. Many were new.

"You must be famished," said his mother, casting him a look of inquiry.

"We ate this morning," said Somerled, "but 'tis unlikely we will turn away food if offered."

His mother smiled. "Just as I remember. And how is Angus?"

"My brother is well."

"Is he still in Morvern with the MacInnes Clan?"

"He is now chief of that clan but he is not always in Morvern. He sails with me most days but, at this moment, he is on Kintyre."

"It heartens me to know you are together, especially since Bethoc has decided to join her errant husband where he is confined in the King of Scots' castle at Roxburgh."

"Aye, when I met with David, he told me of my brother-in-law's confinement but the way he explained it, MacHeth is more a guest than a prisoner."

"You met with King David?"

"I did." At her raised brow, he added, "I will tell you about it in good time."

They took seats around the hearth fire, holding their palms to the heat from the flames. High above them, a small, covered hole in the roof accepted the trail of rising smoke. The hot spiced wine arrived soon thereafter and Somerled and his companions wrapped his chilled hands around the mugs.

"Cook will be preparing your favorite lamb stew," said his mother. "She has been anxious to see you and will want to serve the meal herself. News comes to us of you but not often enough, so tell me all."

"First," said Somerled, "where is my son, Gillecolum?"

"With his tutor. I will call him when you are ready."

Excitement rose in Somerled's chest. "Now, if you please. When I last saw him, he was a wee lad. My eyes are hungry to see how he has grown." Somerled conjured in his mind the image of a small boy with blue eyes and hair the color of harvest wheat.

His mother turned to a servant and told him to summon the lad. While they waited, Somerled told his mother in summary all that had happened. "It began in Morvern, as you might imagine, and from there we took back Argyll, Kintyre and the Southern Isles. 'Twas King David who gave me Arran and Bute."

At the edge of the room, a boy appeared with handsome features and an intelligent face, his gaze appraising Somerled.

"Come greet your father, Gille," said Somerled's mother. With a smile, she told his son, "They now call him 'Somerled the Mighty'."

The lad of ten years stepped forward, tall for his age and straightlimbed, his blue eyes growing larger as Somerled rose to greet him.

"I do not remember you," said his son.

"Aye, we will soon remedy that. Come shake your father's hand."

Gillecolum boldly stepped forward, his gaze never leaving Somerled. When he grasped the boy's forearm, he felt the lad's strength. "You've a powerful grip."

"I suppose I need not ask," said Somerled's mother, "but do you intend to take Gille with you?"

"Aye," said Somerled, his eyes never leaving his son, "'tis time."

Over the next few days, Somerled reacquainted himself with his son.

The next morning, after breaking their fast, he took Gillecolum on a long walk to his favorite places.

Stopping at a waterfall, he invited his son to sit on a rock while they watched the falls. "On a rare summer day, this was my swimming hole. Your uncle Angus and I would take turns seeing who could stay under the water the longest."

"Who won?" asked Gillecolum.

"Sometimes Angus, sometimes me."

"I wish I had a brother."

"How would you like a younger brother, one who would look up to you?"

Gillecolum beamed at the suggestion. "Aye, I would like that very much. Do you have one you will give me?"

Somerled laughed. "Well, mayhap not immediately, but 'tis my plan to take a bride who would be a mother to you and, together, we would give you brothers. At least that is my thought. What think you of such a plan?"

"Would she like me?"

"Oh, I think so. Very much. You are my son and any woman I would choose must love you or I would not marry her."

Gillecolum nodded. "Then it's all right," he said with a furrowed brow, as if pondering a great matter. Which, Somerled supposed, it was.

The next day, though it was spitting rain, they went fishing for eels in a burn where Somerled had fished as a lad.

"I know how to fish for eels," Gillecolum proudly announced, staring into the water.

"You do? Then show me," he said, stepping back.

The lad waded a short way into the burn and began to poke around in the mud with the tip of his spear. A cloud of dirt rose to the surface as he disturbed the water in one place. He pulled back his spear and smiled. On its tip was an eel speared and wiggling. "I found their winter nest!"

"So you did. An excellent discovery and a good catch. Do you like to eat them?"

"Nay," the boy said with a look of distaste. "I don't much like the look of them, but Grandmother likes them so I catch them for her."

Somerled took the eel from the spear and dropped it in the bag he carried. "Most considerate of you," he said, realizing how mature his son was for just ten years.

An hour later, with their bag of eels, they walked back to the manor, warriors together who had conquered the burn and brought back trophies for the woman of the house.

"How would you like to sail with me, Gillecolum? It would mean leaving your grandmother, at least for a time, but you would be with me and your uncle."

"I heard grandmother ask you if you came for me. I am ready. I want to go."

Somerled put the bags of eels and his spear in his left hand and wrapped his free arm around Gillecolum's shoulders. "I have long wanted you by my side, Son. It pleases me greatly to know you would take your place there."

A few days later, Somerled watched as Gillecolum searched the tidepools on the shore with Maurice and Liadan.

Somerled's mother, standing next to him, said, "He has heard many stories of your victories in the last few years and I have made certain he knew of his father's triumphs. Because of them, he is in awe of you."

Somerled had thought often of his son, trying to imagine how he had grown with each passing year. "A few months with me will disabuse him of the myths."

"I will miss him," said Somerled's mother, "but I agree it is time he was with you. He needs his father...and possibly a new mother? Is the young woman with you a prospect?"

"Nay, she is my self-proclaimed guard and the sister of one of my warriors."

His mother laughed. "I see Gille will be well-entertained."

"He'll not be bored. Did he mention my conversation with him the day we fished for eels?"

"He did and he is most anxious to have a younger brother, though I don't think he understands such cannot be quickly delivered."

Meeting his mother's sharp gaze, he said, "I do hope to take another wife and want Gillecolum to meet my choice of a bride."

His mother turned from watching Gillecolum, who was searching the tidepools, to face Somerled. "You have chosen a woman?"

"Aye."

"Who, pray tell, is it?"

"Ragnhild of the Isle of Man."

"The Norse princess?"

"Aye, and sought after by every man of any stature from Orkney to Scotland. But her father has yet to accept any man's suit, including my own, though I have twice asked for her hand."

His mother lifted her head to gaze southeast beyond the rocky shore of Ulaid toward the Isle of Man. "Olaf, King of Man, is the younger son of Godred Crovan, the King of Dublin who died before you were born. 'Tis said Olaf is a wily one. With the death of his two older brothers, I suppose he had to be."

"That and his small stature, for he is no warrior. Olaf is known for his shrewd alliances forged with every kingdom that could pose a threat to him. I am hoping he comes to see me as one of them so that he will grant me the hand of his daughter. Once, I could offer her nothing but that has changed."

"It would mean much for the task you have set for yourself to have such a bride," said his mother. "From what I have heard about the princess, I believe I would like her."

"Aye, you would. But an alliance with her father is not the only reason I want the match. I love her."

His mother gave him a knowing smile. "Then I have no doubt Somerled the Mighty will find a way."

Somerled fixed his eyes on his son who proudly held up a starfish, smiling at his prize. "Father, look!"

Somerled nodded, smiling. "Well done!" It warmed his heart to know his son had come to accept him. Now, he had only to introduce the lad to Ragnhild.

Isle of Man, 11 December 1137 A.D.

ANTICIPATING WHAT MIGHT come of this visit to the Isle of Man, Somerled's gut tightened. Would Ragnhild receive his message with a glad heart?

He had lingered a fortnight in the north of Ireland, visiting his friends and Maurice's kin. All the while, Gillecolum had remained by his side. Now, the boy stood next to Liadan facing into the wind as the galley sailed into the harbor.

When they beached the galley, Somerled beckoned Maurice to him. "Take this note to the princess. If she says aught of wanting to see me or appears pleased with what she has read, tell her I am here and request she come hither to the ship, that I have someone for her to meet."

"As you wish," said the Irishman. "Do we stay the night?"

"Possibly. I would see Olaf if he is receiving. By the look of the long-ships in the harbor, it appears he is here. One flies his royal banner."

RAGNHILD RACED FAIRHAIR along the cliffs, the December wind from the Irish Sea knifing through her mantle. Despite the bitter cold, she would not trade the freedom she felt when racing over the hills for a seat next to the hearth fire.

Nearing the castle, she slowed Fairhair to a walk to admire the view. Overhead, the scattered gray clouds could not overwhelm the golden light from the morning sun. Shading her eyes, she saw a familiar man waiting by the gate, looking in her direction. Drawing closer, she recognized him as one of Somerled's companions, Maurice MacNeill, her father's foster brother from Ireland.

Drawing rein as she arrived next to him, she slid from the saddle. "Good day to you, sir."

He bowed before her. "Princess, you may remember I am Maurice MacNeill. I bring a message from Lord Somerled."

A smile crossed her face. "What is it?" He had not forgotten after all.

From his mantle of deep green, he pulled out a small rolled parchment, tied with string, and handed it to her.

She opened the missive and read.

Love made to wait grows. – Somerled

She read the one line three times. It might be short but her soul thrilled to his words that spoke of love, love delayed yet growing. Clutching the precious parchment to her bosom, she asked forlornly, "He did not come himself?"

"Would you be happy if he had?"

"Oh, yes."

The Irishman smiled. "Then I have Somerled's permission to tell you he awaits you at his ship in the harbor where he has someone he wants you to meet."

Ragnhild shielded her eyes and gazed down to the harbor where some of her father's ships were anchored. Among those beached on the sand was a galley, smaller than a longship. Her heart sped to think Somerled was here but not wishing to appear too eager, in a calm voice, she said, "I will come as soon as I have returned my horse to the stables." She watched Maurice walk down the hill toward the harbor and turned to go, so excited she could hardly breathe.

"Fairhair," she said to her horse, leading him to the stables, "it seems we are to have a most welcome guest." Ragnhild had waited and wondered and hoped a message would come, desperate to know he thought of her. She had never expected the man himself to appear yet here he was and with words of love for her.

Who was it he wanted her to meet?

She handed the reins to a groom and hurried out through the postern gate, not wanting her father to know Somerled was here. A guard would bring him word soon enough.

She would have taken more care with her appearance to meet the man who made her heart race but to do so might draw the interest of her father or Affraic. No, Somerled would just have to take her windblown and ruffled.

The galley beached at the harbor's edge was the same one she had seen off the coast of Man years before, only now its red sail was doused, ready to set should the ship leave in haste. A signal to her had she not wished to see him, he would have swiftly sailed away. Did he doubt so much her heart was his?

Somerled grinned at her from the deck of his ship where he stood, hands fisted on his hips, his fair hair confined at his nape.

"I received your message, Lord Somerled," she said, coming closer. His crew discreetly turned away, busy with their tasks. Did anyone else know what he had written to her? She doubted it. Mayhap his men knew he was glad to see her but 'twas likely he would share his emotions with only those who needed to know. To a man like her father who would arrange her marriage for gain or strategic alliance, such a sentiment would mean little—to her, it meant everything.

"The words are true," he said, jumping down to the sand and taking her hands in his, "every one." His touch sent shivers through her.

Lifting her hands to his lips, he pressed a kiss to her fingers. "I have missed you, Fair Princess, and worried lest another had stolen your heart. I had thought just to send the message but then I knew I must come. I had to look upon your beautiful face."

She could feel her cheeks heat even in the cold but this was no time for timidity. "And I have missed you, my lord, more than you can know."

He turned back to his ship and called a name. Then to her, "I have someone I want you to meet. I hope the two of you will do well together."

She did not have to ask to know this person was significant and that her reaction would be important for any future she and Somerled might have together.

A boy climbed down from the ship. As her gaze roved over him, she knew, without a doubt, the tall fair-haired lad was Somerled's son.

"Your son?" she asked.

"Aye. Gillecolum, make your bow to the Princess of Man."

The boy must have been given instruction for he executed a perfect bow and, rising, said, "My lady."

She smiled. What else could she do in the face of so much charm? "I knew you had been widowed, my lord, and that you had a son. I am happy you have brought him to meet me." To the boy, she said, "Gillecolum, you are a most handsome lad and clearly resemble your famous father."

The boy smiled, obviously happy for any comparison to the man he so admired.

Somerled put his arm around the boy's shoulders. "You honor us with your kind words, Princess. I have just retrieved Gillecolum from Ireland where he has been sojourning with my mother."

The boy gazed up at his father with a look of adoration.

"Ireland is not far," she said. Then facing Gillecolum, she asked, "Would you like to come into the castle and have some refreshments?"

The boy nodded enthusiastically.

To Somerled, she said, "'Tis sure my father will ask you both to stay the night. He lacks for male company just now as Christmas approaches and we women are dominating the hall with our preparations. He has his garrison commander, of course, and the isle chieftains but not one, such as yourself, who travels far and brings news. Such a man's company would be most welcome." Then with a glance at the Irishman with his ebony hair and beard, smiling down at them from the deck of the ship, she added with feigned sarcasm, "Do bring the king's foster brother."

"May I also bring Liadan? She is in my care until I return her to her brother."

Satisfied at last to know the lovely girl's place in Somerled's life, she said, "Of course. I am sure she would be happy to spend some time in the castle."

THE KING MUST HAVE BEEN apprised of their arrival for he met Somerled at the castle door and invited him, his son and Maurice inside. As Ragnhild had predicted, the king appeared happy to see them. "Come in, come in. 'Tis a chill day and the fire burns brightly."

Somerled had decided he would not again raise his desire to wed the princess with the King of Man. Let Olaf wonder at his intentions. Instead, he would allow Olaf to believe he had come solely on a matter of business. In truth, there was a matter of importance he wanted to discuss. Rumors had reached him in Ireland of a storm brewing in the north of England, one that might embroil them all.

Inside the great hall, Somerled scanned the large chamber, now rendered festive with torches set into iron brackets and greenery mixed with red berries adorning them, the tapestries and the tables. The scent of fresh herbed rushes lingered in the air. Doubtless, 'twas Ragnhild's doing.

The deerhounds, sleeping near the hearth fire, rose to greet Somerled as he and his companions handed their mantles to a waiting servant.

Gillecolum had told Somerled he liked hounds and spent some time ruffling the wiry fur of the two who came toward him, wagging their tails.

The king offered his hand to Maurice. "I am favored with two visits in one year!"

The Irishman shook the king's hand. "You can thank Lord Somerled for that."

Somerled then proceeded to present Liadan to Olaf. "Liadan was with me at Irvine," he reminded the king. It took a few minutes to explain why she was with him now but Olaf seemed satisfied.

Finally, Somerled introduced his son. "Gillecolum has been in Ireland and is just now joining me."

The boy met the king's inquiring gaze as they faced each other, for Olaf was the same height as Somerled's son.

"He's a fine looking lad," said the king, smiling at Gillecolum. Then to Somerled, "You were married?"

"Aye, Gillecolum's mother died in childbed."

Out of the corner of his eye, Somerled saw Ragnhild turn aside to speak to the servants, and heard her ordering them to bring hot mead for their guests.

He and his companions followed the king to the circle of benched seats set around the hearth fire.

"The queen is above stairs with her ladies," said Olaf, "but she will join us for dinner. Now is a good time to tell me, what brings you to my kingdom?"

He did not look at Ragnhild, who had joined them at the fire, when he answered. She knew the answer was that he had come to see her but, for her father, he could honestly say, "The civil war in England."

Maurice knew the real reason Somerled had come to the Isle of Man but his expression disclosed nothing. As yet, Gillecolum had no idea of Somerled's feelings for the princess.

Olaf seemed surprised at his answer. "England? What care we for that?"

"I assume you are aware that the six-month truce King David negotiated with Archbishop Thurstan in Stephen's absence has just expired. If the rumors be true, David is preparing to again invade Northumberland for his niece, the Empress Maud."

Olaf's brow furrowed and his hand swept over his beard as if in contemplation. "Well, then, we have much to discuss. Has David said aught of it to you?"

"Nay, but I fear he will. I am his ally, bound to come at his call. For such an invasion, he will need an army of warriors."

Olaf pursed his lips. "My wife's father, Fergus, Lord of Galloway, is sworn to the King of Scots. And though I am David's ally, I have told him I will not fight in England's wars."

Somerled laughed. "I should have thought to say that. But David gave me too much to expect nothing in return."

Cups of spiced mead were handed around by the servants. "The lad's is watered," Ragnhild whispered to Somerled. Her nearness brought with it the smell of her rose perfume and the memory of their kiss.

He lifted his gaze to her and, for a moment, their eyes met and neither looked away. A powerful urge to take her hand and run outside swept over him. Instead, he thanked her for her thoughtfulness and patted his son's shoulder. "'Tis best."

"If David invades England," said Olaf, drawing Somerled's attention to him, "it will not be merely for his niece's sake. To my way of thinking, he seeks to secure lands he believes are rightfully his, promised to him by old King Henry."

Somerled shook his head with regret. "It comes as no surprise that King Henry promised David lands that Stephen now thinks to take back.

I fear the English monarchs only remember the promises that suit them. Stephen gave his oath to Henry to support his daughter, Maud, but was quick to forget it when he seized the throne."

IMPRESSED WITH THE WAY Somerled adroitly spoke of matters of state, Olaf sat back and listened to the young lord expound on what he thought might happen.

"I imagine it came as a great surprise to Stephen to see the Scots king leave off his abbey building and go to war, but David has done so before and I believe he will again."

Olaf nodded his agreement.

Ragnhild, who had joined them, put in, "David's intention to hold Cumbria has never faltered. And then there is the matter of Northumberland he wants for his son whose mother was an English noblewoman, an heiress."

"Aye," said Somerled, "and with Stephen now busy in the south of England, as I hear he is, it cannot be long ere David crosses the border. Only this time, I expect him to summon all his forces, including the men of Argyll and the Isles."

Olaf shifted his attention to his daughter, who was listening intently to the young lord with a look of concern on her face. Did she worry for Somerled's safety? Mayhap if Somerled went to war with David and managed to survive, Olaf would consider him for the princess. Somerled had said nothing of his desire to wed Ragnhild but the day was still young.

"How many men might you be able to muster for David's invasion?" he asked Somerled.

"A thousand or more," he said with a glance at Maurice, who nodded. "Though they must sail from diverse parts of my kingdom and then there is the travel to meet the Scots king. It will take time."

Olaf had not missed the young lord's use of the word "kingdom". Indeed, from what Olaf had heard, Somerled's conquests had made him king of an independent realm. "If David seeks to expand his army by so many, I expect he will want to add the Galwegians."

Ragnhild said, "Fergus' men are an ill-disciplined gang of Picts but they are fierce fighters. David will be hard-pressed to control them. Fergus does not even try."

"David has his Scots, too," offered Somerled, "all are savage fighters, save for the Norman knights. 'Twill be a vast army if he carries through with it."

Olaf was enjoying his conversation with the young lord and the way his daughter traded comments with him. Since Fergus had returned to Galloway, there had been few with whom he could speak of political matters. How pleasant it would be to have Somerled and his companions remain at Castle Rushen for the coming celebration. "If you four can remain with us for Christmas, I would be pleased to have you as my guests," he said to Somerled.

"I would eagerly accept but I promised my crew they would return to Islay for the season of Yule."

Olaf read disappointment in his daughter's eyes.

Maurice explained, "We are hoping to finish the construction on Islay this month ere the worst of winter descends."

"Well, at least stay the night and let us entertain you this eve," said Olaf.

His daughter looked at Somerled with anxious eyes. "We will make it worth your while."

"We thank you," said Somerled, inclining his head to the princess, "and heartily accept."

As they rose from their seats, Ragnhild said, "We have lodgings for your galley's crew away from the cold, and there will be room for them to dine in the hall this eve."

"Thank you. And, may they hunt this afternoon if they are inclined to do so?"

Olaf nodded to his daughter and she gave the requested permission. He was proud of the princess. As a chatelaine, she was unsurpassed. And she easily entered into conversations many ladies would not for lack of knowledge. Today, she appeared to be putting out a special effort for this particular guest, which did not surprise him. "Who knows?" he told Somerled. "Your men might so enjoy themselves they may decide to stay here for Christmas."

AFTER THE MEETING ended, Ragnhild's gaze followed Somerled as he went off to secure the lodgings for his men, his young son following on his heels. She had begun to think of the two of them as hers though she had no leave to do so. But hearts do not always wait for permission to give of themselves.

She turned to attend the cooks, who were beginning to prepare the evening meal. It was one she had requested so that Somerled and his men would dine well that night. She tried to put out of her mind the possibility that he would depart on the morrow and might soon go to war.

If Somerled could not remain for Christmas, she was determined to give him a feast equal to the one they would have in celebration of the Savior's birth. One he would remember in the months ahead.

Since Somerled had expressed a desire to see the abbey later that day, she sent a message to Abbot Bernard to expect them and an invitation to dine with the king this night. She also sent messengers to her father's garrison commander and the island's chiefs asking them to come with their wives to meet their special guest.

She had already made sure that the hall had a merry appearance with new herbed rushes and garlands of greenery. Illuminating all were the torches and candles. She had told the minstrels, who often entertained her father, to come prepared to play songs of the season. The castle bard would sing ballads that would delight. Christmas was only a fortnight hence so it would be a practice performance, one that would please their guests.

Excited for the meal she had asked the cooks to prepare, she instructed them as to details they would not ordinarily see to. She doubted Somerled would dine so well on Islay even at Christmas.

Because it was still Advent, the main dishes would be fish: trout baked with leeks and thyme, salmon poached in a mint and parsley sauce with dried berries and broiled pike covered in cinnamon wine sauce. Vegetables would accompany the fish: onions cooked in a rich gravy with savory herbs, and buttered beets. All would be followed by apples baked with butter, cinnamon and sweet salt. There would be mead to drink.

On the morrow, she would not send Somerled away hungry. After

Mass, he would be served a morning meal of porridge with nuts and dried berries, eggs and bread and butter. She would make sure their satchels were filled with oatcakes, dried fish and apples and their skins full of the monks' fine ale when they sailed.

Somerled would not soon forget the hospitality shown him on the Isle of Man. And she hoped he would not soon forget her.

SOMERLED'S MEN WERE PLEASED to be invited to dine with the King and Queen of Man. With hours still remaining before sunset, after furling the sail and securing the ship, they donned their heavy cloaks and went off to explore the isle, some carrying bows and arrows to hunt. Ragnhild had promised him a tour of the abbey, which Maurice and Liadan also wanted to see. Though he would have preferred to be alone with the princess, he did not think an abbey full of monks would produce that result, so he told his companions and his son they were free to come along.

The princess was waiting for them when they returned to the castle, a dark green woolen mantle over her gown. "My father is a devout man and very proud of the abbey," she said to the four of them.

"There are many abbeys in Ireland," said Gillecolum. "The one in Bangor is where I took my lessons."

Ragnhild smiled at the lad. "In Ireland, the abbeys are ancient and many of stone. Ours is fairly new and made of timber though my father has plans to see it in stone."

Somerled offered his arm and Ragnhild took it entwining her arm with his. She felt right tucked in close to him. Even the dismal weather could not dampen his joy at their reunion.

"How is your arm?" she asked, speaking, Somerled knew, of his wound gained at Irvine.

"It is healing well with only small scars."

She leaned into his right arm. "I am glad, for I worried."

"For me?" he asked.

"Yes, for you, my lord."

They walked to the abbey, Somerled's son and two companions following him and the princess. The wind grew colder as the day waned.

"Do you mind the cold?" she asked.

"Sometimes. The mild winter you have here on the Isle of Man is nothing like the weather in the north or the wind at sea that can leave the deck awash in cold salt water, even in summer."

"I do recall the times my father has encountered bad weather when I was with him. It happened near Islay once."

They reached the large abbey garden first. It was surrounded by trees and laid out in plots protected by wattle fences. Behind the large garden, the abbey rose two stories high peeking above the trees. As they ventured closer, Somerled observed a small orchard.

A gray-robed monk met them as they entered the arched doorway. "Good day, Princess," he said, welcoming them inside. "I will let Abbot Bernard know you are here."

Ragnhild turned to Somerled, Gillecolum, Liadan and Maurice as the monk departed. "There are twelve monks here in addition to the abbot. That small number accomplishes much."

A moment later, the gray-haired, tonsured abbot appeared, both his hair and short beard nearly the color of his robe. Though Somerled did not favor the Roman Church, he knew they did good work and this abbot had a benevolent face.

"Princess, how nice to see you!" said the abbot. "Are these with you the guests who are the cause of the celebration this eve?"

"They are. Allow me to introduce them. This is Somerled, the Lord of Argyll, Kintyre and Lorne, his son, Gillecolum, Maurice MacNeill, the king's foster brother, and Liadan MacGilleain of Islay."

Abbot Bernard offered his hand in welcome. Taking it, Somerled said, "I have been eager to see your abbey."

"They are hoping you might show them around," said Ragnhild, as she laid back her hood. Her flushed cheeks and windswept hair drew Somerled's gaze. He had missed the sight of her lovely face.

"The monks finished another batch of ale a sennight ago," said the abbot. "It should be ready to drink once we have seen the abbey. You are welcome to try it."

"Aye," said Somerled, casting a glance at his companions. On their faces were eager acceptances of the priest's offer. "I think we would like that." Since ale was served with nearly every meal and contained only small amounts of spirits, it was suitable for his son, too.

Abbot Bernard led them first to the large dining hall filled with light from the tall windows at one end and beckoned them to the open hearth where they reached their hands toward the flames to warm them. Somerled purposely took a place next to Ragnhild, their shoulders touching.

Gesturing to the long table in the center of the room with a bench on either side, and a chair at the head, the abbot said, "After Lauds, we break our fast here with bread, cheese and ale before going about our work."

He next took them to the church. "This is the Church of St. Mary, the oldest part of the abbey and its heart." The church had been built in the shape of a cross with an altar at the far end of the chancel. Windows set high in the wooden walls allowed shafts of light to fall on the altar. "Here, we pray and hold services for the people."

The princess explained, "My father established the abbey to promote the Christian faith, to educate the island's young and to give alms to the poor."

"And we do all three," put in the abbot, "as well as produce ale, raise cattle and grow vegetables and herbs."

"Aye," said Somerled, "I can see you are busy. I have always thought that abbeys bring civilization to the places they inhabit, helping the people to understand God. The Gaels have them but we follow the Celtic tradition of Patrick and Columba."

"It might interest you to know that it was Patrick who brought Christianity to this isle," said the abbot. "And both the castle and the abbey are named for St. Russin, who, along with your Columba, settled Iona long ago."

Somerled nodded, unsurprised but happy to hear it. "I know that Patrick traveled to many places, Columba, too. Iona is a sacred place to my people." He raised his eyes to the timbered beams above him and then to the arched windows and felt the quiet stillness, the solemn majesty of the place.

After that, the abbot took them to the room where they made the ale, the rich earthy smell filling the air. Several monks were busy mixing ingredients for the next batch.

"What's it made of?" asked Gillecolum.

The abbot smiled down at Somerled's son. "Malted grains, water and yeast for fermenting. Sometimes we add heather or spices, too."

Gillecolum nodded, pursing his lips.

"Come," said the abbot, "I will show you a small room where I entertain visitors. There, we will share the new ale."

The light was subdued in the corner chamber to which the abbot led them, being provided by small windows high in the walls and a brazier whose fire had burned down to coals. Still, the room was warmer than the others they had seen and inviting.

A monk awaited them next to a table set with mugs of ale, which Somerled and his companions promptly accepted. He handed one mug to his son and then another to Ragnhild. "For you, Princess."

She took it, gazing into his eyes.

The sweet, fruity taste brought a smile to Somerled's face. "Very refreshing."

"I will see you have some to take with you," she said.

"This is good," said Maurice, "better than what we often drink."

"And better than what we have on Islay," put in Liadan.

The abbot was obviously pleased. "We work hard to make it the best. I will send some to the castle for tonight's celebration."

"We are fortunate that the monks produce enough for all," said Ragnhild.

As they were leaving, Somerled thanked the abbot. "Your abbey has inspired me, Abbot Bernard."

On the way back to the castle, he again walked next to Ragnhild, "One day," he said to her, "I hope to found an abbey, mayhap on Kintyre."

She turned to him, her green eyes sparkling. "I believe you will."

He knew she would favor such an idea. He had not mentioned it to the abbot but, when the abbey was built, Somerled would invite Culdee monks to dwell there.

CHAPTER 13

BUSTLING ABOUT THE HALL, checking the preparations for that night's feast, Ragnhild was careful to see all was done well. It might be a long while before she would again see Somerled's face. A face she had come to love.

He was everything she had longed for but never expected to find, a man of even temperament, quiet courage and love for his people. Yet she knew all too well his life could be forfeit in King David's war. And though her fate would be decided by others, still she prayed Somerled would be the man chosen for her.

By the time their guests began arriving, it was full dark outside with the shortened days of December. Though some chieftains arrived by ship, those who came by land carried torches to light their paths. All gave thanks for the warm hearth fire, the mead and the monks' ale that awaited them. Merry sounds filled the hall from the minstrels' pipes, rebec, lyre and lute.

Somerled, his son and his companions descended the stairs to the hall, their attire changed to that fitting to dine with the king and his chieftains. She was glad of it for she wanted the leaders of the Isle of

Man and their wives to think well of him.

She had chosen her own gown with care. The golden bliaut and the circlet of gold holding in place her long hair were the same ones she had worn in Scotland to meet King David. She had not worn them for Lord Fergus, as Affraic might have preferred, but she would wear them for the Lord of Argyll, Kintyre and Lorne.

"Good evening, my lord," she greeted Somerled, "and to you, Gillecolum, Liadan and Maurice."

"The hall is beautiful," remarked the auburn-haired young woman in her blue bliaut.

"And smells of a feast like to enthrall a man," put in Maurice.

"Will we eat soon?" asked Somerled's son.

She chuckled. "Aye, lad. As soon as all the guests are here, the servants will bring out the food. I promise you the feast will be worth waiting for. It was with you and your father in mind that it was prepared."

Somerled gave her a look of approval.

As the chieftains entered the hall, Ragnhild attended to her hostess duties, introducing Somerled and his companions to the ones he had not met previously. Abbot Bernard arrived with his monks and were hailed by all. Many of the sons and daughters of the chieftains who lived close were being educated by the monks and thus they were held in high esteem.

Once everyone had arrived, Ragnhild directed Somerled, Abbot Bernard and the highest ranking chieftains and their wives to the high table where they would join her and the king and queen. The other chieftains, the garrison commander, the monks and Somerled's men, she directed to the trestle tables set at right angles to the dais. Liadan, Maurice and Gillecolum she gestured to seats reserved for them at the end of the trestle table nearest the dais.

At the head table, Queen Affraic sat on the king's right with Maurice on her right and Chieftain Truian and his wife Fritha next to Maurice. On the king's left sat Abbot Bernard. Next to him was the seat Ragnhild would occupy. On her left, by her own plan, was Somerled. And, on his left, Chieftain Conyll and his wife Eithne.

Her father signaled the musicians to pause and asked Abbot Bernard to give thanks. The abbot rose and bowed his head.

"O Lord, thou giver of gifts, light of the world, our blessed Comforter, we are grateful for another year of peace and a good harvest. Thank you for this bounty, and its sweet refreshment."

With that, the abbot took his seat and the minstrels began to play again. Servants set platters of steaming food on the tables from which rose enticing smells. Ragnhild was happy to hear the exclamations of delight at the food.

Somerled cut a succulent piece of salmon from the platter before them and laid it at her end of the trencher. Then he began tasting the fish and the onions he set on his side. "You are to be commended for the dishes, my lady," he said between bites. "They are most pleasing to the taste."

"I am glad you find the food to your liking. Were you to come for Christmas, there would be roast beef and honeyed chicken. Knowing you could not stay for that day, I wanted to provide you with an Advent feast."

"And you succeeded. I have not dined so well since King David's court. But the best part is to be with you, to see your face again, to share the day and evening with you." Beneath the linen-draped table, he took her hand. "Mayhap later we can be alone for a moment."

"I would like that," she said, his words bringing a smile to her face. "For me to be with you is a longed-for pleasure."

She imagined him eating on his galley or in the woods. He seemed a man who could adapt to harsh circumstances if he must to achieve his goal. But surely Christmas would see him celebrating with his Highlanders. "Will you spend Christmas on Islay?"

"Aye, most likely. After we build the chieftains' hall and lodgings for the lord and his men, I want to raise a chapel. Do you like the idea?"

"I do," she said. "'Twould be a fine addition, a place to pray."

"The island in Findlugan's Loch is sacred ground, having served the saint and his monks centuries ago."

"I was on Islay once with my father, that time when we encountered rough seas. It was long ago but, even now, I remember the isle's beauty."

"You would like it there," he said. "The loch is private. All manner of waterfowl, birds and deer claim it as home. It will be the place the clan chiefs gather."

Ragnhild tried to imagine the isle, the loch and the buildings Somerled spoke of. "Will the structures you build be of timber or stone?"

"Timber with thatched roofs with the possible exception of the chapel. For now, I will build in stone only the strongholds needed to protect the sea lanes. Those will be Norman in design, much like Castle Rushen," he said, sweeping his gaze around the hall.

"You spoke of King David's summoning you to war. Do you think it likely?"

"Aye," he said, turning his goblet in his long fingers, the silver catching the light from the candles. "Unless King David changes his course, I think it inevitable."

"If you will allow, I worry for your safety."

He smiled at her, his piercing blue eyes intense in the candlelight. "I will not only allow it, Princess, I encourage it. Nothing would please me more than to know your thoughts are of me when I am gone."

She could not look away. "I will do more, Lord Somerled. I will pray for your safe return for it means much to me."

The look he gave her spoke of his happiness at her words.

The connection between them had grown stronger, a cord that would forever bind them to each other no matter what would come. Her heart moved for this man and no other. She could not bear to think of his falling in battle.

During the meal, as the minstrels played, a juggler entertained them. Ragnhild watched the juggler even as she felt keenly Somerled's presence beside her. She wished they could be alone so he could kiss her again. From his looks, she thought he might be thinking the same thing.

Afterward, a bard came forward to stand before the king. "Your Grace, if you allow, I have composed a poem for your guest, Lord Somerled."

"Say on," said her father.

Accompanied by the lyre, the bard began to recite.

Great Somerled stands in the prow
Winds swirling, waves crashing, there is no fear now.

Lord of Argyll, Kintyre and Lorne, calm now the seas.
The foe flees before him, broken against the breeze.
Great Somerled, keep free our shore.
Invaders fear; they will come no more.
His galley skims o'er the crested wave.
Great Somerled, the warrior brave!

A roar of "Somerled!" arose from his men and was echoed about the hall. Some got to their feet and lifted tankards of ale in salute. Ragnhild knew many on the isle were grateful for Somerled's coming, aware he was the one helping to keep the sea lanes free and the pirates from their shores.

The shouts died down as Somerled stood and bowed. "I thank you for your welcome and gracious ode." Resuming his seat, he turned to her. "Did you have something to do with this, Princess?"

Ragnhild averted her gaze. "Only to challenge the bard. The verses were his." Then turning back to him with a hopeful expression, "Do you like it?"

"I can hardly complain of such gallant verses though they nearly made me blush."

She chuckled as she shifted her gaze to the table where Gillecolum was sitting, a wide smile on the boy's face. "Your son seemed to like the poem. His was the loudest shout."

"Aye. He sees only a father he has long missed."

"I believe he sees more, as do I."

After the evening concluded, Somerled asked her if she might step outside with him. Making sure they were not seen, she found their cloaks and led him through the castle door, nodding to the guard as they passed.

"There is a place at the side of the castle where long shadows will afford us privacy."

"Lead on," he encouraged.

Once they arrived at the place where their presence would not be detected by the guards on the ramparts, she turned to him. "Will you kiss me again?"

"Aye, if you let me."

157

She nodded and he pulled her close, his mouth descending on hers. This kiss was much different than the first. With their mouths joined, sweet pleasure took hold of her. She greedily returned his kiss, slipping her hands around his neck to hold him to her.

When he broke the kiss, he did not let her go but continued to hold her close, pressing her head to his chest under his chin. "How can I live without you, my love?" he whispered. "It will take all my fortitude to leave you on the morrow."

She pulled back so that, inches from his face, she could look long into his eyes, dark with desire in the night's shadows. "I do not want to be parted," she said.

"Worry not, Princess," he said. "I will find a way for us to be together."

THE NEXT MORNING, Somerled thanked the king for his hospitality and proceeded outside into the mist to bid the princess farewell. She stood at the castle door dressed in green wool the color of her eyes. Her red hair, confined to long plaits, made him want to reach out and touch them. His heart ached to think he might not see her for some time, mayhap not ever again.

"I had food delivered to your ship for your travel," she said.

"My men and I are most grateful." Placing a small velvet package into her hand, he said, "I brought you this from Ireland. 'Tis a gift of the season."

Her brows drew together in a look of dismay. "But I have nothing for you…"

"That you welcomed my kiss was gift enough, my lady." He bowed and turned to go before he would be unable to do so.

She called him back. Unwinding a green riband wrapped around one of her long plaits, she offered it to him. "May this be a reminder that my prayers go with you."

He tucked the silk into his waist. "I will treasure it, Princess. 'Twill be a reminder not only of your prayers but of you."

Somerled was in high spirits as he joined his son to descend the hill to the harbor where Maurice and Liadan waited by the galley. It seemed no one else had claimed Ragnhild's heart. He only wished that would be enough but he knew better.

"What did you give the princess, Father?" his son asked.

He tousled the lad's hair. "A trinket for her horse." He hoped the princess liked his gift, a black leather browband with white Celtic scrolling that would dip to a point when placed on the horse's forehead. Such a handsome horse, much loved by his mistress, should have a unique adornment. Ragnhild had been his first thought when he had seen it in the marketplace. He believed she would be pleased with the gift.

Once all had boarded his galley, they left the mist-filled harbor and rowed into the Irish Sea where a strong wind filled the sail, allowing them to pick up speed as they headed north to Kintyre. He'd been away longer than he had planned but he wanted to stop there before going on to Islay to see how his brother fared and to convey to him their mother's good wishes.

By the end of the day, they had reached Dunaverty Bay and beached the galley just as the sun was setting. On the western horizon, the gray clouds were silhouetted against a lavender and gold sky.

Assured the galley was secured, Somerled climbed down and saw his brother approaching. "I brought someone who is eager to see you," he said to Angus.

His brother looked up to where Gillecolum stood on deck, poised to jump down. After considering him for a moment, Angus shouted, "My nephew! Come here, Gille, and let me look at you!"

"I sail with my father now," the boy proudly replied as he vaulted over the gunwale to the sand.

"How you have grown!" exclaimed Angus, gazing down at the lad. "Aye, you are a man now." Then turning to Somerled, Angus said, "How goes the building on Islay?"

"Well enough that I could leave it to pay a visit to our mother who was anxious to hear news of you."

Maurice joined them to shake Angus' hand. "Aye, the building goes well enough for our leader to make a stop on the Isle of Man after that."

Somerled's brother gave him an inquiring look. "And how is the princess?"

"Busy with preparations for Christmas," was all he would say. He did not wish to share his time with her but his memories of that night were firmly implanted in his mind and heart.

"And our mother?" inquired Angus. "She is in good health?"

"Aye," said Somerled. "You will have to make the trip to see her."

The crew, released to enjoy themselves, hurried up the beach to join the men returning from the day's labor.

Liadan, garbed in tunic, trews and short boots, left the ship to join Somerled, Gillecolum, Maurice and Angus as they walked toward Ruairi's house where Angus was staying while Ruairi and his family were in the north.

"How goes the work on the castle?" asked Somerled.

"The stonemason de Mares directs the work cutting stone," said Angus. "He praises the sandstone on Kintyre."

"Ah, that is good," said Somerled, running his hand through his hair, tangled from the wind. "Mayhap the spring will see the start of construction." He wondered how d'Harcourt was faring in the north where he had sailed with Ruairi to look at castle sites. "I hope to be in Morvern in the spring with our Master Mason."

After dinner with his son and companions, he joined his men around the bonfire to talk of their work and his growing concern about the civil war in England.

"Cutting stones is hard work, carrying them more so," said one. "But it builds strength and I like to think that, one day, I'll see those stones I carry in a castle rising from that rock." He shifted his gaze to the looming headland just waiting for the castle.

"When we left Islay for our trip to Ireland," said Maurice, "the hall where the chiefs will one day gather was coming along nicely."

The men nodded their approval, their faces set aglow by the flames rising into the night. All had their mantles drawn about them. Somerled waited until the conversation quieted to raise a difficult subject. "I must tell you I believe the King of Scots may invade England next year. And, if he does, we will likely be summoned to join him."

"Let us hope if that happens," said one man, who Somerled knew to be a farmer, "he does not call upon us until the spring seed is sown."

"Aye, we can pray for that," said another.

The men would do their duty but, by their dour expressions, Somerled could see none were pleased at the thought of fighting a war in England when they were still fighting Norse pirates in the Isles.

"If you go to war for the Scots king, we go with you," said Maurice.

"Aye," said Angus.

The men gathered around the fire nodded their agreement.

Somerled was touched by their loyalty. "As soon as winter is over," he said, "we will travel north to deal with any Norse who linger in the Isles with plunder in mind."

The next morning, Somerled said goodbye to Angus and his men and sailed with Maurice, Liadan and Gillecolum back to Islay where they would spend the rest of the winter.

The voyage, though short, was not pleasant due to harsh winds and pelting rain. By the time they reached Loch Indaal, they were sodden and happy to be ashore. Barnacle Geese, still there in large numbers, sent their clamorous calls into the air from where they roosted on the flat, muddy land near shore. Otters, indifferent to the weather, gamboled together in the bay.

Somerled's crew beached the galley and they all headed inland, taking the well-trodden path to Findlugan's Loch. Fallow deer in thick winter coats stared at them from the brown hills. As they came over the rise, Somerled gazed down at the loch surrounded by wind-swept peat bog, grasses and gently rolling hills.

In the distance, he saw buildings standing on the largest of the islands in the loch.

Anxious to observe the progress of the construction, with his young son at his side and Maurice and Liadan following, he strode toward the north end of the loch, passing curlews wading near shore, their long down-curved bills searching for food in the mud.

The wintering ducks and geese apparently approved of the new human tenants as they were floating on the rippling waters of the loch in great numbers.

Once he was close enough to see what had been accomplished since he'd been gone, Somerled stood amazed. From the largest island rose the tall wooden great hall with a new thatched roof. New, too, were outbuildings and what looked like a small stone chapel with a thatched roof.

Smoke rose into the air from three of the roofs ere it was swept away in the wind.

"Do you think Domnall has returned?" asked Liadan, betraying her interest.

"Since his ship wasn't at Loch Indaal," replied Somerled, "we will have to wait and see. If he is here, he may have entered on the east coast, sailing up the sound." He watched his charge for signs of disappointment, but she gave none. "They must have been hard at work to have done so much," he said, gazing in awe at what appeared to be a small village on the island.

In time, he would build other, more magnificent strongholds in Argyll and the Isles but none would be more significant for the future of his lordship than this secret place. Here the council of chiefs would meet. Here new lords would be installed. And here, peace would be celebrated and God would be praised.

He took out Ragnhild's green riband and fingered the soft silk, bringing to mind the image of her handing the riband to him. Mayhap it would be here, too, that the woman who held his heart would join him.

"They wanted to meet your goal to be finished by winter's onset" said Maurice, "and it seems they have done so."

"Father," said Gillecolum, pointing to the smoke rising from the buildings, "they have lit hearth fires. Can we go inside and get warm?"

Somerled looked at the earnest expression on his son's face and smiled. "Aye, we shall. 'Tis a good idea. Forgive me," he said, turning to Liadan, "for not thinking of you and the lad." He glanced at his men standing behind them. "My crew surely feels the same."

"I minded not pausing to admire all that is here," said Liadan, taking Gillecolum's hand as they crossed the wooden path from the shore to the large island. His men, who crossed after, remarked at how much they liked the raised path that allowed their boots to stay dry when they were so often wet.

They were met by Duncan MacEachern, the village smith from Keills, whose powerful chest appeared even larger draped in his brown woolen mantle. Beaming his pleasure, he said, "Greetings, Lord. Welcome back! As you see," he gestured behind him, "the men have done much in your absence."

"You and the men are to be commended," said Somerled. Then putting his arm around Gillecolum's shoulders, "Duncan, meet my son. I have just retrieved him from Ireland."

A handshake was exchanged and the smith said, "A fine lad, indeed."

"Now," said Somerled, "lead on. We are eager to be where a fire burns."

"Since winter is upon us and the principal structures are up," said Duncan, walking ahead of them toward the great hall, "we build inside, finishing the walls and the furniture. The village men have offered their carpentry skills. Most of those have left for the day but they will return tomorrow."

Inside the great hall, Somerled was surprised to set his foot on stone, the same gray-green stone used to construct the chapel. As they shed their mantles, he inhaled the smell of newly cut timber and the wood smoke from the hearth fire. Windows high in the walls on each side allowed the afternoon's pale light to flood the large space.

The men who had been working laid down their tools to greet him, obviously proud of their accomplishments.

"I thank you all for what you have done here," said Somerled. "I could not have hoped for more. Even a chapel."

"Aye," nodded Duncan. "The priest at Keills has agreed to hold services here until another of his brethren can be found."

"I can always bring one back from Ireland," offered Maurice.

Somerled acknowledged the offer with a smile. "A Celtic priest would be good." Then to Duncan, "Will the hall be warm enough for the men this winter?"

"We keep the fire burning through the night," said Duncan, "so the men can sleep here on pallets."

Somerled nodded. "That is good, a warm place to shelter."

"Already there is a table with benches," remarked Maurice, glancing toward the long table before them.

"That will become the high table," explained Duncan. "There will be two more, longer tables when we are finished. Then all the men and those who come from the village to help us can eat here."

Liadan scanned the room. "'Tis bare. The women of Keills could do much to make this a more welcoming space."

Duncan spoke up. "They have already helped a great deal to make the lord's lodgings comfortable. There, you will find a large bed with a goose feather cushion, warm furs and pillows."

In his mind, Somerled envisioned Ragnhild spread out across the large bed, her long red hair strewn across the pillow, waiting for her lord. He sighed, hoping the vision would, one day, be reality. For now, he must be concerned for his men. "Are there lodgings for my men besides the floor of the hall?"

"Aye," said the smith, "we are building them but they are not quite finished. And we thought to have a guards' house on the shore of the loch."

"A good idea," said Somerled.

"Have you food?" asked Liadan, gazing at the bare table.

"Aye, we do," one man spoke up. "Geese cleaned and ready to roast over the fire and fish caught this morning. The women of Keills brought us apple tarts and root vegetables."

Somerled's stomach rumbled when Liadan asked about dinner. He had been hungry even before the long walk from Loch Indaal. Likely, his crew was as well.

"I assure the men eat well," said Duncan with a hint of pride.

"You are a good man," said Somerled, patting the smith on the back. "Tell us what we can do to help."

"I'll get the men started with dinner and, while the geese are roasting outside, I want to show you the other buildings." With a look of satisfaction at all they had accomplished, Duncan said, "I think you will be pleased, my lord."

"I am already pleased. And I am eager to join the men in finishing all we planned. It will soon be time to gather the chiefs."

CHAPTER 14

The Isle of Man, January 1138 A.D.

CHRISTMAS AND NEW YEAR'S had come and gone with only a few days of frost and much celebration yet, despite this, Ragnhild's mood had been more subdued than in past years. Not even the Feast of Epiphany was as gay a celebration as it had been before, at least not for her. One man's absence cast a gray pall over all, much like the sky overhead.

The antics of young Godred, her half-brother, who was now two and walking on unsteady feet, never failed to cheer her, however. And Abbot Bernard's message of hope at Epiphany had been a comfort, as was his friendship. They played chess by the fire on days with much rain and he read to her from the Gospels.

Both Earl Rognvald, whose attention was apparently still given to his cathedral building according to his message, and Uchtred of Galloway sent her gifts she had not expected.

Rognvald must not have forgotten her hair as he had sent her an exquisite comb carved from antler bone and embedded with silver. Uchtred had sent her a book adorned with beautiful pictures and colors telling a story of King Arthur. His accompanying message expressed the hope he would be there in the spring to read it with her.

They were splendid gifts but neither touched her heart like the browband Somerled had brought her for Fairhair. How could he know a gift for the horse she loved would be more treasured than a gift for herself? She could put away a comb and place a book on a shelf, but the browband Fairhair wore was before her eyes every day—a constant reminder of Somerled's thoughtfulness and a constant reminder of the man himself.

Clever man.

The short days and often dismal weather kept her inside. But whenever the sun broke through the clouds, she and Fairhair left the castle grounds to ride across the hills to her favorite place where she would gaze at the stormy Irish Sea and wonder about the golden warrior who had come one summer and taken her heart with him when he sailed away.

Isle of Islay, late April, 1138 A.D.

SOMERLED WALKED among the yellow wildflowers blooming on the hillside nearest the loch, letting his fingers trail through the tall grass. It was that glorious time of year when, though still cold, the light was brilliant, the geese were feeding on new grass, preparing for their long journey north, and the midges were yet to arrive. That in-between, gentle season.

On the loch, new sights and sounds replaced the departing geese. At dawn, male thrushes sang for their mates. In the muddy shallows, mating frogs made their presence known with their low rumbled croaking. Water lilies at the edges of the loch gave bloom to delicate flowers. The osprey that lived in the trees fished for trout. And a stately gray heron, hunched over the water, silently watched for fish or mayhap a frog.

All around him, the isle had stirred to life from its winter sleep, making him wonder if Ragnhild was greeting the spring with thoughts of the future.

He and his men had completed the headquarters at Findlugan's Loch and the Islesmen returned to their plowing and seeding of new crops. But, for Somerled, there were castles to build, a fleet of galleys to construct and Norse pirates to hold in check. He could not remain in one place.

To Liadan's great joy, Domnall had arrived the day before, bringing news of Norse pirates pillaging the coast of Moidart in the far north of Argyll. Remembering their conversation, Somerled knew he must soon leave Islay.

"When word reached us at Ardtornish of the attacks," said Domnall, standing with Liadan and Gillecolum just outside the new hall, "I gathered two ships of warriors and sailed after them. We fought them on Moidart's western shore and chased them north."

"Was Sweyn Asleifsson one of them?" Somerled asked.

"I did not see him. That is, he was not among the dead. The pirates still alive after the battle did not stay long enough for us to sort them out."

Liadan swept her gaze over Domnall. "Were you hurt?"

He smiled at her concern. "Nay, just a scratch here and there."

"What about the Morvern men?" asked Somerled. "Did we lose any?"

"Aye," said Domnall with downcast eyes. "Two. Others were wounded but there is a healer at Ardtornish who is tending them."

"Was my brother, Diarmad, among them?" asked Liadan, giving Domnall an anxious look.

"He was among those fighting but not among the wounded. 'Twas his galley that sailed with me, bringing some of the warriors."

Liadan nodded, sighing in relief. "He is my only brother now."

"Aye, lass," said Domnall. His tone was caring, so unlike the warrior Somerled knew. "But take comfort Diarmad is well."

Somerled cast Domnall an assessing gaze, wondering if he'd spoken to Liadan's brother about his sister's future. There would be time for them to talk later. "What you say makes me think we should always have a healer with us. We will soon leave here and sail north. We can ask for volunteers along the way. Mayhap an older healer has a young apprentice he has trained who is willing to sail with us. Or, there might be warriors among us who are learned in tending wounds."

"Aye, 'tis needed," said Domnall.

"I know a little of herbs and poultices for wounds," offered Liadan.

"You do, lass," said Somerled, "and I thank you for treating my arrow wound. 'Tis now healed." Not wishing to discourage her, he did not mention he would be loath to take her into battle.

Later, after dinner, Somerled drew Domnall outside to ask if he'd spoken with Liadan's brother about her.

"I did," replied Domnall. "He was warm to the idea but asked me to wait until next year when he hoped to return to Islay. He told me, quite directly, that I could use the year to woo her." Then chuckling, he said, "I thought it best not to hit my future brother-in-law so I agreed and told him I would watch over her even though she sails under your protection."

"Does Diarmad know she has declared herself my guard?"

"Aye, he found it amusing. He knows his sister well. In truth, he was the one who taught her how to use a sword."

"It was good he did," said Somerled, "or she might not have survived the battle at Keills."

Two days later, Somerled sent a messenger to Kintyre to let his brother know he was leaving Islay for Morvern and, once there, would send Ruairi south so that Angus would be free to join Somerled. On his way north, he planned to stop in Knapdale at Castle Sween to visit Ewan MacSuibhne. Somewhere north of there, Somerled expected he would catch up with Goubert d'Harcourt, his Master Mason, and see what his thoughts were on the construction of the castles.

It was yet another bright spring morning when Somerled and his companions, Domnall, Maurice and Liadan, along with his son, Gillecolum, bid farewell to Duncan MacEachern.

The smith assured Somerled he would take care of the headquarters on Loch Findlugan. "Worry not, Lord. All will be ready when you return."

Knapdale, Argyll

THEY SAILED TWO GALLEYS out of Loch Indaal, Somerled's and the one Domnall had taken north. With every hour he had sailed, he thought of the distance his travel was putting between him and Ragnhild. But his mission required it and he hoped she would understand.

Sailing south out of the great sea loch, they turned east, rounding Islay, before heading north into the Sound of Jura. Some distance into the sound, with Somerled's galley in the lead, they entered Loch Sween, the narrow sea loch in Knapdale where Castle Sween was located.

He watched as the castle came into view. There was none like it in Argyll, a stone fortress built in the Norman fashion, reminding Somerled of Castle Rushen on the Isle of Man.

The hillsides of Knapdale were green with spring, like those on Man when he'd first glimpsed Ragnhild, yet Somerled was keenly aware no jewel-eyed princess would be galloping over them on her white horse. He ignored the longing that rose in his heart and prayed she would still be unwed when he was in a position to claim her.

As they beached the galleys on the small swath of sand just south of the rocky ridge on which the castle rested, he noticed two other galleys. Ewan had more than these two but mayhap the others were on voyages. He hoped Ewan was not on one of those ships.

Somerled, his son, and his companions climbed the hill where he was pleased to find Ewan standing at the arched castle entrance. "I am glad to find you at home."

"I was expecting you. Recognized your red sail from afar. 'Tis about time you paid me a visit." With a nod toward Maurice, Domnall and Gillecolum, Ewan said, "Good day to you all. To Maurice, he said, "I have not seen my fellow Irishman for some time."

"I've been busy about Somerled's work," said Maurice.

Ewan nodded. "From all I hear, your mission to drive the Norse from Argyll never ends." To Somerled, he said, "Your French mason has come and gone."

"Was it a good visit with him?" Somerled asked. He was anxious to know if the stonemason had endured his sea travel and was still enthusiastic about the castles.

"Aye. We talked much about what he was to see. I will tell you about it over some ale and cheese." It was only afternoon but Ewan loved to eat, as his round belly and full cheeks attested. His shaggy red-brown hair framed what was a perpetually cheerful face. Older than Somerled by a decade, Ewan loved to entertain his Highland friends. His wife, Mary, was always accommodating. Having the only stone castle in Argyll, and being on the route to the north, they often received visitors.

Somerled then introduced his son to Ewan, who was delighted to meet him. "I like having lads about and my son, Michan, who is your age, will be happy for your company. And the lady?"

"It may be difficult for you to believe," said Somerled, "but this young lady is sister to Diarmad MacGilleain, one of my galley captains. She guards my back."

"And spies for Lord Somerled," put in Liadan with a canny smile.

Domnall frowned.

Ewan raised a brow. "Spy, is it?"

"And a good one, too," said Somerled.

"I know your brother," Ewan told Liadan. "So, 'tis not hard to believe what you say. Diarmad's sword is never unsheathed except he draws blood." To the five of them, he asked, "Are you all well?"

As they walked through the gate to the castle's inner bailey, Somerled answered for them. "Aye, we are and eager to visit the sites for the castles. Will you come with us?"

Ewan grinned. "I was hoping you'd ask." It had been Ewan's idea that he should help oversee the construction of Somerled's castles so his willingness to accompany them came as no surprise. He would help Somerled find the best places to locate fortresses to guard the sea lanes and make sure the castles were placed as they should be.

Ewan gestured them to the door of the great hall and, once inside, led them to a trestle table where food and ale were being set out. "Tell your men the kitchens will have food for them and they can bed down in the great hall if you are staying the night."

"If that is an invitation," said Somerled, "we accept," taking a seat with the others.

Just as Somerled was lifting his ale to his lips, a woman swept into the great hall, her dark hair in two plaits hanging beneath her cream-colored veil held down with a simple fillet of gold. The crimson tunic she wore was long and flowing with flaring sleeves.

"Ah, Mary is here. Come, love. Our friends have arrived."

"Good day to you," she said, crossing the hall to their table, her brown eyes sparkling. Mary was not beautiful but handsome with her long dark plaits. By the looks she gave her husband and those he returned to her, Somerled was convinced she and Ewan were much in love. A pang in his heart reminded him of his own love, now far to the south.

"Ewan has been awaiting your arrival for a sennight," said Mary, "ever since the hillsides broke into full bloom."

Somerled set down his ale and introduced Mary to Gillecolum and Liadan. Like Ewan, Mary had met both Domnall and Maurice before.

"You've a fine looking son," she said, smiling at Gillecolum. "My son, Michan, is around here somewhere. You should meet him." Then with a glance at Liadan, "I did not know you traveled with a young woman."

"Liadan is sister to Diarmad MacGilleain," Ewan explained to his wife.

"Ah," said Mary, "that handsome young man with a quick wit. He has the same auburn hair."

Liadan smiled. "I hope to see him when we reach Ardtornish."

Somerled was pleased with the girl from Islay. While Liadan had lost her parents and younger brother and been separated from the remaining one for some time, still she could smile. He glanced at Domnall whose eyes were fixed on the auburn-haired lass. Liadan laughed at Domnall's stories but, whether she felt more than friendship for Somerled's cousin, he could not say.

They dined with Ewan and his family that night. Somerled was glad to see Ewan's son and Gillecolum had become fast friends.

The next morning, Somerled explained his intention to stop at Jura and Lorne as well as the Isle of Mull before setting their course for Ardtornish Point on the north shore of the Sound of Mull in Morvern.

Mary kissed her plump husband and, with the dark-haired Michan, by her side, wished him Godspeed. Ewan waved to his wife and son and climbed aboard Somerled's galley as they departed the shores of Loch Sween, taking advantage of the southwesterly winds.

Ardtornish, Morvern, May 1138 A.D.

IT TOOK THEM a fortnight to reach Morvern with their visits to Jura, Lorne and Mull where Somerled spent time with the villagers, inquiring into the status of the settlements and the families. He wanted to share his plans with the people and ask their opinions. Having ploughed the fields and sown their crops, the villagers were hard at work weeding and pruning and planting new apple and pear trees. Still, they took time to meet with their lord and his men.

The conversations were lively and his presence was greeted with enthusiasm. It was gratifying to know that, while they may have local chiefs, they still considered him their lord, the one who had united them against a common foe.

As he left Mull, his parting words reminded all, as he had on Jura and in Lorne, that they must keep sharp their fighting skills. "In the next years, we will still fight to maintain the freedom we would pass on to our children."

Heads nodded and one man said, "Aye, Lord, we never forget. Every man jack here can wield a sword and a bow. We keep the smith busy." Somerled did not doubt the truth of it. Like him, most carried swords and daggers and their bows were always close to hand. The archers of Argyll were renowned for their skill.

Once they left the coast of Mull, they pressed on, sailing north, finally entering the Sound of Mull between the Isle of Mull and Morvern. On the north shore of the sound, they pulled up their galleys on the narrow strip of shingle at Ardtornish Point where there was already a galley resting on the shore.

Somerled jumped down from his galley and stood gazing up at the timber castle rising from the grass-covered promontory above him.

Gillecolum joined him to ask, "Is that the castle?"

"Aye, though not quite what I was expecting." He had hoped to see the beginning of a stone edifice but, for now, timber would have to do.

Mayhap the mason had even suggested timber first with stone to follow.

A white-tailed sea eagle flew overhead, a fish in its bright yellow beak. Somerled and his son stopped to watch, the wind blowing their hair around their faces. "Come on," urged Somerled, "let's see it from the top." Together, they scrambled up the hill.

His companions, slower to act, trailed behind them.

At the top of the rise, he paused and, with his back to the castle, looked across the sound.

"What's that land, Father?" Gillecolum asked.

"The Isle of Mull." The long shape of Mull was silhouetted against what was now a cloud-filled sky. The blue-gray waters of the sound surrounded the point where they stood on three sides.

To the west and running inland was Loch Aline, where, at the headwaters, he had been fishing for salmon in the River Gear Abhain when the men of Clan MacInnes had come for him. To Somerled, it seemed a very long time ago, for much had transpired since that auspicious day.

From here, he could see down the entire length of the sound in both directions. No ship could pass without his knowing of it. Whoever held this point would control the main routes to the Hebrides and much of Argyll's jagged coast so favored by the pirates. Control of this place would allow Somerled to strike fast at the Norse raiders who had dominated the sound before he had risen to challenge them.

"What say you?" his cousin, Domnall, asked, joining them. By his side was Liadan, who Somerled had seen his cousin help down from the galley. Domnall gazed up at the castle. "Is it not grand?"

"Aye," said Somerled, looking over his shoulder at the tall keep. "Like a mushroom springing up from damp soil. A good beginning."

Maurice reached the top of the rise to stand with them, gazing at the view from the point jutting into the sound.

Ewan came last, puffing and more slowly given his girth.

Behind him, Somerled heard his name shouted. He turned to see Ruairi MacInnes coming through the castle door, his young son running in front of him.

"Are you pleased, Lord?" asked Bran, arriving in front of Somerled and giving Gillecolum a curious look.

Somerled smiled at the boy. "I am. Did you build it?" he asked in exaggerated wonder.

"I helped my father," Bran said, raising his chin. "And I have been practicing with the sword you gave me."

Somerled drew his son to him and said to Bran, "You will have to practice with my son, Gillecolum."

Bran greeted Gillecolum in friendly fashion. "That would be grand! So much better than my sister."

The boys laughed and went off to compare swords.

Passing the boys, Ruairi extended his hand and Somerled shook it. "We have been wondering when you might get here."

"Aye," said Somerled, "we took time to check on the settlements. I'd introduce you to my son, Gillecolum, but it seems he's off with Bran."

Ruairi said, "I know you have longed to have the boy with you."

"Well, we are together now."

Maurice stared up at the timber castle. "You did well," he said to Ruairi.

"The men have worked hard, and, as you can see, the keep is up but we have yet to add the palisade and some of the outbuildings." Turning to Somerled, Ruairi said, "The people of Morvern remember all you did for them and are happy to help. I knew your priority was shelter for the men so the keep and the great hall were our first concerns."

Somerled nodded. "You were correct. Did the stonemason suggest timber?"

"Nay, 'twas me. If we began with stone, you would only see a foundation. But, given the timing, the mason agreed we could cover it later in stone."

"Aye," said Ewan, "'twill be easy now that you have the basic castle. That is how my ancestor did it at Castle Sween."

Somerled nodded. "We have made a good start on controlling the sound." Shifting his gaze to the Isle of Mull, he said, "What do you think of a few more castles on the other side?"

"'Wouldn't hurt," said Ruairi. "Mull has frequently been a target of the Norse pirates."

Somerled silently agreed. "Is d'Harcourt here?"

"Nay. Once Liadan's brother, Diarmad, returned from Moidart, I sent him back there with the stonemason. I did not want to leave here until I was certain the castle was complete for your arrival."

Somerled glanced at Liadan, who wore a disappointed look. "Worry not, lass, we'll catch up with your brother."

"Come in out of the wind," said Ruairi. "I have a map you can use to site your castles and Aileas is preparing refreshments." As they turned to walk to the castle, Ruairi said, "Ceana is helping her mother or she would have been the first to greet you. She wears that riband you gave her nearly every day, claims it is the color of her eyes."

Somerled laughed. "'Tis easy to win a young girl's heart. The grown ones are more difficult. They take time and much patience. But love that grows slowly is often the surest."

Domnall shot a glance at Liadan. She averted her eyes.

The great hall at Ardtornish—like the hall at Loch Findlugan—smelled of newly cut timber. Trestles and benches, enough for the crew of their two ships and Ruairi's, filled the hall. The hearth fire burned steadily adding the smell of oaken wood smoke to the air.

"Are there bedchambers?" Somerled asked.

"Aye," said Ruairi. "Above stairs." He pointed to a narrow set of stairs at the end of the hall.

"I like it, Father," said Gillecolum, joining them with Bran in tow. "And it sits high above all." Somerled knew the boy was comparing the one at Loch Findlugan. Ardtornish might present a grander, more strategic view and its keep more a castle, but Findlugan would be the center of power.

Somerled draped his arm across his son's shoulders. "'Twill be one of many, Son. In the next years, God willing, we will see them all."

They availed themselves of ale, cheese and kippers, while Ruairi unrolled a hand-drawn map of Argyll and the Isles. Somerled and his companions gathered around to study the places marked off. "From the Mull of Kintyre in the south," Somerled said, pointing with his dagger, "to Ardnamurchan and Moidart in the north, we will build castles at every critical spot to guard the sea lanes."

"That is a great number of castles," said Maurice.

Somerled's brow furrowed. "Aye..." He studied the map, mentally assessing the most critical areas. "At least a dozen, I expect."

"Do you really need one in Moidart?" asked Domnall.

Somerled looked again at the map and remembered the land they spoke of. "Moidart may be wild and untamed yet I believe a castle on the shore of Loch Moidart is essential. 'Twill be an important guard over the small isles and waters south of the Isle of Skye."

"All those castles will take years," said Ewan, "especially if you wish to build in stone."

Somerled was undaunted. "Once we have dealt with the Norse raiders and peace reigns in the Isles, we will have time. It must be done, else the pirates will not take seriously our intention to stay and our intention to build—not just castles, but a kingdom."

"I believe you will do it," said Liadan, her pretty face smiling up at him.

In Somerled's mind he heard Ragnhild's words, spoken on the night he'd first introduced himself to her. *I believe you will accomplish the task you have set for yourself, Lord Somerled.* Melancholy swept over him as he thought of the lass he wanted by his side. He missed her, often pulling the green silk riband she had given him to press it to his lips.

Shaking off the feeling, he asked Ruairi about Morvern. "Are the people there still committed to the cause?"

"More than ever. Morvern is yours, Lord. Have no doubt."

That evening was well spent in the great hall of the new castle. Somerled, his hosts, his son and companions and the galleys' crews dined well on the venison the afternoon's hunt had provided. Aileas had planted a kitchen garden and the herbs that were sufficiently grown to be harvested added flavor to the roasting meat. The meal was simple and hearty and much appreciated.

Somerled looked at Ruairi over the flickering candle and wondered if he and Aileas wished to return to Kintyre or would prefer to stay here. Angus was the MacInnes chief but Morvern was Ruairi's home as well. "Ruairi, I can find a man to oversee the building of the castle at Dunaverty if you and Aileas want to remain here."

Ruairi cast a knowing look at his wife. They had obviously discussed the possibility. "We have enjoyed our visit here, Lord, but we will be content to return to Dunaverty should that be your decision."

"If you still feel the same in the morning, you can sail south to

Kintyre and send Angus north to meet me at Moidart where I go to find my wandering stonemason." They shared a laugh at that for d'Harcourt was a bit of a character.

By the time dawn cast its golden rays through the narrow window in Somerled's chamber, he was up and dressing, eager to be sailing. He'd shared the lord's chamber with Maurice, Domnall and Gillecolum, who were still asleep on their pallets. Ewan had been given a small chamber of his own. "Wake up you lazy-bones! If we're to stop on Ardnamurchan's coast and arrive in Moidart while there is still light, you'd best be moving!"

His son rubbed his eyes and raised himself on one elbow. "Father?"

"Aye, Son. Time to rise." Gillecolum's gaze took in Somerled fully clothed and jumped from his pallet to struggle into his tunic and hose. "Good lad," Somerled encouraged him.

Maurice and Domnall had downed enough ale last evening while laughing at Ruairi's ill-timed humor and idle tales to keep them dreaming until noon. Ruairi, too, most likely. Somerled would have none of it. The day was young but 'twould not be so for long.

One brief nudge with his boot to Maurice's side and a bit of water poured onto Domnall's face had his companions groaning. "Go away," moaned Domnall, covering his face with a pillow.

"I am for breaking my fast," announced Somerled. "If you two wish to travel with empty bellies, sleep on. But when next called, you had best be ready to sail or your galley will arrive a day behind mine." Turning to his son, he said, "Come, Gille. Food awaits."

Ruairi might be sleeping in, but Aileas was bustling about the hall with servant girls helping her. Ewan MacSuibhne was already diving into a bowl of porridge.

"Morning, Somerled," said Ewan as he reached for his ale.

"And to you," said Somerled.

A fire blazed in the hearth against the morning chill. Aileas handed him a bowl. "'Tis porridge with dried berries and hazelnuts. The villagers keep us well supplied."

"My thanks," he said, taking a seat. "The food is much appreciated. I want to get an early start. Is Liadan awake?"

Aileas smiled. "Aye, she'll be here in a moment. She's helping the children dress." To Gillecolum, she said, "They wanted to join you for the morning meal and see you off."

In-between bites, Gillecolum nodded enthusiastically.

As he turned to his porridge, Somerled asked Aileas, "Did you and Ruairi make a decision as to whether to stay or return to Kintyre?"

"Aye, we'll go. We have come to love our cottage on Dunaverty Bay and, with your blessing, Ruairi wants to supervise the castle rising there. We'll take today to see matters are in good hands here and sail tomorrow."

Happy at their choice, Somerled said, "You and Ruairi have done well here. With you two at Dunaverty Bay, I will not worry over that castle."

Maurice and Domnall eventually appeared in the hall, bleary-eyed and seeking food.

"Best eat fast," said Somerled, with a wink at Aileas. "We sail within the hour."

By then, Liadan had returned to the hall and set porridge before the two men, none too gently. "Aye, you're late."

Domnall gave her a remorseful look. To Somerled, it appeared his cousin was pleased she took notice.

Minutes later, Somerled, Ewan and Gillecolum stepped outside into a windy morning with a gray, cloud-filled sky that made the waters of the sound appear like slate. They walked down to the beach where his crew was just arriving, going about their chores to prepare to sail.

"Morning," Somerled said in greeting.

Several replied with "Morning, Lord." Their groggy voices told him they were still waking up.

A sudden movement on the water caught Somerled's eye. He gazed beyond the beached galley into the sound. Some distance from shore, he glimpsed a longship sailing toward them. From the top of the mast flew the royal standard of Scotland, a red lion rampant on a field of bright yellow.

Watching the banner wave in the morning wind, a foreboding came over Somerled. He feared he was about to find out how dearly his alliance with the King of Scots would cost him.

CHAPTER 15

AS THE LONGSHIP was beached, Somerled recognized the man who jumped over the gunwale and thought him spry for his age. At Irvine, he had met Edward Siwardsson, David's high constable, an older Anglo-Saxon, whose tall height and fair hair made him appear Norse.

Siwardsson offered his hand. "I have been chasing you from Islay where I expected to find you, Lord Somerled."

Somerled met the man's strong grip. "Dare I ask why you travel so far to seek me out?"

"'Tis King David. He sent me to summon you as he prepares for war."

Somerled had known the summons from the Scots king would come one day. Yet, now that it was here, his heart sank for all it meant. "Let us retire to the castle where we can discuss your mission."

At the castle door, Somerled was met by the rest of his companions and Ruairi. As Ruairi did not know the high constable, Somerled introduced him. "He is here to deliver a message from King David."

Maurice exchanged an ominous glance with Somerled and he gave a slight nod.

Ruairi beckoned them enter and asked a waiting servant to fetch ale. The two children and Gillecolum stood off to one side, their expressions curious.

The servants brought ale and tankards. Once Somerled and the men claimed seats on the benches at a trestle table, Aileas came forward to inquire if they wanted food. None did.

Anxious to hear from David's high constable, Somerled was direct. "Has the king invaded England then?"

"The situation is ever changing, my lord. Mayhap you did not know that the Empress Maud's half-brother, the Earl of Gloucester, has risen in open rebellion to Stephen. Other nobles, too. With that good news, in the middle of April, King David crossed the border and captured the Bishop of Durham's castle at Norham, overlooking the River Tweed. It had a good effect on the northern noble, Eustace Fitz John, who then changed sides and joined David, turning over his castles to us.

"David is assembling a vast army to accompany his next foray into England. I went first to the Lord of Galloway for he, too, is summoned to come with his Galwegians, some of them already with the king's men in Scotland. And, from Galloway, I came to you." The high constable's eyes, as blue as Somerled's own, fixed him with an intense gaze. "You will heed the king's call?"

Somerled did not hesitate. "Aye. Honor demands it, for I am pledged to do so."

"Good. How many of your Highlanders will come, do you think?"

"At least a thousand, mayhap more. But it will take time to reach them and more time for the warriors to sail south. Only the beach at Loch Indaal on Islay can accept the number of galleys and longships the men of the Isles will bring. And then we'll need near a sennight to sail to Scotland's coast. Where are we to meet King David?"

"His castle at Carlisle in Cumbria. I will await you there. You can sail up the Solway Firth, which is the way I came, and thence to the River Esk. It will take you to the River Eden where the castle sits on its southern bank. Lord Galloway will already be in Scotland with King David, who will be coming from his castle at Roxburgh, gathering men and taking any castles in the hands of the English as he marches south."

Somerled knew it to be a huge undertaking but 'twas duty that called and he would not shy from it. "We'll begin the call to the men of Argyll and the Isles this day."

The king's high constable rose from his bench.

"Will you stay the night, Lord Siwardsson?" asked Ruairi.

"Nay, I must return to Carlisle and get a message to David." Then, offering his hand to Somerled, he said, "The king will be pleased when I tell him of your response."

Aileas must have anticipated his departure for she came and thrust a package into Siwardsson's hands. "Food for you and your crew, my lord. You've a long way to go."

"My thanks, my lady." He took the package and, inclining his head, turned to leave.

Somerled followed him to the door. "Godspeed, my lord."

"And to you!"

When the high constable had gone, Somerled turned back to Ruairi and his companions. "There is much to do and little time to do it. Domnall, you will sail north to Moidart and sound the call ere you return to Islay. Tell Diarmad to remain in the north with the stonemason unless our French mason has seen enough and wishes to sail to Kintyre where the castle at Dunaverty has begun. Ruairi, you will sail to Kintyre, as planned, stopping at Knapdale and Jura to issue the summons there. Once at Dunaverty, you must get word to the men on Arran and Bute to join you as you sail to meet me on Islay. I will return to Islay, stopping at Mull and Lorne to sound the call. Tell all the galley and longship captains they are to set sail for Loch Indaal and camp on the beach there. And, if any can spare healers, they should bring them. We will likely have need of their skills." He paused, looking at each somber face. "Any questions?"

Ruairi, Domnall, Maurice and Ewan shook their heads.

Liadan raised her gaze to him. "What about me, Lord?"

"You will accompany me to Islay where you will stay until we return from our service to King David."

"But—" Her expression was forlorn mixed with rebellion but Domnall visibly relaxed when Somerled told her his decision was firm.

"I will not risk your life in this war, lass, no matter how well you fight. Your brother would have my head. Besides, I need you to prepare a healing area in the great hall for any wounded we bring back with us.

The women of Keills can assist you for their men will join us as we sail to Carlisle."

Liadan raised her head. "Aye, Lord, I will do it."

"And me, Father?" asked Gillecolum.

"You will also sail with me to Islay, Gille, to help Liadan."

His son nodded, no regret in his eyes. Mayhap he understood that the battle they headed to was not a place for a youth.

Ruairi turned to his children. "You will come with your mother and me to Kintyre where you will await my return."

The instructions issued, all but Ruari and his family departed, for they would sail the next day.

The North Shore of Loch Indaal, Isle of Islay

ON A PARTICULARLY WARM afternoon in June, Somerled stood above the shore at Loch Indaal seeing a sight he had only imagined before. The wide crescent of sandy beach that caressed the azure waters of the great sea loch was filled with galleys and longships, at least thirty, and more coming. He had imagined this scene of his Highlanders and Islesmen gathering but he did not think it would happen so soon or for such a cause. That so many would rally to his call for a war that was not theirs made his throat tighten and his eyes fill with unshed tears.

"Did you doubt they would come?" asked Angus, coming up the rise, the wind blowing his hair away from his face.

"I did not know if they would, but I had hoped…and I prayed."

"They are not here for the Scots king, Brother. They are here for *you*."

Courage, loyalty, honor. These were the qualities Somerled prized in his men. If a kingdom could be forged by such men, would it not stand strong for hundreds of years? "I will let them make camp and enjoy the fellowship of their friends and fellows tonight. Make sure all the chieftains know that tomorrow at noon, I will address them in the great hall at Findlugan's Loch."

"Aye, I will let them know. They will be keen to hear what you have to say."

Somerled walked down the hill, his brother at his side. "We must thank those who have come."

Once on the beach, Angus took off on his mission and Somerled wended his way through the small groups of warriors, greeting each one who raised his head. Some, sitting in front of tents sharpening their weapons, looked up and smiled as he passed.

Somerled stopped to talk to those he had not seen for a while and those he had yet to meet. Some, he noted, were younger than he and some as old as his father would have been had he lived. He was glad Gillecolum was not yet old enough to go to war.

A few practiced their archery and knife-tossing skills with targets erected for that purpose, preparing for the fight to come.

He felt the heavy weight of command resting on his shoulders as one who loved his men and now must lead them into the largest battle they had ever faced. He asked God to direct his path and vowed he would not leave a generation of Gaelic warriors to be buried in English soil. Thus, he would be careful with his words to their chiefs.

That night, he slept in a tent on the shores of Loch Indaal, wishing to be one of them. But the next morning, he rose with the golden dawn and, rousing his companions, took the path inland. Angus, Domnall and Maurice did not complain at sharing leadership in this critical hour. Ruairi he had asked to remain at Dunaverty, but Ewan MacSuibhne of Knapdale had brought a longship of forty warriors.

In the great hall, Liadan was directing the women preparing the meal for the chieftains who would come later. "Lord," she said, looking up at him, her gray eyes earnest, "all is nearly ready. Can I ask, why did you want to bring them here and not speak to them on the beach?"

"You show insight at asking that question, Liadan. In truth, I could have addressed the chiefs there. But I wanted them to have the long walk back to the beach to reflect on what I will tell them, else they might quickly dismiss my words or have them questioned before they have owned them. Too, I wanted them to see the place we will gather in the future."

"Ah, I see. Yea, Lord, you are wise."

BY THE TIME THE SUN was high in the sky, the chieftains had arrived at Findlugan's Loch. They expressed surprise at how quickly the settlement had been constructed and how pleased they were with the great hall. Somerled waited until they were seated with food and ale and then he rose to address them.

"First, let me express my gratitude for your coming." As an aside, he added, "'twould have been embarrassing for me to stand on the shores of Loch Indaal with nary a chief's ship in sight."

The chieftains chuckled; a few smiled.

"You may well ask why I called you to the great hall and did not speak to you on the beach." They nodded, as he expected they would, for he had anticipated Liadan's question. "I wanted you to see this honored place. We will gather here in future times to decide matters of importance, to choose a lord when I have gone. It will be the heart of the lordship. Thus, I welcome you to send your banners to decorate the walls, for it is your place as well."

Then looking at the face of each man, he said, "And I wanted you to have the long walk back to Loch Indaal to reflect upon my words. We respond to King David's call, as we must, for it is the price of his favor. Those of you from Arran and Bute know your isles are now under my protection because of David's gift."

There were nods all around. Satisfied, he continued, "I am mindful that we go to fight on foreign soil. David calls us to a civil war that is not of our making...not our war. We must take great care to spend no man's life needlessly."

A few "Ayes" were muttered.

"Lord, where do we go from here?" a chieftain from Mull inquired.

"We sail southeast, to the Irish Sea and then to the Solway Firth. From there, we will sail up the River Esk to the River Eden that flows by our destination. David's castle at Carlisle. But where we will engage the English after that, I do not know."

"All that traveling on land and 'tis the season for midges," a chieftain from the Isle of Jura jested in a sarcastic tone.

They did not face midges on the sea, so the small, biting creatures would be an added annoyance. The insects would be the least of their problems but he would not have his men complaining. "Aye," Somerled agreed, "but think of this: at least we'll not be contending with snow."

A boisterous discussion broke out between the gathered chiefs about weather and warfare.

When they quieted, Somerled began to speak of what more concerned him. "We have thrown off the burdensome yoke of the Norse and driven their pirates—who rape and pillage and kill—from our shores. We must not appear to be like them. Hence, there will be no plundering of Scots villages or English towns. I know some warriors, even the Scots, will expect it; we must not indulge. We will follow David into England and then come home to our coast and our isles. See that your men obey this as I will hold you accountable for their actions."

He waited until the somber expressions of the men told him they had understood the gravity of his words. Then he asked, "How many of you have healers in your ranks?"

Six hands went up.

"Good. We may need them. Lastly, while I will give commands and expect you to heed them, I will also carry a hunting horn into battle. One blast for 'Attack'; two blasts for 'fall back'; and three for 'retreat'."

"Retreat, my lord? How can you mean it?" inquired the youngest among them.

Somerled fixed him with a steady gaze. "I do not know what we will find in England, whether David will prevail or the English will drive him back and engage in slaughter. I trust the horn will help us stay together, acting as one. I want to spare our warriors to grow old on our isles, on our soil. There will be mounted Norman knights on both sides, wearing hauberks and wielding swords. Those of you who have taken mail as spoils in our battles, can wear it. But mark my words, mail will be heavy on a long march. Most of us will have only leather or padded armor."

With that, the chieftains rose as one, shouting, "We are with you!"

Somerled raised his sword high in the air. "For Argyll and the Isles! For home!"

The sound of metal sliding from sheaths rang in the air as the chiefs raised their swords, echoing Somerled's cry. "For home!"

Somerled sheathed his sword and heaved a sigh of relief, his heart racing now that he'd delivered the message and they'd agreed. "We sail on the morrow!"

The next morning, the wind was up and the weather fine as their forty galleys and longships sailed out of Loch Indaal, heading southeast toward the Irish Sea.

Two days later, the great fleet rounded Galloway and reached the Solway Firth. Somerled stood at the starboard gunwale gazing south at the Isle of Man, a long gray silhouette against the blue sky and waters. He pulled the green riband from his waist and held to his lips, smelling the faint scent of roses. The Princess of Man was there on that isle. Could she see the sails of so many ships? Mayhap not as her father's castle faced south.

The Isle of Man

IT BEING A GLORIOUS DAY, Ragnhild had ridden Fairhair to the northwest of the Isle of Man to visit a chieftain's wife who had just given birth. It was as Ragnhild turned south to return home that she paused on a hill. Shielding her eyes, she gazed north across the Solway Firth toward Galloway. Dozens of longships and smaller galleys were sailing east toward Scotland's coast. A few had red sails. Could one of them be Somerled's galley?

She watched for a moment as the cloud-like sails passed by, then urged Fairhair into a gallop, racing back to Castle Rushen, determined to tell her father of what she had seen. Mayhap he or Abbot Bernard had heard of these ships heading toward Scotland's coast and knew the reason for them.

"Father!" she called out as she burst into the hall. "I have seen ships and galleys, mayhap as many as forty, heading toward Scotland's coast."

Her father turned from one of his guards with whom he'd been speaking. "It must be Lord Somerled's fleet," said her father. "Both he and Fergus have been summoned by King David to join him as he prepares again for war with Stephen."

Ragnhild sank into the nearest chair. "War. I remember now. He spoke of it being likely." Ragnhild did not worry for her friend, Fergus' son, Uchtred, for he would not follow his father to David's war in England. But she did worry for Somerled, the man who held her heart.

He must survive the coming battle. He must return to her. Remembering her promise to him, she jumped up and headed for the door.

"To where do you go in such haste, Daughter?"

"To pray, Father, with Abbot Bernard."

CHAPTER 16

Carlisle, Cumbria, Scotland, July 1138 A.D.

GRAY CLOUDS HOVERED over Cumbria as Somerled and his army of Highlanders and Islesmen secured their ships on the banks of the River Eden and climbed the hill to David's castle at Carlisle. Even before Somerled reached the keep, rising from a grass-covered hill, he marveled at the great number of men-at-arms camped on the wide green banks of the river. Yet, the number of tents was not as great as he had expected.

And then he recalled the king's main army was not here but with him marching south from Roxburgh.

The stone tower, built in Norman fashion, was just seven miles from the English border, a strategic position that had determined its history. Somerled learned from Maurice that the first castle, constructed by William Rufus, son of the Conqueror, was built over an old Roman fort. Both had been of timber. King Henry had ordered the site to be fortified with a castle and towers but they were not completed when he died five years ago, allowing King David to reclaim Cumbria and finish the stone castle at Carlisle, now secure behind a surrounding stone wall.

The adjacent rivers provided the moat's water.

As Somerled watched the tents before him, Angus, Domnall and Maurice approached. "We will be hard pressed to find a place for our own tents," said Angus.

"Any place away from the Galwegians would be best," offered Maurice.

"Aye," said Somerled, crossing his arms over his chest and remembering Ragnhild's words about them being like Picts. "But they won't be here. Edward Siwardsson told me they are already with King David's men." Then facing Maurice, he said, "While Angus and I go to the castle to meet with Siwardsson, scout out a place for us to camp. We may only be here a few days."

"As you wish," said Maurice and he turned to go.

To Domnall, Somerled said, "Speak to the chiefs and let them know we rest here for only a short while. They can fill their skins with water but should not wander far until we set up camp."

"Aye, Cousin," said Domnall. "I will keep them together until you return."

Somerled dipped his head in acknowledgement and set off for the castle with Angus at his side.

"Who are all these men?" Angus asked as they wended their way through the myriad of tents and men.

Somerled eyed the mixed throng, so very different in clothing and armor. "Those with horses and swords and more elaborate tents with pennons flying are likely mail-clad knights or Norman barons aligned with David. However, I do not see many knights among this crowd. I assume they are with the king." He gestured to a large gathering of men with no armor save the padded vests worn by Somerled's warriors. "Some Scots dress as Gaels with no armor other than what we ourselves wear. They carry targes, the same round leather shields borne by our archers. Many will have spears and silvered axes if not swords."

"What of Prince Henry, David's son?"

"He will be clad in a knight's attire, fighting at his father's side."

That the king's son fought with him told Somerled that should he survive the coming battle, one day Gillecolum would be fighting by his side. He vowed to train the lad well so he would be a force to be reckoned with.

They had crossed the moat and arrived at the castle gate. "Lord Somerled of Argyll and the Isles to see Edward Siwardsson, the king's Lord High Constable," announced Angus.

"Ah, the Islesmen. You are expected." He turned and preceded them into the great hall, cool even on a July day, for while the windows in the stone edifice allowed in sunlight, the stone remained cold.

Siwardsson was standing at a wooden table, looking down at a map. As they walked toward him, he looked up. "Lord Somerled! You arrive at last!"

"You remember my brother, Angus, from Irvine," said Somerled. "When you came to Ardtornish, he was on Kintyre."

"Aye," said the high constable, shaking Angus' hand. "I recall the resemblance. Would you have some ale?"

"Ale would be most welcome," said Somerled. Angus nodded and a servant poured the three of them full tankards.

Somerled was parched and thankful for the drink. "Does the map signify our destination?"

Siwardsson again bent over the parchment. "Mayhap. Word has come that with the Earl of Gloucester again rebelling against Stephen, David means to seize his chance to gain ground for his niece. He is marching south toward Durham. In two days, we can meet him at Hexham in Northumberland."

"Do we leave on the morrow?" asked Somerled, thinking of his men who would profit from a short rest.

"We can leave the day after and still arrive at Hexham before the king. Those camped here at Carlisle will be following after us to join David."

On the day appointed, Somerled's more than one thousand men and those that had been camped on the riverbanks set out for Northumberland. As they marched eastward, the men of Argyll and the Isles, unused to so much travel by land, expressed their longing for the sea and fresh fish.

At the end of each day, they set down their weapons and bundles to cool their aching feet in a nearby burn and, with the coming dusk, pulled their blankets over their faces to keep the midges away. They carried enough food for the present but, eventually, they would have to hunt.

Siwardsson had timed their arrival well, for they had but a few days wait at Hexham until David, riding south, came upon them. Prince Henry was at his side, looking much like a Norman knight, a pennon fluttering from his lance.

The army behind the Scots king and his son was a mixture of warriors from the kingdom of Scotland and Northern England. Some were mounted Norman knights in hauberks and silvered helms, carrying swords and long shields. These contrasted sharply with the fierce unarmored Galwegian spearmen and Lothian Scots, who carried short swords and axes. The latter, Siwardsson told him, were the descendants of the Anglo-Saxons who fled England after the Conquest to dwell in southeastern Scotland.

He gazed at the vast array that composed the Scots king's army and asked Siwardsson, "How many would you say have come to David's call?"

The aging Anglo-Saxon surveyed the throng of men. "Ten, mayhap fifteen thousand before adding your Highlanders and Islesmen."

"Never have I seen so many," said Somerled. Taking his leave, he strode toward David, inclining his head as he arrived in front of the king. "Your Grace, Argyll and the Isles have answered your summons."

The king smiled. "Siwardsson sent me a message telling me you were coming, which pleased me greatly. If you can beat off the fierce Norsemen, for certes you will acquit yourselves well in the battle with Stephen's army." Then turning to his guard, David said, "We'll camp here tonight."

Though supply wagons trailed behind King David's army, still, the men hunted, for fresh meat was preferred above salted pork. Once the camp was set up, they gathered around the night fires, some men roasting hares caught that day and some sharing a deer they had brought down.

Somerled decided it was time he met David's nobles and generals. With Angus by his side, he went from tent to tent, introducing himself. All were cordial and some, who had heard of him, expressed approval of what he had done, for the Norse pirates were feared by many.

Somerled was amazed at the high rank of the generals who had responded to David's call—every man a seasoned warrior.

After that, he joined his men to eat, Domnall on one side, Angus on the other and Maurice and Ewan on the other side of the fire with Ruairi.

Somerled had just finished his meal of roast venison when Siwardsson came. "We are called to the king's tent."

Turning to his brother, Somerled said, "Let the chiefs know I will speak to them once I have heard what David has to say."

"Aye, I will tell them," said Angus, who, along with Ruairi, Domnall and Maurice, had been acting as messengers to the chiefs.

Somerled and the king's high constable headed into the center of the camp where the king's tent flew the Lion Rampant flag, the royal banner of Scotland. As he walked through the opening to David's tent, the candles flickered in the breeze caused by their entry.

King David stood behind a table, frowning as he stared down at a parchment. Peering at the object of David's interest, Somerled realized it was not a map he recognized. There were only lines, vague shapes and arrows. A battle plan, he supposed.

Surrounding the king were his commanders that Somerled had only just met. On David's right stood Prince Henry, looking very much the heir to the Scots kingdom with his noble bearing and confident stance.

On the king's left was one of his nephews, William Fitz Duncan, a general and the Earl of Moray, as well as an English baron. On their way to meet David, Siwardsson had told Somerled that in the month prior, Fitz Duncan had led the Galwegians to victory over the English at Clitheroe, raising hopes for the battle to come.

Somerled recognized others gathered there, among them Eustace Fitz John, a Norman baron of Northumberland, who recently switched sides and surrendered his castles at Alnwick and Malton to David.

Malise, Earl of Strathearn in central Scotland, had joined David's ranks and now stood with Lord Fergus of Galloway and the Galwegian chiefs, Ulric and Donald.

Somerled recalled what King Olaf had said about the men of Galloway. While their lord was as finely dressed as any of the noblemen, his warriors were wild-looking with their half-shaved heads and bare legs.

They wore only tunics and, at their waists wicked-looking daggers. Most carried long spears as well.

Only two others were, like Somerled, blue-eyed and fair-haired, Siwardsson and another Saxon lord.

To Somerled it seemed an odd collection of notables. He wondered how David intended to unify thousands of men from such diverse backgrounds and lead them into such a significant battle. Surely, they did not all consider themselves Scots. Somerled's own men would not have thought of themselves that way, nor would the English barons who had sided with David. Many northern nobles had been forced to make a choice between loyalty and the reality of their situations. If they supported the wrong side, they would lose their land as well as their titles.

"Ah, Somerled," said the king, "I am glad you are here. You have met my nobles and commanders, of course?"

"Aye, I've had the pleasure," Somerled said, giving them a curt nod.

"We but talk strategy, though one cannot be precise until we see what the English and their Normans have in mind. I've sent spies to survey the land south and see what can be learned." The king, again considering the drawing before him, said, "My intention is to take the English by surprise if we can. The vanguard," he said, pointing to the first line on the parchment, "will be led by Henry and his knights, reinforced by a bodyguard of mailed men-at-arms under Eustace Fitz John and the men of Galloway."

One of the Galwegian chiefs muttered an oath. David ignored it.

"Behind them," the king continued, "in the second line, will be your Highlanders and Islesmen, Lord Somerled. I will command the third group, consisting of Saxon and Norman knights. In the rear will be the men of Moray."

Somerled was curious as to why the king would place such well-armored men in the rear, but he did not ask. He did wonder about his archers, however. "Your Grace, if I might ask..."

David looked up. "Yes?"

"My Islesmen are known for their skill with a bow. Might you not want them with the vanguard?"

The king appeared to consider the idea. "What you say is true yet I would prefer to place some of the Saxon archers with Henry and his mounted knights and have your men follow them. Once Henry has opened a hole in the English ranks, your arrows will find their targets more easily."

Before Somerled could respond, the Galwegian chiefs took great offense at the lines of battle the king had proposed. "We fight better than any Frenchman!" shouted Ulric. His reference to Frenchmen was how many described the Normans but, spoken by Ulric, it sounded more like a curse.

While Lord Fergus remained silent, Malise, Earl of Strathearn, joined in the Galwegian chiefs' objection. "Whence comes the king's confidence in the Normans? I wear no armor but there is not one among them in Stephen's army who will advance beyond me."

"Rude earl!" exclaimed Alan de Percy, baseborn son of the great Alan, and a distinguished Norman knight. "You boast of what you dare not do." Turning to David, he said, "Sire, if the Galwegians fail, the rest of the army will lose heart. 'Twould be a fatal error."

"We will not fail!" cried Donald, the other Galwegian chief. "Remember Clitheroe where Fitz Duncan prevailed because of us."

"Why, my king," pleaded the Earl of Strathearn, "do you listen to foreigners when none of those with armor would outdo the earl who wears none?" He meant himself, of course, an arrogant man Somerled did not trust.

"Enough!" shouted David. The king appeared to be wavering, mayhap worried lest his fragile alliance of commanders might falter. "The Galwegians may lead the attack under their own commanders with the mailed knights in the second line."

Somerled bit back a curse.

Prince Henry averted his eyes but, before he did, Somerled glimpsed a look of disapproval on his face.

"That puts you, Somerled," said David, "in the third line."

Though he disagreed, and knew his chiefs would like it not, Somerled did not argue with the king, who was obviously trying to keep the Galwegian wolves at bay. "As you wish, Your Grace."

The meeting ended with some of the Scottish lords grumbling under their breaths as they departed the king's tent.

Somerled was about to leave when he heard Henry tell his father, "With your permission, I will add the Cumbrians and men of Teviotdale to my numbers."

The king nodded. "Probably wise." Then to Somerled, "I will add the men of Lothian to your numbers in the third line."

Somerled nodded. Though he would have aligned the warriors differently, he did not question further David's orders. At least his Islesmen would not have to rush the English knights in the company of the overly confident and wild Galwegians. He much preferred to follow Henry who appeared well-trained and in full command of his mailed cavalry.

Derlinton, North East England, August 1138 A.D.

IT HAD TAKEN THEM weeks to cover the nearly fifty miles between Hexham and Derlinton, which lay twenty miles south of Durham, close to the River Tees. The delay was owed not only to the army's unwieldy size but to the stop at Durham. While the king paid a visit to the castle, the Galwegians plundered the surrounding towns, enraging Somerled.

"'Tis unseemly for a Christian king to allow the wild Picts to prey upon innocent villagers," he spit out when reports reached him of their savage acts. He and his companions were discussing the recent events in the tent erected for them. He thought of Gillecolum and Liadan, left behind on Islay, relieved they were safe. "I will speak with Lord Fergus."

He was not the only commander to refer to the Galwegians as wild Picts, for that was their reputation, much deserved. It rankled that the Lord of Galloway permitted his men to behave in such a manner when Somerled would not allow such actions to be named among his own warriors.

"I doubt you will find a receptive audience with that one," said Maurice.

"Still, I must try," said Somerled. "Failing there, I will speak to David."

Somerled found Fergus lounging in his tent with the two Galwegian commanders imbibing the wine they had brought with them from Galloway. "My lord, a word if I might."

With a jerk of his head, Fergus sent Ulric and Donald out of his tent. "What is it, Lord Somerled?"

"Tales have reached me of your men ravaging the countryside, burning, raping and pillaging. Such actions bring dishonor to the Scots king and are beneath those of us from the western shores. Innocents are not our enemies; they are not even King David's enemies."

Fergus pursed his lips and stared at his goblet. "Aye, mayhap 'tis something your Islesmen disdain, but my Galwegians are not of your ilk. That is why they make good warriors. They even drink blood when they think it improves their ability to conquer."

Somerled realized he would get nowhere with such a man. "I see." He would waste no further words. Inclining his head, he said, "Then I will ask no more of your time." As he slipped through the tent's opening, the sound of Fergus' laughter rang in his ears.

In David's tent, he found a worried king, for his spies had returned with sour news. "Sit, Somerled," said David. "You might as well hear this, too. Soon, the entire camp will know of it."

The spy, a Norman from the look of him, was bedraggled and dirt-covered but no less eager to convey his news. "The English morale, being low and some unwilling to fight, Thurstan, Archbishop of York, who has the defense of the north in the absence of Stephen who is engaged in the south, has devised a clever plan."

David's eyes narrowed. "Say on."

"He has assured the northern barons of victory and offers absolution and Heaven to all who fight. To rally the men, he has designed a standard the Normans will carry into battle with the clergy in every parish appearing in procession with their crosses, banners and relics."

"It sounds like a crusade," remarked David.

"Aye," said the spy with a chuckle. "I imagine it will appear just so."

"Who leads them into battle?" asked Somerled. "Surely not the old archbishop?"

"Nay," said the spy, accepting a cup of water offered by David's servant. "From what I could tell, 'tis likely to be William d'Aumale but Walter l'Espec, Sheriff of York and a Norman warrior of great experience, was ever present."

"What of this standard you referred to?" asked King David.

"'Twas Thurstan's idea, apparently. It's to be a ship's mast mounted on a wheeled cart with a silver pyx at the top, holding consecrated bread of the Eucharist. From the yard, banners will hang representing the saints of York, Beverley and Ripon."

Somerled inhaled sharply, greatly concerned, for he knew how the English revered their Roman saints and being promised Heaven, they would believe it and fight all the harder. He cast a glance at David, wondering what effect this would have on the Scots king who also gave allegiance to the Church of Rome.

"Holy Jesus!" David exclaimed. "That conniving Thurstan."

"Where are the English now?" Somerled asked.

"Near York and advancing north," said the spy.

"Several days away," muttered David. "Time enough." He rose then and told the spy to eat and rest, that his king may have another assignment for him in the morning.

When the spy had gone, David turned to Somerled. "You came to see me?"

"Aye, though it seems a lesser concern at this point. I wanted to lodge my objection to the way the Galwegians have been pillaging the countryside as we marched south."

The king heaved a sigh, looking fatigued. "You are not the first to bring me news of their crimes. Alas, I like it not, however, Fergus will take no action to stop them and, at this point, I want the wild men of Galloway ready to set upon the English."

"You will not hear of my men doing such despicable things. Having been slaves to the Norsemen, they would not prey upon another people in like manner. They are fierce in battle but they will not rape or murder the innocent. Moreover, I have strongly admonished my chiefs that I will hold them responsible should their men disobey me in this respect."

David's mouth formed a small smile. "This from the man who tore out his enemy's heart?"

"'Tis not the same, Your Grace."

"You speak truth, yet my own Scots burn villages and take plunder. 'Tis the way of war. Your stance is rare." He reached out and touched Somerled's shoulder, an older man to a younger leader. "I dislike war but I must hold the English accountable for their oaths and their charters to my family. Northumberland is my son's inheritance and my niece was robbed of a crown. If the unruly Galwegians can help me secure both, so be it."

Somerled left, disheartened. He had not wanted to be a part of England's war any more than King Olaf and he vowed if he survived this one there would be no more. The gnawing in his stomach was accompanied by a foreboding that told him this Scots ship of war had a torn sail with a crew not pulling oars together. It might shatter in rough seas, which the battlefield, for certes, would readily provide.

Two miles from Northallerton, England, 22 August 1138 A.D.

WHEN THE DAWN CAME, a heavy mist covered the ground like a veil drawn over the land. Through the wavering mist, Somerled glimpsed the blooming heather, a reminder of home. He pulled the emerald silk riband from his waist and thought of the princess he might never see again.

Closing his eyes, he imagined her face and remembered her promise to pray. Mayhap her prayers would carry him and his men through this day. It was his fervent hope.

The night before, he had conveyed the king's battle alignment to his close companions and his chiefs and they, in turn, to the men. "Harken to my orders as I will likely have to shout above the fray. Listen for my horn. Given so strange a mixture of warriors, I cannot say what may happen or what I may command. I seek but to save the lives of our men wherever I can. Remind them to keep out of range of the English arrows, which may be fired from longbows."

Once Somerled's men were roused from sleep and ready to march, weapons to hand, they followed the rest of David's army south down the Great North Road and crossed the River Tees.

The standard borne by the Scots was a simple affair, a long lance affixed with a wreath of blooming heather.

Before they reached York, in the heavy mist, they came to a sudden halt when they blundered into the English army. Somerled turned to see King David sitting atop his bay horse, his face a mask of shock. He had planned a surprise attack but surprise was no longer an option.

With quickly shouted orders, both forces fell into battle order on two low hills about six hundred feet apart. Somerled ordered his best archers and the Lothian Scots on his left to stand ready. Behind them, he stood with the rest of his men, carrying shields, swords, axes and spears.

The Galwegians took their agreed upon place in the front of the army, Prince Henry, his knights and the Saxon archers behind them and to the right.

Once David's army was aligned in the agreed upon ranks, Somerled gazed ahead to the English commander, whose name, William d'Aumale, was whispered among the Scots. A Norman with lands in both England and France. D'Aumale ordered the wagon carrying the archbishop's standard to be placed in the center of the English forces.

Somerled stared at the banners of the saints waving in the early morning breeze. The standard would be a conspicuous rallying point.

With the standard in place, most of the English knights and retainers were ordered by d'Aumale to dismount and their horses sent to the rear with a small contingent of mounted knights.

Somerled wondered why they had done so. Was it for fear the horses would be panicked in the face of the fierce Galwegians? For certes, the roar of the Scots army would have struck fear in the hearts of the Norman knights as they peered into the fog. Or did d'Aumale wish to prevent his knights from a hasty retreat? Whatever the reason, they were now on foot behind the English archers and clustered tightly around the standard.

Behind Somerled, David dismounted and ordered his horse and those belonging to his guards sent to the rear of the Scots lines.

Before the battle began, two Norman knights in silvered helms and mail came to the Scottish lines, bearing a white flag.

King David came forward to hear what the Normans had to say.

The Normans' stated purpose was to parlay a peace. It was all so civilized. Somerled knew it was the custom of war but he could not imagine trying with the Norse pirates he and his men fought. The pirates would only laugh.

He strode to where Prince Henry sat atop his horse with his mounted knights. "Who are they?"

Never taking his eyes from the two, Henry said, "Robert Bruce, Earl of Annandale, and Bernard de Baliol, a baron. Both are Norman nobles who hold estates in both England and Scotland."

"On behalf of King Stephen," said Bruce, "we offer you a grant of the earldom of Northumberland in favor of Prince Henry if you give your word to take your army back to Scotland."

King David frowned his displeasure. "Northumberland is my son's inheritance; it is his as a matter of right. Yet there is more I would have. Stephen stole a crown from my niece, the Empress Maud. We want it back."

"You know we cannot give you that," said Baliol.

With bitter words, the two Normans renounced their allegiance to the Scottish Crown they had earlier given and, without another word, turned to go.

David's warlike nephew, William MacDonoquhy, still flushed with pride from his victory at Clitheroe, shouted to Bruce's back, "You are a false traitor, Bruce!"

An aged Norman warrior, who Somerled was told was Walter l'Espec, appeared in front of the English army and delivered a speech, at the end of which he said to the commander, "I pledge my troth to conquer or to die!"

One of the English clerics said in a booming voice, "Illustrious chiefs of England, by blood and race Normans, before whom France trembles, here are the Scots, who fear you, undertaking to drive you from your own estates!"

The English, Normans and peasants kneeled while the priests gave them absolution, telling them that were they to make the ultimate sacrifice, their sins would be forgiven in the afterlife.

Somerled shook his head at so grand a promise made by mere mortal men. To Somerled, the strategy behind the spectacle was clear: men would fight for family and country but they would fight even harder if they believed that their deaths would assure entrance to Heaven.

The priests' words were followed by a loud chorus of "Amen!" and the English quickly stood.

As if David's forces had been waiting for this spectacle to finish, the Scots king gave the command to attack and the battle began. A sudden rush and cries of "Albion!" rose in the air as thousands of fierce Galwegians, daggers and spears to hand, charged toward the English army and their Norman knights.

Somerled cringed at what happened next for it could have been foreseen. The air resounded with the hiss of arrows as the English archers fired. The Galwegians blocked the arrows with their shields and continued to run toward the Normans, screaming like the wild men they were. The Norman knights, clinging to their standard, did not move.

When the arrows did not stop the mad rush of the Galwegians, the English archers began shooting at the lower extremities of the howling men. With moans and grunts, the first ranks fell under this fire but the Galwegians behind them leaped over their fallen comrades and rushed toward the English who could not fire their arrows fast enough.

Ulric and Donald in the fore of the rush had fallen yet the men of Galloway rallied without them and kept up the attack. Some got through to break the line of English archers. Yet, for many Galwegians, if they survived the arrows, they were slashed to pieces when they reached the firm-standing Norman knights.

The Galwegians might have been prideful and foolhardy but Somerled gave them credit for courage.

As the other lines closed up, Somerled and his men drew closer behind Prince Henry and his mounted knights and the Saxon archers. Henry lowered his lance and shouted, "Attack!" The knights charged as one toward the English, breaking through their ranks as if they had been spiders' webs. So deep did Henry's knights penetrate, they dispersed the English knights that had been taken to the rear.

Somerled saw his chance. When the Saxon archers with Henry began to run toward the opening the prince had created, Somerled blew once on his horn, sounded his war cry and ordered his archers forward but with this caveat: "Two men's shields to cover one archer!"

The ploy worked. The arrows of his archers made it through with only a few of his men hit while the Saxon archers, who were exposed, fell in great numbers.

The English were quick to close up the rent in their lines created by Henry's charge.

Somerled blew twice on his horn, ordering his archers back. Except for covering the archers, neither his Highlanders nor the Lothian Scots had yet to fully engage. Somerled was loath to send them into the middle of the battle, which had devolved into a confused mass of men, bloodied from swords and spears. Except for a miracle, any man falling into the writhing mass of bodies was destined to die.

David ordered the armored Scots forward only to have them fall on the blades of Norman knights who rammed their weapons through the Scots armor at the shoulder joint.

Somerled watched as the Galwegians began another foray. The English, pushed in from all sides around their standard, were having difficulty staying upright. However, one English soldier, more clever than the rest, suddenly elevated a human head on his spear, shouting, "Behold the head of the King of Scots!"

Of course, 'twas not David, for he and his guard were behind Somerled and his men but the ruse spread through the ranks of the Scots with great effect.

The Galwegians, disheartened, began to flee, falling back on the Lothian Scots. When it was clear the men of Galloway would not charge again, the Lothian Scots abandoned the field.

Somerled shouted to them that the king lived but, in the noise and confusion, none heard. He raised his horn, about to order his men into the fray, when King David shouted, "Stand your ground!"

Somerled turned back to see a look of anguish on the king's face. David was shouting, trying to rally his men and dispel the myth of his death but so great was the tumult, he could not be heard. His guards, crying of their concern for the king's safety, brought forward David's horse and urged him to mount.

Bareheaded, David rode among the ranks of his army, continuing to try and stir his soldiers but to no avail.

Compelled to retire from the field, David assumed command of his cavalry and covered the retreat.

Somerled gave three blasts on his horn for "Retreat" and followed King David, ordering his men to protect the king's back.

The Scots were in full retreat.

The battle had been intense but lasted only a few hours. By the time the mist cleared, the sun shone down on the bodies of fallen Galwegians, Scots, Saxons and Normans, lying bloody on the grassy field. Somerled, relieved his own men lived, thanked God there had not been more deaths.

CHAPTER 17

SOMERLED FOLLOWED DAVID as he led the remains of his army to Carlisle, his expression gloomy, his words few. The sky above mirrored the king's mood, gray and cloud-filled, but Somerled was grateful they'd had no rain. The weary battle march back to Carlisle would have been worse if their paths had been muddy quagmires.

David's spies had brought word on the first night that they were not being followed, which surprised them all. With that good news, the men looked only forward as they marched back to Scotland and not over their shoulders.

Arriving in Carlisle, David let loose his fury as he addressed his men, who he considered responsible for so many deaths. After a scathing rebuke, he exacted an oath from the survivors that they would never again desert him in war.

Embarrassed, and mayhap shamed by their actions and too hasty retreat, the army fell into fighting amongst themselves, Scot attacking Saxon, Norman attacking Norman and the Galwegians angry at all for the loss of so many warriors, including their chiefs.

Somerled's army of Highlanders and Islesmen did not share in the self-flagellation of David's men. They had listened to their chiefs and to Somerled and were happy to be alive and headed home. A few of his men had taken English arrows but his healers had been tending them from the first night they made camp. Somerled gave thanks when he was told all would live. For himself, he was just glad to be able to return to his son and the woman he loved.

With the stone keep of Carlisle Castle rising above them, Somerled walked with his brother among their warriors camped on the banks of the River Eden. "I did not think 'twas possible," said Angus, "for us to return unscathed."

"Nor did I," replied Somerled, "but then it never occurred to me most of my men and I would never enter the battle. Only the cowardice of David's soldiers put the army in retreat, delivering us."

Somerled had been with King David twice since they arrived at Carlisle and each time he appeared haggard and worried. The cause was not difficult to discern. They had yet to hear from Prince Henry and Somerled knew the king feared his heir was dead. As a father, Somerled felt for the king who loved his son.

The next day, Somerled had gone to see King David to seek his approval for their departure, when a great clamor arose outside in the bailey. He and the king went to the nearest window and looked down. There, sitting atop his horse with a dozen mounted knights behind him, was Prince Henry.

"Thank God!" exclaimed David and rushed down to the keep's entrance where Henry and his knights were dismounting. Somerled followed for he wanted to hear how Henry escaped.

Embracing his son, the king pulled back to look into Henry's face. "You are well? You are whole?"

"Aye, Father. But the losses—"

"I know, my son. Too many. But God bless you. How did you survive so many English knights?"

By this time, a crowd had gathered, murmuring in amazement that Henry was here, for all were anxious to learn what had happened.

"Once we broke through their lines, we pursued their knights who had been taken to the rear of the English lines. Soon, we were surrounded by the enemy. Many of our knights and their horses fell to Norman blades. Some were taken prisoner and must be ransomed. When I saw our army withdrawing, I told my men to throw down their banners and follow the English Normans that turned to pursue you. We looked like the Normans in our mail and helms. In the confusion, none suspected we were Scots."

"God has answered my prayers," said the king. "Tonight, we will celebrate your return."

That night, there was feasting and revelry in Carlisle and the king smiled as he entertained his nobles, notwithstanding the great losses of the battle. It was the first time Somerled had seen the king happy since they had left the battlefield. Perhaps it was just relief, for he had only the one heir and Prince Henry was much loved.

As the evening drew to a close, Somerled rose, thinking to find his companions and seek his tent. To David, he said, "With your permission, Your Grace, I would take my Highlanders and my Islesmen home on the morrow."

"Aye," said David. "You have done what you could. I would ask no more. Godspeed to you."

"Thank you, Your Grace. If I might ask, where do you go from here?"

King David stared straight ahead, a slight smile on his face. "I will take what is left of my army and go north to Wark on the Tweed. I've a mind to raze Walter l'Espec's castle to the ground as I failed to do earlier. It will give my men something to look forward to instead of this constant bickering amongst themselves. And then I must turn my attention to negotiating terms of peace with Stephen." Shifting his gaze to his son, who was drinking with his knights, David added, "I will not allow Stephen to keep Northumberland, which is properly Henry's. I may not have won the battle but I will yet have my way in this."

Somerled bowed as he took his leave, never doubting that David would salvage a great deal out of his defeat.

A short while later, Somerled stepped onto the deck of his galley and experienced a rush of relief. Angus, too, must have felt the same for he greeted Somerled, saying, "'Tis good to be leaving, aye?"

"Indeed, it is, Brother." Somerled waited until his men were assembled on the banks of the River Eden or standing on the decks of their galleys and longships, and then he began to speak.

"Brave men of Argyll and the Isles!" he shouted to the more than one thousand men arrayed before him. Their conversations ceased as they looked up. "You have proven your courage and your loyalty in coming to my call. For that, I am grateful. And I thank the Almighty for answering my prayers, for you live to make old bones. Your chiefs are bold men; you can be proud of them. I look forward to their helping me build castles that will forever guard the sea lanes and a fleet of galleys to keep the Norse from our shores."

"Aye, Somerled, we are with you!" cried one chief.

Shouts of "Somerled! Somerled!" followed, their voices echoing off the river bank and the walls of the castle rising above it.

"Godspeed!" Somerled yelled back. His eyes misted over. He loved every one of them.

Their fleet of nearly forty galleys and longships that had dotted the River Eden for weeks were now pushed into the river like giant seals sliding off a rock. Once in the water, applying their great strength and skill, the men rowed hard for the mouth of the River Esk where it emptied into the Solway Firth.

Somerled's galley led the others, his spirits rising as he smelled the open sea and felt his soul being restored.

Sailing southwest in the Solway Firth with Galloway off the starboard and the Isle of Man coming into view off the larboard, Somerled's thoughts turned to the Princess of Man. He longed to see her, to look into her emerald eyes, yet he would not leave his fleet nor could he delay his men's return.

Immediately behind him were three other ships, a galley commanded by Ruairi and two of the longships they had acquired from the Norse, one commanded by Domnall and one by Maurice. Ewan had told him he would find his own way back to Knapdale.

"We sail to Kintyre?" asked his brother.

"Aye, to Dunaverty where I would see the progress being made on the castle. There, we will leave Ruairi ere we sail to Islay. I want to visit Keills where I hope to commission the first of our galleys. Then we will gather Liadan and sail north."

Angus nodded and gave the orders to the crew.

Somerled stood at the gunwale, gazing toward the Isle of Man, thinking of Ragnhild. He would send her a message letting her know her prayers had been answered. He said his own prayer, asking God to let him be the one to claim not only her heart but the woman herself.

The Isle of Man, August 1138

THE DAYS OF AUGUST were waning. Ragnhild felt it in the morning chill and the early twilight that descended on the isle. She rose in the dark each morning. Though she was tempted to remain under the furs until sunlight poured into her chamber high in the keep, Cecily was quick to remind her she could not.

"'Tis nearly eight, my lady. Did you not wish to break your fast with the king before going to the stables? The queen will still be abed but King Olaf is already afoot."

Ragnhild stretched her arms and yawned as she sat up and dropped her legs over the side of the bed. "I suppose I must. Father will expect it."

"And young Godred will be looking for you," Cecily reminded her. "He scarce leaves his nurse ere he is asking for his Aunt Hilde."

Ragnhild smiled to herself as she thought of her half-brother, Affraic's young son. The small dark-haired boy looked more like his mother than the king. The child had an uncommon proclivity to activity, never silent, never still. "All right. You persuade me."

Cecily held out Ragnhild's sapphire woolen gown and helped her into it, pulling the laces tight. Then her handmaiden replaited her hair as she stood at her window looking out toward the Irish Sea.

The rising sun cast a soft glow across the horizon. Cumbria lay on the other side of the sea and she wondered if Somerled was still there, if he still lived. She could not accept that he had died in battle yet there had been no word from Scotland of King David's invasion of Northumberland. *Surely it is over by now.*

By the time she had finished eating and greeting young Godred, the sun was warming the land. Bundled in a warm woolen mantle, she set off for the stable, eager to greet Fairhair, who whinnied as she entered. As he chewed on a large chunk of apple from the first of the season's crop, she slid his bridle over his head. Her eyes focused on the brow-band Somerled had given her, the Celtic scrolling on black leather. "A worthy adornment for so handsome a horse, a gift from my love, a king in his own right."

Fairhair ate the rest of the apple from her hand then nudged her shoulder as if asking for more.

"Nay, no more, for we ride while the weather is fair." And, with that, she allowed the groom to saddle the palfrey and assist her into the saddle. She rode out of the castle bailey into the cool morning air, planning to greet the farmers that were harvesting winter grain and beginning to plant for the spring.

A few hours later, she returned and, once Fairhair was back in his stall, she went into the great hall to reach her hands toward the hearth fire to warm them. As she spoke to her father, giving him a report on the harvest, the castle door opened and a man she recognized as one of Lord Fergus' guards hastened inside.

He bowed before the king and handed him a rolled parchment, sealed with red wax. "A message from Lord Fergus, Your Grace."

Her father invited the man to sit. "There is ale if you are thirsty," he said, gesturing to a flagon and tankards sitting on a nearby table.

"Thank you," said the messenger and poured himself ale.

She watched with interest as her father broke the seal and unrolled the parchment. A minute later, a frown crossed his face. "The news is not good."

Her brows rose in anxious inquiry. "What is it, Father?"

"Fergus speaks of a great battle north of York in a place called Northallerton. Thousands were slain on the Normans' swords and lances. Many of Fergus' men were killed with English arrows, including the leaders of Fergus' army. Alas, King David retreated in defeat."

Ragnhild's hand rose to her chest as if to hold in her rampaging heart. "Does he speak of Lord Somerled?"

"Nay. He only mentions King David's wrath at being deserted by so many of his soldiers and his joy that Prince Henry managed to survive."

"Lord Somerled would never desert the Scots king."

Her father gave her a sympathetic look. "'Tis possible he no longer lives, Princess."

Her father handed her the message and she read it twice, searching for any clue as to the fate of her brave warrior. Would Fergus have spoken of Somerled if he had died? Or, only if he lived?

She sank onto the bench in front of the crackling fire, staring into the flames. She knew her father could force her to marry another, but she could no longer guard her heart. For some time, she had known she would love no other man save Somerled. Had God answered her prayers? Did her love yet live?

Dunaverty Bay, the Mull of Kintyre, late August 1138 A.D.

SOMERLED'S GALLEY SLID over the sand as the four vessels arrived at Dunaverty Bay. The sunset over his left shoulder cast its golden rays across the waves crashing onto the foot of the great headland jutting into the sea. His gaze was drawn upward to the huge rock that would become the foundation of his stronghold. Already, large stones were piled a few feet high.

The construction of the castle had begun.

Loud female shouts called his attention back to the beach. More wives had joined his men, taking up residence on Kintyre, and they now rushed forward to embrace their returning husbands.

"None were lost!" Somerled yelled as he met the crowd of women and children and the older sons and few men left behind to guard them.

"Is it true, Lord?" asked Ruairi's wife, Aileas. Ruairi had his arm around her and their two children were hugging their father's waist.

"Aye," said Somerled, jumping down to the sand, "though King David was none too pleased at the Scots who deserted him and fled."

"The Scots ran away?" asked eight-year-old Bran, incredulous.

"Aye, lad, when a clever Norman raised a man's head on a pike and claimed it was the king's. The deception had its intended effect."

The boy curled his lip and his face took on a grimace as if smelling something foul. "Dirty trick!"

The men who had remained behind with the French stonemason to work on the castle came forward to welcome Somerled back. With them was Aubri de Mares, d'Harcourt's assistant mason who he had left in charge of the castle's construction.

"I see the castle is rising," Somerled said to the grinning de Mares.

"*Oui*," said the ruddy-cheeked mason. "Did you doubt it, Lord?"

"Nay, but I am pleased. You have done well."

"You missed nothing save a long walk with midges," said Domnall to one man who remained behind and asked what he had missed.

"And the slaughter of the Galwegians," added Maurice. "A grisly sight."

"You kept our men out of the fight?" asked another man who had stayed behind.

"All save the archers," said Somerled. "We were consigned to the third line and never called into the battle, which was just as well. 'Twas confused chaos made worse by the Roman archbishop's raising a standard in the midst of the English forces rendering it a holy cause for the Normans who clung to it like a bear's foot to honey."

"You must be hungry," said Aileas to Somerled and the small group of men standing around him.

Somerled glanced at his brother and Maurice and Domnall before nodding. "Aye, food would be good if you have any to share."

"We've plenty of trout and salmon caught this morning. I'll go to prepare it. Come when you are ready." With that, she kissed Ruairi on the cheek and, calling the two children to her, turned to walk back to their cottage.

"I am in need of a wash," said Somerled to Ruairi, "else I will arrive at your table smelling of English mud and kelp." He thought to bathe in the burn that flowed through the woods nearby.

"Best we all bathe," said Ruairi, "or my wife will be holding her nose."

Somerled's companions agreed and fetched their satchels from the ships before they all headed inland. In addition to his bath, Somerled trimmed his copper beard close to his face. It had grown long with his sojourn in England.

As planned, they dined with Ruairi's family and the stonemason. Aileas and the children made the cottage a home and, not for the first time, Somerled felt the longing for one of his own. Now that David's war was over, he would set his sights on the future.

"The trout and salmon are delicious," he remarked to Aileas. "The herbs and butter add much. 'Tis nothing like my cooking."

"My brother speaks truth," said Angus. "He oft forgets to take the fish from the fire."

That began a round of teasing but Somerled did not mind, for he was used to it. Moreover, he was glad they had come home to teasing and laughter instead of somber mourning.

Content that the mason, de Mares, was doing a good job, Somerled determined to leave for Islay with his two galleys and one longship the next day.

He was anxious to embrace his son.

Isle of Islay, early September 1138 A.D.

THE HEARTH FIRE BURNED steadily as Somerled sat at a table in the great hall, finishing his letter to Ragnhild. Gillecolum sat nearby bent over something he was carving out of wood. The boy had grown taller since he'd taken the lad from Ireland.

After weeks away in Scotland and England, their reunion had been sweet. Gillecolum was now in those difficult years between boyhood and manhood when he needed a father most. No longer did he play with wooden swords, now he practiced with a steel blade.

Somerled's letter to the Princess of Man was short. Though his thoughts of her were tender and full of love, he did not seem to be able to write more than the barest of facts. He could not very well tell her that he intended they would be wed within the year, though he did. How he would accomplish that he did not yet know but he knew in his heart she would be his and not that far off. So, instead, he spoke of the outcome of the Battle of the Standard, as it was coming to be known. He thanked her for her prayers, telling her they were answered, that he and his men had survived. For that was the most important part. If he lived, there was hope for them. Ragnhild, being no fool, would understand the significance of that.

He had just sealed the letter with red wax using the new seal Duncan MacEachern, the Keills blacksmith, had made for him—a galley complete with sail inside a circle with a sprig of heather—when Maurice entered the hall.

Somerled rose, wondering what time of day it might be. He had lost track of time with his thoughts of the princess. What he could glimpse of the gray sky outside through the window did not tell him much.

Maurice's mouth twitched up on one side. "I see you have written another letter. For the princess?"

"Aye," said Somerled, rather sheepishly, still reluctant to admit what was apparent to all. "Now, I must find a way to take it to her."

"I'll do it," offered Maurice. "'Twill give me another chance to visit my kin on the way." At Somerled's unspoken question, Maurice said, "Aye, I will visit your mother and let her know you and Angus live and that Gillecolum is thriving."

Somerled's son looked up and grinned.

"Thank you, Maurice. It will mean much to her to know we survived England. I have to assume the reports from Scotland have spoken of the king's defeat and the death of thousands. She will be worried."

"Aye, she will be."

Somerled handed his friend the letter for Ragnhild. "I must sail to Morvern and then to Moidart to see what the stonemason d'Harcourt is doing."

"If you take Liadan with you," said Maurice, "you might as well take Domnall. He will want to call upon her brother, Diarmad."

"I had planned to do so. Domnall would have insisted."

Maurice ran a hand through his dark hair, grown longer with their sojourn in England. "Who can blame him with so bonny a lass not yet betrothed?"

"True. Ere we sail north, I want to speak to the shipwright in Keills who is known to Liadan to see if he might be willing to build some of our galleys. Rents can be forgiven for such assistance. Will you join us in Moidart?"

"I will, though it might be more than a sennight ere you next see me."

Somerled gave Maurice a curt nod before each went his own way.

Having delivered all of the Islay men home hale and hearty, Somerled's talks with the shipwright in Keills went well. He was happy to build galleys for their growing fleet and promised to solicit others on the isle to help.

A few days later, Somerled sailed north with two galleys. Maurice had taken the longship south to Ireland. Domnall captained one galley but Liadan sailed with Somerled, Angus and Gillecolum. The young couple had grown closer with Domnall's return, and they would have enough time together in their visits to Knapdale and Morvern on the way to Moidart. There was no reason to tempt fate if Liadan was to be a virgin on her wedding night.

The Isle of Man, September 1138 A.D.

"WHEN WILL YOU LEAVE?" Ragnhild heard her father's garrison commander ask, his deep voice carrying to where she stood in the shadows having just come in from the stables.

"In a few days, as the weather permits," her father replied. "I will take the princess with me and visit my tenants on Skye before calling upon the Earl of Orkney. Rognvald has sent me a most gracious invitation."

Ragnhild froze. What could her father have in mind? And why take her with him to Orkney? She could think of only one reason. No word had come from Somerled or any news, for that matter, as to what might have happened to him in England. She despaired to think her father might count him among the dead. She could not allow herself to do so.

"Shall I speak to the captain to ready your longship?" inquired the garrison commander.

"Thank you. While my forty men will be sufficient for a visit with tenants and to call upon the earl, best to tell them to be prepared for battle should we cross with pirates."

The commander dipped his head. "As you wish, Sire." With that, the commander departed through the door to the outer bailey on the opposite side of the hall.

She crossed to where her father stood. "You are planning a voyage?"

"I am," he said, smiling at her. "'Tis time to call upon my tenants and to visit that elusive Earl of Orkney. You will come?"

Ordinarily, Ragnhild would the thrilled to be included in one of her father's voyages but this one boded ill for her if her father expected her to accompany him to the murderer's den Rognvald called home. "If you wish it, Father."

"I do. You have not sailed with me since we called upon King David. 'Twill do you good to venture outside of Man."

Ragnhild thought of the stark Orkney coast of high, rugged cliffs, the rest of it flat, and sighed. "Very well, Father." She would go but she would find a way to thwart any marriage plans involving Rognvald.

It was only days later when a longship arrived in the harbor one morning that she knew was not her father's nor any Norse ship for the stem posts were plain and the rudder was in the stern where Somerled had cleverly moved all of his. *Could it be him? Did he live?*

Shielding her eyes, Ragnhild stood in front of the castle, gazing down the hill, the grass still green from the last rains. In the harbor, a lone figure jumped down from the beached longship. She recognized him as the Irishman who was Somerled's man. His curly dark hair and beard and his Celtic dress gave him away as her father's foster brother, Maurice MacNeill.

Her heart sank to think he might have come alone because his lord no longer lived.

The guard at the palisade gate, by now familiar with the Irishman, allowed him entrance.

She met him halfway down the hill.

"Princess," he said, dipping his head, "I come with a message for you from Lord Somerled."

"He lives!" she exclaimed, relieved beyond all measure. "I am happy he survived King David's war when so many did not, but I am disappointed not to see him. Is he injured?"

"Nay, he is well, my lady. He has sailed to Argyll's north coast and to Moidart where his stonemason is surveying castle sites. He was forced to leave there when he received King David's summons."

Her disappointment was too keen to hide.

Maurice held out a parchment, sealed in red wax. "He sent this, my lady, knowing you would be worried since he was in the battle where thousands died. He did not want to leave you wondering about his fate."

Accepting the letter, she asked, "Will you stay the night?"

"I cannot, for Somerled is expecting my return. Is there a message for him?"

"A moment," she said. Breaking the seal on the letter, she opened it to read.

Princess,

Some months past, I sailed to Scotland with forty galleys and longships at King David's summons and fought with him in England. 'Twas the price of his favor and could not be denied. I oft looked at your green riband and thought of you and your prayers that I welcomed but did not deserve. Surely, God has answered them, for all of us lived to return.

– Somerled

He did not speak of love or any future they might have together. She looked up to encounter Maurice's expectant gaze. "You may tell him I am grateful for his kindness in sending you so far to deliver his message." She thought carefully of the next before adding, "And you may tell him my father leaves in a few days' time for Skye and then he will pay a visit to the Earl of Orkney for Rognvald has extended him an invitation."

"I see." His brows drew together. "And do you sail with him?"

She met his inquiring gaze. "I do."

He bowed. "Then I bid you Godspeed and farewell, Princess."

She watched him walk down the hill to the gate and from there to the harbor, knowing the underlying message had been conveyed. If Somerled was ever to claim her, it must be now. He had once spoken of love. Did he still feel the same or, with the passage of time, had his heart changed?

CHAPTER 18

Loch Moidart, Argyll, September 1138 A.D.

THE HEATHER-COVERED PROMONTORY, overlooking the joining of the River Shiel and Loch Moidart, that was sometimes rendered an island by the tide, was the place Somerled intended to locate his most northerly castle.

Standing there now with Gillecolum, it seemed to him that of all the windswept places in his kingdom, Moidart might be the most beautiful. For certes, it was the most wild, the most untamed and the most remote. And yet, it was not for those reasons he had chosen the site.

He humbly admitted he was not the first to recognize the strategic importance of the location, for here stood the remains of an ancient hillfort, a guardian of the past. From this spot, he could command the waters west to the Sea of the Hebrides and north to Skye and from Loch Shiel east to Loch Sunart, avoiding the dangerous waters off Ardnamurchan Point. And, if that were not enough, there was sand enough close by to beach his ships.

"Is this the place you would build a castle, Father?" asked Gillecolum.

"Aye, lad, what do you think of it?"

"It reminds me of Ardtornish because it will sit high and look out on the sea loch."

"Aye, you are correct. The sites for most of our castles have that in common. Do you know why?"

"So that we can see the enemy coming?"

Somerled placed his hand on his son's shoulder. "Well said. To see the Norse pirates coming from afar is to be forewarned. And it may not always be the Norsemen that trouble our shores."

"Somerled!" Angus shouted up the hill. "You are wanted in camp!"

"Is the stonemason ready for me?" Somerled yelled down.

"Aye with maps and drawings aplenty."

Somerled and Gillecolum retraced their steps back to the camp in the woods. Liadan's brother, Diarmad MacGilleain, and his crew had raised the tents before he and Domnall had arrived with their galleys.

Liadan's reunion with her brother had been touching. Each had longed to see the other's face and tears fell in abundance. In the days since their arrival, Domnall had oft spoken to Diarmad, making Somerled think mayhap they had come to some agreement, for they were easy in each other's company.

Inside the main tent, Somerled found the French stonemason, Goubert d'Harcourt, with Angus, Domnall, Diarmad and Liadan. They were gathered around a table studying a map much like the one Ruairi had shown Somerled at Ardtornish.

"So, what think you of this site for a castle?" he asked them.

D'Harcourt ran his fingers over his small, pointed beard. "*Un bon choix*, my lord. Assuming there is stone enough to be had, it should not be difficult to erect a Norman tower here."

"Excellent," said Somerled, pleased they could move forward. "Then tell me of the other sites you have seen while I was delayed with the King of Scots."

D'Harcourt looked down at the map. "Where there is already a timber castle, or hillfort, as you call them," he pointed to several places on the map, "the building will go easier. Others, like the site at Dunaverty Bay on Kintyre, will, because of their locations, take more men and more time."

Somerled had known all that to be true. "May I leave you here to supervise the construction, at least the beginning?"

"*Bien sûr*, I will stay, but we need to find more masons, else the castles you want will take decades."

"I expect you are right but I will find the skilled men and you can train others. God willing, we will have time. The Norse pirates still plague certain isles but not like they once did."

When the sun had risen high in the sky, a longship sailed into the loch, approaching the promontory where he and Gillecolum had stood earlier that day. Somerled watched it hove into view. When it was nearly to the beach, Maurice waved to him from the deck.

"'Tis Maurice," said Angus who had joined him and Gillecolum on the beach.

"Aye and about time." Somerled strode to meet the Irishman as he climbed down from the deck. Gillecolum and Angus followed, close on his heels.

"I bring news," said Maurice, "but first ale and food!"

Over a dinner of fresh trout, Somerled finally persuaded Maurice to divulge the news he'd been hiding. "Well?"

"Your mother is in good health and very happy to hear you and Angus survived David's war with the English. She asked about her grandson and I told her Gillecolum thrives 'neath your watchful eye."

Somerled raised his brows, sure Maurice was toying with him. "And?"

"Oh, yes. The Princess of Man thanks you for sending me, your trusted companion," he said with a wink, "to convey your message. Though, to be honest, I do not believe she thought much of it."

Maurice's teasing hit Somerled as truth. He'd known he had not written words to satisfy a maiden's heart.

"Yet, she must think much of you to confide the next," said Maurice.

"Tell me," Somerled said, narrowing his eyes on the Irishman.

"She divulged that her father was to sail north for Skye in a few days' time, taking her with him, and afterward, he plans to call upon the Earl of Orkney at Rognvald's invitation."

All eyes turned to Somerled. He did not need to ponder the significance of such a move overlong. "'Tis time to claim my bride."

"What will you do, Father?" asked Gillecolum.

Somerled smiled because he knew his son liked the princess.

"Do not doubt, Gille," said Angus. "Your father will think of something clever, for he means to give you a new mother and the princess is his chosen lady."

Offshore of the Isle of Mull, September 1138 A.D.

RAGNHILD SET HER FACE to the wind, inhaling the smell of the sea. It had taken the king's longship a sennight to arrive where they anchored off the west coast of the Isle of Mull. They'd made several stops to see old friends and greet her father's tenants. She had enjoyed their visits along the way and was glad her father had included her in this voyage, though she worried about its end.

She gazed toward the west where the Isle of Coll was silhouetted against the light from late afternoon sun. It was cool on the water but she was warm in her hooded, fur-lined mantle.

Here, she felt Somerled's presence, for these were waters over which he claimed authority, though Coll and its neighbor, Tiree, were among her father's isles. If Maurice had delivered her message, Somerled knew the time might be short in which to ask for her hand. Why had he never done so? He had never spoken of marriage, though she hoped what she had seen in his intense blue gaze was not only love, but a desire to call her his own.

"Sail ho!" called out one of her father's crew.

She shifted her gaze to the north where a galley with a red sail was rounding Mull, heading toward them. *Somerled's ship?*

"I know that galley," said her father. "'Tis Lord Somerled's, or one of his, with that strange rudder in the stern."

When the galley drew close, Somerled waved. "Hail, King Olaf!"

"Have we sailed to your front door, Lord Somerled?" asked her father in an amused tone.

"Nearly so," Somerled answered back. "I come from my new castle at Ardtornish, timber now but one day stone. Where are you bound?"

The ships were alongside each other now. Her father leaned against the gunwale, his head just peeking over the rail. "We sail to Skye. Join us!"

"Aye, I might," came Somerled's reply. "What say you to sojourning tonight with me at Ardtornish? We've a banquet's fare if you are hungry."

Ragnhild observed her father hesitating. "Why not accept, Father? Skye is too far to reach in what is left of the day and I would like to see his castle."

Olaf nodded and leaned back to Somerled. "Very well, we accept."

"Excellent! Follow me into the sound. You can anchor off the point and ride my galley to the shingle." He gave Ragnhild a quick glance before ordering his men to row for the sound. She knew the minute their eyes met that he had planned this interception and the evening to follow.

SOMERLED HAD THOUGHT of a way to force the King of Man into finally consenting to his request for Ragnhild's hand but as yet, he'd divulged it to no one. Now that King Olaf and his daughter were settled by the hearth fire and the crew of Olaf's longship was enjoying ale at one of the trestles, he enlisted his brother, his cousin and Maurice in his cause. Even his son.

"Gillecolum, go speak to the princess and her father. Make sure they are comfortable and let them know I will be with them shortly." He was certain the lad would charm them both. "Liadan, make sure the cook is preparing a feast fit for a king. Even the men who row Olaf's ship and those who keep watch will dine well. The ale must flow freely for I do not want their senses sharp this night."

"And for us?" asked Domnall.

Maurice and Angus, too, gave Somerled an inquiring look.

He had already made sure the lord's bedchamber was ready for Olaf and another prepared for the princess. "While the king and his men sleep, just before dawn, I need you to alter the King of Man's longship."

A sly smile grew on Maurice's face. "Does this have anything to do with the extra tallow and butter you asked for earlier?"

"Aye. I need you to bore holes in his hull, sufficient to make him think he is sinking. Put most of the holes in the bow so the forward motion of the ship drives out the plugs and drives in the water. Make sure we can reinsert the plugs with pitch to make the ship seaworthy again. Meanwhile, stuff the holes with butter and tallow. As he departs on the morrow, I will follow them out of the sound. Maurice, you and Angus will sail with me. Domnall and Diarmad will follow in the two other ships. Rounding Ardnamurchan, where the wind and waves have been at odds, the tallow and butter will be forced free."

"Suddenly, all is clear," said Domnall. "You will require the hand of the princess as a condition of coming to their rescue."

"Aye. Just so."

"You take a great risk," said Maurice. "Even if he agrees and we can reinsert the plugs, there is much that can go wrong. Or he may consent and, later, be angered and recant, not to mention the anger of the princess."

"I have considered that. And you are right. But I believe he will give me what I ask. And I am convinced the princess wants our marriage. My crew will be prepared to save all if need be and I have enough longships to replace the one we damage if it comes to that."

"Why not just ply him with wine at dinner and when he is in high spirits, ask for her hand?" asked Angus. "Would that not be simpler?"

"I have asked for her hand more than once but, aye, I will do so again tonight, for I want him to know I first asked fairly with honor. But if he resists, as he has on other occasions, then our plan will proceed."

"'Tis your funeral, Brother," said Angus, "but we are with you."

"Lord knows you have led us into stranger ventures," said Domnall.

Maurice smiled again. "I rather like it."

The dinner had taken some forethought but, in the end, the roast venison, fresh trout and Liadan's instructions to the cook as to how to use herbs for seasoning made for a succulent feast. The bread, too, was fresh and hot. He had to pry a case of wine free from his French stonemason with a promise to invite him to the wedding if he was successful but it had been worth it. And the local bard was paid well enough to bring a few of his friends with instruments for music.

The evening proceeded well with everyone enjoying themselves. Somerled would have liked to spend all of it with Ragnhild but tonight was for her father. If he succeeded, he and Ragnhild would have a lifetime together.

Olaf took a long draw on his wine, having indulged in several helpings of food. "You set a fine feast in this new castle of yours, Lord Somerled."

"It commands a grand view of the sound," put in Ragnhild.

"One day, the timber will be covered in stone," Somerled replied, "but with so many castles to build, in some places, such as Ardtornish, we build first in timber to quickly gain a stronghold."

"I must commend you for you are a man of your word," said the king. "As you once promised, now you deliver."

Somerled had arranged for Liadan to ask Ragnhild if she would like to see the night sky and, once dinner was finished, the princess was quick to agree and the two women left the castle.

"Now that we are alone, or nearly so," said Somerled, for Olaf's men were enjoying themselves at a nearby trestle with Somerled's men challenging them to a dice game, "I would ask again for the hand of the princess."

Olaf sat back and smiled. "Predictable, yet rewarding to know you are so constant."

"You have no idea." Somerled waited, hoping the king would make his plan unnecessary.

Olaf turned his goblet in his hand. "Sail with me to Skye and, after that, we can discuss this further."

Somerled did not trust Olaf, for he knew the King of Man planned to sail to Orkney. He called for more wine to fill Olaf's empty goblet. "I will gladly accompany you to Skye, for the isle has always interested me as a place where the Norse pirates build their longships, but I would have your answer first."

"Alas, you must wait," said the king. "As for the building of Norse dragonships, rumor has reached me that my tenant, Leod, is turning a blind eye to MacLier in Strath who may be about such business. If true, I will have harsh words for Leod and soon see MacLier gone from Skye."

The castle door opened and Ragnhild and Liadan entered, their cheeks rosy from the night air, their words full of wonder at the stars they had glimpsed. "So many!" exclaimed Ragnhild. "And a shooting star, too! Oh, Father, you should have seen it." She tossed Somerled a smile full of promise and his heart responded, such was her effect upon him.

The king rose from the table. "I think 'tis time for me to retire. I thank you, Somerled, for your gracious hospitality. 'Twas a delightful evening. Now, I would seek my bed for we've a day's sail ahead on the morrow."

Somerled let out a sigh. *So be it.* With Olaf preceding them, Somerled walked the princess to the stairs. He paused at the bottom stair and she turned to look at him. "Princess, can you swim?"

"What an odd question, my lord! Of course, I can swim. You need ask when you know I grew up on an island?"

"I wanted to be sure. I would not want you flailing about in the water should a wave wash you off your father's ship."

She laughed and then whispered, "You do care..."

"Aye, I do. And, know this, what I do on the morrow I do for us. Trust me no matter what happens."

She paused and blinked. Before she could ask, he wished her good night and turned to rejoin his men.

He did not sleep above stairs that night, but with his men and Olaf's in the great hall. He wanted to make sure they were prepared for the sail to Skye with their weapons ready. "Liadan may come, if you permit, Diarmad, for the princess will be aboard her father's ship. If there is trouble on Skye, I would ask your sister to guard my lady."

"Aye, she'll come," said Diarmad, his auburn hair and gray eyes so like his sister's. "'Twould be difficult to hold her back."

Near dawn, Somerled woke his companions and they set out for the shore.

RAGNHILD SLEPT WELL in the chamber assigned to her in Somerled's new castle. She paid no mind to the smell of new oak wood. It was a welcome change from the cold, damp stone of Castle Rushen that could be musty after a rain. If she were his wife, she considered happily, she might dwell in many such castles of timber.

She awoke as shafts of sunlight fell across her face, warmed at the thought Somerled was in this place with her, even if not lying next to her. That thought brought a smile to her face. She recalled Somerled's last words. He was planning something for them, something that would require her trust. *What does he intend to do?*

The morning passed without issue. Liadan came to help her dress, which she appreciated for her laces would be tighter for the lass's assistance. "I should have some gowns made like yours," she told the young woman. "They would be easier to don without my handmaiden."

"No matter, my lady, I am happy to help."

"Have you been with Somerled long?" she asked, curious to know more.

Pulling the laces tight, Liadan said, "Since he saved my village of Keills from the Norse pirates. I offered him my sword to guard his back and my eyes and ears as his spy. It is an honor to serve him."

Ragnhild could well imagine Liadan would be grateful after Somerled had saved her village, but a sword? "You can wield a sword?"

The beautiful girl fingered one of her long auburn plaits, then smiled. "I can," she said proudly, "though not dressed like this." She looked down at her blue bliaut. "My brother Diarmad, who sails for Lord Somerled, taught me to use a blade when I was young."

The girl was only a year or two younger than Ragnhild. Still, she appeared wiser in some ways and less worldly in others. "I am sure Somerled values your presence."

"He is very fond of *you*, my lady."

She smiled. "I do hope so."

After a meal of herring, bread and berries to strengthen them for the voyage, her father helped her climb onto his longship and set off with Somerled's two galleys and a longship accompanying them. Her father told her while they ate that Somerled was going to sail with them to Skye.

It was windy on the Sound of Mull as they sailed northwest toward the open sea, causing Ragnhild's cloak to whip around her as she stood at the gunwale in the bow of the ship.

They had just turned due north to round Ardnamurchan, heading toward the small Isles of Rum and Eigg, when the ship began to slow, falling behind Somerled's galley. The captain shouted orders to ease the sail to let it flag and then trim it to capture the wind. It did not help. The ship seemed to become heavier, more sluggish, as it wallowed and rolled, going nowhere.

Water from the hold suddenly came surging up through the deck boards.

Alarmed, the captain shouted, "Sire! We are sinking!"

Where Ragnhild stood in the bow, shivering, the water was deeper, now climbing up her legs to her knees. Her gown was sodden but she had gathered her cloak to her waist, realizing of a sudden why Somerled had asked if she could swim. He had also told her to trust him and she would.

Her father, standing amidships, fighting to keep his balance in the rising water, shouted to Somerled, "Save us, for we are sinking!"

"Do not fear, King Olaf, I will save you. But first, I must have your vow to give me Ragnhild's hand."

Her father turned to her with furrowed brow. "What is this?"

"I do not know, Father, but I tell you now, I would be happy to be Somerled's bride."

Her father looked aghast at the water rising around him, panic on his face for he was so much shorter than the others. Then in a stern voice, he said, "Very well, Daughter, you have sealed your fate." To Somerled, he cried, "I like not what must be your treachery, but I agree. You have my word to give you my daughter in marriage. Now, Christ on the Cross, save us!"

Somerled promptly brought his ship alongside and took her, her father and all his men aboard while Maurice, Somerled's brother and a member of Somerled's crew scurried onto her father's ship with tools and buckets in hand.

"Your ship will be fine in no time, Olaf," said Maurice, beaming at her father who huddled, shivering on Somerled's deck. "Still, it could have been so much simpler if you had just agreed to my lord's request the first time he made it long ago."

Ragnhild heard the words on the wind and rejoiced. Somerled had asked for her hand "long ago"?

Once she was secure on Somerled's ship, he replaced her mantle with his own and took her in his arms. Ignoring his watching crew and those of his other ships whose crews cheered loudly at their lord's boldness, he kissed her. The cheers grew louder.

His piercing blue eyes softened as he pulled back and met her gaze. "I love you, Princess. I told you once my intentions were honorable and I am ever constant once my heart is given. There is no other woman for me and never will be."

She threw her arms around his neck and returned his kiss in full measure. "My heart is yours, Somerled."

Disgruntled at what had been done to his ship, her father grunted as he shed his sodden mantle. "I should have realized this day would come."

"I've other longships from which you may choose, King Olaf, should you want another," said Somerled. "But as I told you when we met at Irvine, I had no intention of forsaking my quest to make Ragnhild mine. 'Tis well you have finally given me her hand, else I might have been tempted to abduct her, for patience has its end and I have waited long for this moment."

Olaf gave Ragnhild an accusing look. She did not shrink from it. Instead, she smiled up at Somerled and he tightened his arm around her.

Beneath his bushy red brows, her father regarded Somerled. "I expect you to hold up your end of the bargain. You will fight with me when there is a need and there may very well be when we get to Skye."

"Aye," said Somerled, "why do you think I brought three ships? I promised you such an alliance from the beginning."

CHAPTER 19

The south coast of Skye, October 1138

SOMERLED AND OLAF agreed to sail along the southwest coast of Skye where pirates seeking to hide their shipbuilding would find safe harbors in the many coves cut into the jagged coast. The Norse called Skye the misty isle, which was true enough from Somerled's trips to that part of the Hebrides. Though, today, the isle was favored with full sun, he had most often viewed its Black Cuillin Hills shrouded in a cloud-like mist.

Reports had reached Somerled some time ago that suggested Norse pirates were using the isle as a base to build dragonships. Though Skye was one of the isles in Olaf's Kingdom of Man, Somerled doubted the king visited often. And while Olaf thought to issue any pirates on Skye a command to leave, Somerled was convinced they would not go easily.

Somerled was pleased Ragnhild had decided to remain on his galley where he could protect her. She had retrieved her bow and quiver of arrows and stood next to Liadan in the bow. He had already spoken to the two women to make sure they stayed out of any battle that might ensue. "If we meet trouble on Skye," Somerled told Liadan, "you and

Ragnhild stay in the bow." The bow was the least vulnerable part of a ship, the stem higher and more difficult to break through. "You will be safer there and I will leave Maurice to stand guard but, if he falls or needs help, unless I can break free, Ragnhild's safety is yours to guard."

As he knew she would, Liadan had taken her responsibility seriously. "Aye, lord, I will guard her with my life."

Olaf sailed on his own longship, now bailed out and made seaworthy under the careful direction of Maurice MacNeill.

Angus and Maurice sailed with Somerled but Diarmad commanded his own galley and Domnall acted as captain of one of Somerled's longships. Between Somerled and his companions, they had nearly one hundred men to add to Olaf's forty.

It was as Somerled passed the Sleat peninsula and entered the sea loch called Slapin that he caught sight of two dragonships on the loch's western shore. He gave the order to douse sail and his men took to the oars, rowing closer. A few warriors in chainmail and conical helms could be seen guarding the dragonships riding at anchor near shore. On the beach, Norsemen engaged in building longships swarmed like bees around three half-built hulls.

Somerled's ships drew nearer and were spotted by the Norsemen standing guard, who shouted to the men onshore. The pirates dropped what they were doing, grabbed their weapons and, splashing through the shallows, rushed to the dragonships.

By this time, the four ships with Somerled and Olaf were coming alongside the pirates' ships.

"Ready your bows!" shouted Somerled, as he raised his own. Olaf's warriors, a few of them in mail like Olaf, joined Somerled's men, obeying the order as one. "Draw!" His men drew back the strings. When the Norsemen running from shore were within range, he cried, "Loose!"

Arrows hissed through the air and found targets in the Norsemen attempting to climb onto their ships. Many fell into the water but those following them took refuge behind their shields and ran on.

"Prepare the grappling hooks!" Somerled called out to his ship captains.

Grapnels flew through the air, snagging the gunwales of the Norse ships. The men pulled the ropes tight, lashing the ships together, forming a more stable footing from which to fight. The four ships commanded by Somerled and Olaf had the dragonships surrounded.

Shouting his war cry, Somerled slid his sword from its scabbard and leaped onto the closest Norse ship with his shield in one hand and his sword in the other. His brother and his men followed on his heels, all except Maurice, who stayed behind to guard the women.

Somerled slammed his shield into a pirate's head, dazing him. With the moment given him, Somerled slashed upward, across his opponent's body and then downward. The pirate gripped his bleeding belly and fell to the deck.

More pirates, wielding axes and blades, scrambled onto the dragonships, taking the place of their fallen comrades.

Somerled confronted them with gleaming sword, delivering death. Blood splashed onto his tunic and face as he cut them down. At one point, he had to sweep his sleeve over his eyes to better see.

All around him, men clashed with their swords, axes and spears as the battle raged across the decks of the dragonships. Shouts in Norse and moans of the wounded surrounded them. The dead or wounded pirates were forced over the side into the water.

Olaf's mail-clad warriors cut down many Norse who, except for those who had been standing guard, wore no mail.

Somerled scanned the waning battle, pleased to see they were prevailing. Angus was holding his own and Domnall on his other ship stood tall. Diarmad, a fierce fighter, was covered in the blood of his victims.

Bodies soon littered the decks of the dragonships, which became slippery with blood.

For the moment, the fighting was confined to the decks of the enemy ships but Somerled worried it might spill over onto his galley where the women stood in the bow. His fear was realized when, looking back over his shoulder, he glimpsed two pirates charging toward Maurice.

Maurice, an experienced swordsman, could handle one, but Somerled worried about the other, a hulking brute of a man who attacked Liadan with a vengeance.

Somerled crossed back to his galley and confronted the pirate fighting the gallant lass from Islay. "'Tis me you will fight, Pirate!"

The Norseman turned and tried to buffet Somerled with his shield. Somerled kicked out at the pirate's groin with his boot and the pirate bent over, groaning, but did not fall. Knocking the pirate's shield to the deck, Somerled moved in with his sword, blocking the sword of the Norseman until he saw an opening and thrust his sword deep into the pirate's belly. He crumpled to the deck.

From the shore, Somerled heard his name shouted and turned.

Sweyn Asleifsson.

A faint smile formed on Somerled's face. *At last.*

"Somerled, you dog! Because of you, Rognvald banished me from Orkney. Today, I will have my revenge and your head!"

Seeing Maurice finishing off the other pirate, Somerled climbed over the lashed gunwales back to the dragonship.

Wielding his axe, Sweyn climbed aboard the Norse ship and rushed forward, knocking his own men out of the way to get to Somerled. He raised his sword, his eyes narrowed on the man whose time it was to die.

RAGNHILD HAD NEVER BEEN in the midst of a battle but when Somerled called for bows to be readied she did not hesitate. When he gave the command to loose arrows, she had settled her bow next to Maurice's shoulder and fired into the charging Norsemen. At her side, Liadan, too, sent arrows into the chests of the pirates.

Ragnhild had been gratified to see them fall for she remembered the stories of their killing, raping and burning. The few children who had escaped were now orphans, left to mourn alone. She was glad when her father and Somerled had discovered the den where the pirates made their dragonships. Best to destroy them in their nest like the vermin they were.

She had never seen Somerled fight, never witnessed his command of his men. It was a sight she would never forget. His orders were quickly obeyed, as he fought alongside his men with sword and shield. It was clear why the Gaels named him their champion. He rose above others as his powerful arms wielded his sword with swift efficiency, slicing through the Norse pirates as if he were harvesting wheat. His fair hair, held back by braids on either side of his face, allowed her to mark him when the fighting grew intense and close. Never did he falter or lose his footing, never did he fail.

She pressed her lips together and blinked back tears to think such a valiant warrior was hers, a warrior who was fierce with his enemies yet tender with her.

Silently, she asked God to let him live that they might have a lifetime together.

A few of the pirates began to cross over to Somerled's galley where she and Liadan stood behind Maurice. When two attacked at once, Ragnhild feared for her life.

It was then Somerled ran back to his galley, attacking the giant pirate like a maelstrom, his silver blade slashing and blocking the pirate's thrusts. With a rapid stroke, Somerled gutted him.

Suddenly, an axe-wielding, muscled pirate boldly shouted Somerled's name from the shore. She shuddered as she recognized Sweyn Asleifsson, the gold Thor's hammer still displayed on his chest. His lank brown hair, bleached from the sun, was longer than when he appeared in her father's court but his beard and roughened features were the same.

As Sweyn climbed onto the Norse dragonship, Somerled tossed Ragnhild a smile and crossed back to the deck of the Norse ship to meet the challenge.

The fighting subsided as all turned to watch.

Swaggering with confidence, Sweyn circled Somerled, who turned, keeping the pirate in front of him. Tossing his shield aside, Somerled drew a long dagger from his belt. With knife in one hand and sword in the other, he faced his enemy, his gaze fixed and determined.

Ragnhild inhaled sharply, her eyes never leaving him.

Sweyn lunged.

Somerled gracefully moved aside, avoiding the axe's blade.

Sweyn swung his axe in a large arc, aiming at Somerled's head.

Somerled jerked his head aside and let out a loud sigh. "Let me know when you mean to fight, Sweyn, for this game you play is becoming tiresome."

Sweyn's face turned an angry red.

She suspected it had been Somerled's intention to raise the pirate's ire to make him grow reckless. She remembered him as a dishonorable hothead, the one who had accosted her in her father's stables.

Somerled brought his sword down, the blade close to Sweyn's chest. The pirate tried to move out of range but tripped over a body. At once, Somerled was on him, kicking his boot heel into the pirate's belly, sending him reeling back.

Sweyn managed to remain standing. Gripping his axe, he took up his shield and raised it before Somerled.

Somerled brought his sword down on the round wooden disk, the blow so forceful the shield gave a loud crack, cleaving in twain.

The Norse pirates who had been watching backed away with stunned looks. Their necks were quickly under the blades of Somerled's men.

Ragnhild glimpsed fear on Sweyn's face. He threw away what was left of his shield and regained his footing, pulling a knife from his waist.

Like a golden lion attacking his prey, Somerled unleashed his fury on the Norseman, defeating every swing of Sweyn's axe and the short thrusts of his blade.

Silently, Ragnhild cheered.

Somerled forced the pirate to the gunwale.

She glimpsed a plea in Sweyn's eyes. Somerled must have seen it, too, for he said, "I have twice granted you mercy. There will be none this time."

On Sweyn's face was a look of horror as he attempted to shrink back from Somerled. But there was nowhere to go.

Somerled tossed his short blade aside and, gripping his sword hilt with both hands, whirled in a circle. With great force and a single stroke, he severed the pirate's head. It flew out and rolled, blood spurting over the deck.

Straining to see from where she stood on the galley, Ragnhild glimpsed Sweyn's gold Thor's hammer, gleaming in the sun where it lay on the bloodied deck of the dragonship.

Her gaze flew to Somerled. He was unharmed, thanks be to God.

At Somerled's command, the Norse pirates, who were under the blades of Somerled's men, had their throats quickly slit. The few who escaped this death jumped into the water and fled to shore with Somerled's men in hot pursuit.

When the decks were cleared of dead pirates, the wounded of Somerled's and her father's men were taken to Domnall's longship where a healer could tend their wounds. Only then did Maurice allow Ragnhild her freedom.

Ahead of her, Liadan ran to Domnall, who had come to inquire of her wellbeing. His arm was bleeding but nothing more serious was apparent. Liadan embraced him. "You live!"

"Aye, lass. And does that make you happy?"

Liadan swiped at his shoulder. "Of course, you oaf!"

Ragnhild and Maurice hurried to where Somerled stood on the pirate ship, talking to his brother, Angus, and her father, who thankfully appeared whole. She smiled at her father as she passed him and ran into Somerled's welcoming arms.

"I am covered in pirate blood," he protested.

She held him fast. "I care not, for I am thanking the Almighty you live."

"Very well," he said, pressing her tight to his chest. He smelled of blood and sweat but, those smells would pass. Now that he was hers, she would not be letting him go.

"Your killing of Sweyn was quite a show," said Maurice. "'Twill be the subject of the bards' songs for many a year."

"Aye, and you know I did it only for that reason." Ragnhild felt the laughter rumble in his chest.

"I wonder how many other pirates build ships on Skye's hidden shores," asked Angus, casting a glance at the shore. In the distance, the Black Cuillin Hills loomed over all.

"Well," said her father, "I know one who will no longer be on Skye. I killed the MacLier this day. Perhaps on another day, we will see if there are more but I am content with today's harvest. Some of our men are wounded but we've no dead as far as I can tell. It helped that most of the pirates did not wear mail."

"And we outnumbered them," said Somerled. "Too, I discovered long ago that Sweyn would, in the end, act the coward and plead for mercy."

"I am in debt to you for your ships and your men," said her father, "and for protecting my daughter."

"'Twas the least I could do," he said, looking into her eyes. "After all, Ragnhild will soon be my bride."

Her father cast her a disappointed glance, shaking his head. "And to think you could have married an earl."

Ragnhild smiled. "Why would I wed an earl when I can marry a king?"

CHAPTER 20

The Church of St. Mary, Rushen Abbey, Isle of Man, 1 January, 1139 A.D.

RAGNHILD GAZED UP at the tall door of the church, the sun's light on this crisp morning falling across the oak wood. Years ago, when she had first met Somerled, she was drawn to him but had not envisioned such a day. Yet, in God's good time, it had come to her.

Glancing at the man to whom she would soon be wed, she rejoiced at God's favor, for He had given her a golden warrior, a leader of thousands, whose wisdom and intelligence were prized by all. His people, who would soon be her people, now dominated Argyll and the Southern Isles and, unlike so many, lived free.

As she had told her father, she was truly marrying a king and their children would inherit a kingdom unlike any other, one not bound to Scotland, Ireland, England or Norway, except by alliances of its own making. Not even her father, standing with their guests, could say so much, for he was bound to Norway.

Abbot Bernard smiled and beckoned them closer.

Somerled took her hand and led her forward. With few words, the abbot asked if each gave their consent to this union. Somerled turned to face her and smiled. "I will."

When it was her turn, Ragnhild gazed up into his clear blue eyes. "I will."

She had always thought Somerled a handsome man. She had seen him garbed in royal apparel to meet two kings; she had seen him covered in other men's blood and smelling of sweat; and she had seen him wind-blown and browned from the sun. Until now, he had never allowed her to see him clothed with a mantle of love. But it was there in his eyes when he turned to her and began to speak.

You are now blood of my blood, and bone of my bone.
I give you my body, that we two might be one.
I give you my spirit, 'til our life shall be done.

With tears of joy falling down her cheeks, they exchanged rings of gold that would forever mark them man and wife. From this day onward, except when she was alone with Somerled or their family, Ragnhild would wear a veil covering her hair, indicating she was a married woman.

Abbot Bernard blessed them and prayed for their union, their children and their life together, and for the legacy they would leave. The ceremony was brief, after which, they entered the church for Mass.

And then the celebration began.

SOMERLED HELD RAGNHILD'S HAND tightly as they stepped from the church into the chilled morning sun. Loud cheers erupted all around them as the people of Man and Galloway and Somerled's friends gathered to wish them well. Most, he assumed, admired him for gaining a great alliance and a large dowry. The message of congratulations from the King of Scots hinted at such. Few knew he had been long in love with the jewel-eyed Princess of Man. If they wanted to think him canny for the marriage, it mattered little to him. That Ragnhild was his bride and would share his bed and his life mattered more.

"Father has prepared a great feast for us," she said as they walked back to the castle, the boisterous crowd following.

"My men will appreciate that." Already, Angus, Maurice and Domnall, walking beside Liadan and her brother, were smiling and waving to them. Gillecolum walked apart, beaming at them, for he was glad of the marriage and had told them the night before that it was time he had a mother.

"You know what Gille and I look forward to, my lord?" she said in teasing manner.

"Tell me."

"We hope for peace so there will be no more sad goodbyes and no more hasty utterances of "Godspeed".

"Aye, we will be together now." Then in offhand manner, he asked, "Do you know what I look forward to?"

"I can guess," she said with a sly smile. "'Tis tonight when we escape to my chamber."

He chuckled. "Already you know me well. Yes, but not just this night, my love. It is all the nights we will share for the rest of our lives."

She glanced down at the ring on her finger, happy God had brought Somerled through wars and battles to this day. Then meeting his gaze, she echoed his words, "For the rest of our lives."

EPILOGUE

On the shores of Loch Findlugan, Isle of Islay, Spring 1147 A.D.

RAGNHILD WATCHED, amused, as Dougall, her eldest son, fairer than his two younger brothers, chased after the frog loudly proclaiming its ownership of the lily pad to which it had leaped. Close behind him, as always, Ranald, just one year younger and redheaded like her, circled around to grab the frog from the shallow water into which it had escaped at his coming. Angus, her youngest with the dark blond hair of his namesake, looked longingly after his older brothers but they were sometimes reluctant to include him.

In the years of peace since her wedding to Somerled, their family had grown, along with her husband's many castles and his fleet of galleys.

Dougall chased after Ranald and the look on Angus' face spoke of disappointment as he tried to follow. "Careful, Angus," she warned. "The water is deeper there." Being only three, his short legs would not carry him far.

Somerled stepped behind her, placing his hands on her shoulders. "Do not worry, my love, our boys will find their way. And Gillecolum is ever watchful of them."

She knew she should not worry for her husband spoke the truth. Gillecolum, standing on the shore not far away, acted the older brother to all three of her sons. Nearing the age of twenty and good with a sword, he was a hero to his half-brothers and close companion of his father.

"Did I tell you the news of Rognvald?" asked her husband.

"What, pray tell, has he done now?"

"He is taking fifteen longships and going on a pilgrimage to Jerusalem."

"I cannot imagine the earl doing such a thing, unless it is penitence."

"Aye, it might be, though 'tis said he's making a great show of it." Somerled slipped his hands to her belly, swollen with his child. "Do you think this next one might be a girl?"

"Could be. For certes, I am carrying the babe differently."

"I promised your father that after the child is born, we will bring the brood to Man. Did I tell you that when I first asked for your hand, it was one of my pledges that he would see his grandchildren often?"

She placed her hand over his. "He should have granted you your request then, for he is glad now that you were my choice and is pleased he has three grandsons who can inherit his isles, especially in light of the difficult child Affraic's son, Godred, has become."

"I suppose you are right. Reserves are always a good idea, although our sons will have many lands to carve up between them without Olaf's isles."

Ragnhild sharply inhaled as her youngest son stumbled climbing out of the loch.

Gillecolum, as tall as his father and with the same fair countenance, swept Angus up in his arms. "Come, little one. I have another game we can play, one you will like."

Angus giggled with glee.

Ragnhild watched her adopted son carry her youngest toward Fairhair where he nibbled on grass at the edge of the loch.

Once they visited her father, they would return to Islay to greet the chiefs who would gather after the autumn harvest.

She turned in Somerled's arms, unable to get close for the babe in her womb. "Have I told you that I love you, my lord?"

"Aye, but I will gladly hear it again."

AUTHOR'S NOTE

Somerled is the accepted founder of Clan Donald, though the clan takes its name from Donald, the 3rd Lord of the Isles, Somerled's grandson, who died in 1269. Donald's son was the original "Mac" Donald ("mac" meaning "son of").

Some argue as to whether Somerled's name is Norse or Gaelic. *Sumarliðr* is Old Norse for "summer warrior" (or "summer traveler" in the sense of a Viking). *Somhairlidh*, pronounced Saw-ur-lay, is a Gaelic name. As written in the 15th century documents, it was pronounced "Sorley". It means champion or warrior. While "Somerled" is not a Gaelic name, since so many know him by that name, I have used it. Based upon my research, he was both Norse and Gaelic, what was called a "Norse-Gael" or "foreign Gael". His father *Gillebride* was most likely a Gael or a Norse-Gael and his mother could have been wholly or partly Norse. (All I was able to discern is that she was "fair" and likely of Norse descent.)

Gaelic historians trace his lineage back to the Norse Kings of Dublin and the great *Ard-Ri*, the High Kings of Ireland. His origins also speak of *Colla Uais*, a Celtic prince with influence in the Western Isles before the establishment of the kingdom of Dalriada.

Except for a few key dates, the life of Somerled is shrouded in the mists of time, much of it the subject of legend, of which I have made free use, believing, as I do, that there is always some truth to legend. As the story goes, Somerled's grandfather, Gilledomman of the Isles, had been defeated by the Norse and exiled to Ireland. Though some online sources indicate it is "assumed" Somerled was born in Morvern in Argyll, I think the better view is that he was born in Ireland while his family was in exile. It was from there his father raised an army of five hundred and returned to Argyll to try and regain their inheritance but was defeated. At that time, Somerled would have been a young man, old enough to accompany his father.

The dates for Somerled's birth and emergence as a hero vary widely. For the sake of the story, I have been flexible, placing him in his late twenties. Most sources say he married Ragnhild in 1140 but others say it could have been earlier. We know that David, King of Scots, granted Somerled the Isles of Arran and Bute in 1135. And in 1138, Somerled began construction of his compound on Islay (pronounced "Eye-lah"). In that same year, he heeded David's call to join him to fight the English in Yorkshire (what became known as "the Battle of the Standard").

All sources agree that Somerled successfully cleared Morvern, Lochaber and the northern part of Argyll from the Norse, becoming the Thane of Argyll. Then he turned his attention to southern Argyll and the Isles. His warriors would have included close-fighting Islesmen, archers from Argyll and Irish mercenaries from Antrim. Since we know Somerled fought for King David in 1138, it is likely he had David's support for turning back the Norse tide, building his castles and taking the title he did as Lord of Argyll, Kintyre and Lorne. David would have considered Somerled a minor king, but a king nonetheless.

Long before the Norse invaders arrived, Celtic seafaring was part of the culture. In time, Somerled developed his own fleet of galleys, half the size of the Norse longships and more maneuverable with the moveable stern rudder he invented. They were called *Naibheag*, or "Little ships," sometimes "Birlinns". In contrast, the larger Norse longships used a steering board on the right side, hence the term "starboard", which gave them limited steering capability.

Most of my characters were real historical figures, even Sweyn Asleifsson, "the Skullcrusher". According to the *Orkneyinga Saga*, he came to prominence when he murdered Earl Paul of Orkney's cupbearer about 1134 in a quarrel over a drinking game. He was a pirate whose activities included drunkenness, murder and plundering. Rognvald did, indeed, drive him out of Orkney. Clan Donald tradition states that

Somerled slew a Viking named *Sweno* who had courted Ragnhild. Not exactly the real historical figure but close enough. When the Normans retook Dublin in the late 12th century, Sweyn was killed. I preferred he die by Somerled's hand.

We do not know much about Ragnhild, save for her parentage, the approximate year she married Somerled and the names of her children. That intrigued me from the beginning. What would the Princess of Man have been like to draw the attention of a warrior like Somerled? She was a known beauty and it is said Somerled was smitten, but would she have been more? I like to think she could have been the woman I have portrayed her to be, intelligent and spirited, the daughter of a powerful king, desired for more than her dowry.

From 1140 to 1153, Somerled established a family, built military alliances, extended his influence in the Isles, and adhered to a cautious middle ground in the world of Norse-Scots politics. These were long years of careful preparation—redesigning and building faster, more maneuverable galleys, constructing castles, and training fierce warbands for the inevitable conflicts.

Sadly, in 1153 both King David and King Olaf died, the latter being murdered by his three nephews. In 1156, Somerled defeated Olaf's heir, Godred the Black, by then the ruler of Man and one the people disdained. With the Kingdom of Man now under his lordship, Somerled became *Ri Innse Gall* or King of the Isles. As he envisioned, his was a kingdom independent of both Norway and Scotland.

By 1158, Somerled's dominion covered 25,000 square miles and more than 500 islands. North to south, his control covered 200 miles from the Isles of Lewis and Skye to the Isle of Man. It was unified by the broad roads of the sea protected by his many castles of which there were fourteen in his time (errors in the Internet notwithstanding). Somerled's fortifications were on coastal heights and deep in lochs where his galleys could be beached and his warriors protected to keep the sea lanes clear. Some were timber castles to be later fortified in stone, which may be why some Internet sources wrongly attribute the dates when they were fortified in stone to the original dates for their construction. Alas, I found too many Internet errors to name.

In 1164, in an attempt to forestall King Malcolm's attempt to grab the lands of Argyll, Kintyre and Lorne, Somerled invaded Scotland with 164 ships, sailing up the Clyde to near Renfrew. In the ensuing battle against Walter FitzAlan, then High Steward of Scotland, sadly, Somerled was killed along with Gillecolum. This was so devastating to the Highland cause that there was no serious challenge to the Kings of the Scots for more than two centuries.

Ragnhild gave Somerled three sons, Dougall, Ranald (or Ragnall), Angus, and a daughter, Bethoc. (The *Chronicle of Man* indicates they had a fourth son, Olaf, but he is never heard from.) It was Donald, one of the descendants of Ranald, who would be the progenitor of the Macdonalds. Bethoc, named (presumably) after Somerled's sister, became the prioress at Iona. Somerled, too, founded an abbey—at Saddell on Kintyre—as he had wanted to do. Construction of Saddell Abbey was begun by him but he died before it was finished. It would be his son, Ranald, who would complete it. Somerled was buried on Iona.

You might wonder about the religious beliefs of the people at the time. The Norse, English and Scots, including the people over which Somerled reigned in the west, were all Christians. The Gaels would have followed the Celtic tradition of Columba and the Culdees. (They were not initially Roman Catholic.) As historian A. J. Wylie explains in his *History of the Scottish Nation*, Vol. III.,

> The 12th century, particularly in Scotland and Brittany, was a time when two Christian faiths of different origins were contending for possession of the land, the Roman Church and the old Celtic Rite. The age was a sort of borderland between Culdeeism and Romanism. The two met and mingled often in the same monastery, and the religious belief of the nation was a mumble of superstitious doctrines and a few scriptural truths.

As you know from my story *Rebel Warrior* (titled *The Refuge* in the stand alone, inspirational version), in the late 11th century, despite Queen Margaret's desire to move Scotland more toward Roman Catholicism, Culdee monks existed there into the 12th century. Somerled would have followed the Culdee tradition, which aligned with his Celtic roots, but Ragnhild and her father, Olaf the Red, would have been Roman Catholics, likely because of Olaf's having been raised in England in Henry I's court.

All evidence points to St. Columba, who founded the Iona center of worship in 563, being a Culdee. The same is believed of St. Patrick and St. Findlugan. Columba is given credit as the first evangelizer of Scotland. In the last year of his life, Somerled attempted to persuade the head of the Columban Church, Flaithbertach Ua Brolcháin, Abbot of Derry, to relocate from Ireland to Iona. With Somerled's death, however, the reunification he sought did not occur.

The Culdees represented "the people's church". They did not place great value on formal church hierarchy but emphasized learning and the study of the Scriptures. According to tradition, Columba spent much of his time in reading and writing, and he placed great value in exact copying of ancient texts. Also, unlike the Roman Catholics of the time, the Culdees believed that the Scriptures should be translated into the vernacular languages of the people.

Though marriage was not declared a sacrament by the Roman Catholic Church until 1184, when Somerled and Ragnhild married it seemed reasonable to me that both she and her father would have wanted them to be married on the Isle of Man and before my fictional Abbot Bernard. (My research suggests the actual name of the first abbot at Rushen Abbey was Conanus, but Bernard comes easier to the tongue.)

While Ragnhild would, in time, have many castles to choose from in which to live, she would often be on Islay, as Somerled imagined in my story, because that is where the chiefs gathered and would for genera-tions.

Since the map developed for this story is one I hope to use in subsequent novels in the series, which will move forward in time, I have tried to use place names you would recognize. For example, though the earlier version of Argyll is "Argyle", I used the name from later centuries. Ulaid in North Ireland—the far northwest part—would become part of Ulster. And, while I named the loch on Islay "Findlugan's Loch" after the Irish monk, it would eventually become "Finlaggan" and would serve as Clan Donald's headquarters.

Summer Warrior has its own Pinterest storyboard that captures some of my research, including the maps I used and the way characters and places appear to me.
pinterest.com/reganwalker123/the-clan-donald-saga-by-regan-walker

Follow me on Amazon for notice of future releases in the series.
amazon.com/Regan-Walker/e/B008OUWC5Y

On my website you can sign up for my newsletter. I give away a free book each quarter. And there is a Regan Walker's Readers group on Facebook.
www.ReganWalkerAuthor.com
facebook.com/groups/ReganWalkersReaders

AUTHOR'S BIO

Regan Walker is an award-winning author of Regency, Georgian and Medieval novels. A lawyer turned writer, she has six times been nominated for the Reward of Novel Excellence (RONE) award. Her novels *The Red Wolf's Prize* and *King's Knight* won that award in the medieval category. *The Refuge: An Inspirational Novel of Scotland* won the Gold Medal in the Illumination Awards. *To Tame the Wind* won the International Book Award for Romance Fiction and Best Historical Romance in the San Diego Book Awards. *A Fierce Wind* won a medal in the President's Book Awards of The Florida Authors & Publishers Association. And many of her books have been finalists in numerous other contests.

Years of serving clients in private practice and several stints in high levels of government have given Regan a feel for the demands of the "Crown". Hence her novels often feature a demanding sovereign who taps his subjects for special assignments. Each of her novels features history, adventure and love.

Regan lives in San Diego with her dog "Cody", a much-loved Wire-haired Pointing Griffon.

Follow Regan on Amazon and BookBub.
amazon.com/Regan-Walker/e/B008OUWC5Y
bookbub.com/profile/regan-walker

And join Regan Walker's Readers on Facebook.
facebook.com/groups/ReganWalkersReaders

You can sign up for her newsletter on her website, too.
www.ReganWalkerAuthor.com

BOOKS BY REGAN WALKER

The Agents of the Crown series (Regency):

Racing with the Wind
Against the Wind
Wind Raven
A Secret Scottish Christmas
Rogue's Holiday

The Donet Trilogy (Georgian):

To Tame the Wind
Echo in the Wind
A Fierce Wind

Holiday Novellas (related to The Agents of the Crown):

The Shamrock & The Rose
The Holly & The Thistle
The Twelfth Night Wager

Medieval Warriors:

The Red Wolf's Prize
Rogue Knight
Rebel Warrior
King's Knight

The Clan Donald Saga:

Summer Warrior

Inspirational

The Refuge: An Inspirational Novel of Scotland

www.ReganWalkerAuthor.com

Made in United States
Orlando, FL
03 October 2023

37528701R10153